She made her way mindful of how har and vigilant of her surroundings.

At the bottom, she took a deep breath then started another trek, this one over rocks and dirt and the occasional wayward root. It was a steep climb, and by the time she reached the tree line, Alessandra was slightly out of breath. So she paused to pull in a few gulps of oxygen. And when she did, she realized she could hear a masculine voice. Low enough that she couldn't discern the words. But audible enough that she recognized it.

Rush. Thank God.

Her mind quickly connected the dots. The flash she'd seen was likely his phone, and he'd probably just sneaked off to have a quiet conversation. But the relief at having an explanation was short-lived. Because as Alessandra lifted her foot to move closer again, and opened her mouth to call his name, a light bit of wind kicked up and carried his voice to her. Clearly now, so she could completely make out his words.

"I've really got no choice," he growled. "I have to get rid of her."

The two statements were rough, angry and ominous. And they made Alessandra stumble. For a few seconds after her miniature crash landing, she didn't move. She didn't know if she could.

Do I run? Do I pretend I never heard any of it and go for a more subtle escape? Or do I confront him? Or—

Her tumble of frightened thoughts stopped short as a new sound carried to her ears. It was the crash of a man, pushing through the bushes. Rush was headed her way.

* * *

**Undercover Justice:
Four brothers-in-arms on a mission for justice...**

* * *

If you're on Twitter, tell us what you think of Harlequin Romantic Suspense! #harlequinromsuspense

Dear Reader,

Welcome to the fourth and final installment in my Undercover Justice series. I'm so excited to bring you the elusive Detective Rush Atkinson. Not that I like to play favorites, but I do have a soft spot for this particular hero. He once told his brothers-in-arms that if it weren't for the fact that he was seeking justice for his slain father, he might've slipped onto the wrong side of the law. And I love this about him.

Rush is rough. He's gruff. He's definitely not an easy man, and he's not going to be tamed. Not even by love. But that's one of the things that makes Alessandra so perfect for him. She's a free spirit. And I hope you think they're as tingly, meant to be as I do!

Happy reading,

Melinda

UNDERCOVER REFUGE

Melinda Di Lorenzo

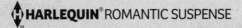

HARLEQUIN® ROMANTIC SUSPENSE

Recycling programs
for this product may
not exist in your area.

ISBN-13: 978-1-335-66204-0

Undercover Refuge

Printed in U.S.A.

Amazon bestselling author **Melinda Di Lorenzo** writes in her spare time—at soccer practices, when she should be doing laundry and in place of sleep. She lives on the beautiful west coast of British Columbia, Canada, with her handsome husband and her noisy kids. When she's not writing, she can be found curled up with (someone else's) good book.

To all those who love a bad boy with a good heart.

Chapter 1

Detective Rush Atkinson was sure of two things. One. Someone was following him. And two. They were going to be sorry.

Gritting his teeth, he stepped a little harder on the gas. The Lada protested immediately. The lumbering old vehicle—built in 1972 and seemingly held together by sheer willpower alone—had a strong preference for moving at a slow and steady pace. It was good on the back roads and got the job done, and it usually suited Rush just fine. Of course, he wasn't usually being stalked up a mountain road. If he'd thought that was even the vaguest possibility, he would've grabbed his second-favorite vehicle. A monster of a motorcycle that he'd pieced together with his own two hands. A source of pride.

"A source of speed, too," he muttered as he took another quick glance in the rearview mirror.

He knew his look wouldn't yield anything. Not on the straight patch of road. So far, he'd only caught glimpses of the car on the wider bends. It was a silver hatchback. One of those hybrid electric vehicles, Rush thought.

Strange choice for a stalker.

He didn't really have time to muse on it. Or the desire to, as a matter of fact. He was supposed to be meeting with his "boss," Jesse Garibaldi—aka the man he was trying his damnedest to put behind bars—in just under five minutes. He should've been early. *Would have* been early, if some fool wasn't tailing him. No way was he going to make it on time now. He'd been trying to give the silver hatchback the slip since the second he realized it was following him.

"For your own good," he grumbled at the unseen driver.

Really, he *was* doing them a favor. Garibaldi wasn't the kind of man who welcomed uninvited guests. Not on this side of things, anyway. Inside the small town of Whispering Woods, he might be thought of as a businessman and philanthropist and an enthusiastic lover of tourists, but Rush knew better. The man was a murderer.

Fifteen years earlier, when they were both barely more than kids, the other man had killed Rush's father and Rush's friends' fathers. Garibaldi had set off a pipe bomb at the Freemont City police station in order to destroy some kind of evidence. He'd been successful, and the three men who died were nothing more than collateral damage to him. A good lawyer had seen to it that he got off. Now, a decade and a half later, Garibaldi was entrenched in the small tourist-driven economy of the mountainside town. A pillar. But all of the goodwill and investment were a front for something more sinister. Using the truly good people of Whispering Woods, Garibaldi had set himself up with a tidy little drug empire. In came the heroin. Out went a series of doctored paintings, laced with the deadly mixture of opiates and paint, and no one was the wiser.

Except us, Rush thought grimly as he swung the wheel and veered off the concrete road and headed onto a small dirt-packed one.

Just a couple of months earlier, he and his partners had discovered Garibaldi's out-in-the-open hiding place. They'd pieced together his method. Now, with two of his three partners holed up in Mexico, and the third on hiatus in Europe, it was Rush's job to put the final nail in the coffin. Something he was eager to do. It was going to happen any day now, too. Garibaldi was organizing something big. A meeting with a buyer, Rush believed.

It was the perfect moment to make the bust. All he had to do was to get his pseudo-boss to trust him enough to disclose the details and include him in the exchange. He was well on the way there. In the short time since Rush had used his connections to secure a position on Garibaldi's crew, he'd already risen from grunt man to enforcer to errand-runner.

Gonna be hard to get any higher than that if you've got a stalker tagging along.

He guided the Lada around a corner and took yet another look in the rearview. He wasn't surprised to see the flash of silver through the trees. He still dropped a curse as he slowed down. Being wrong wouldn't have been so terrible in this case.

Just up ahead, the road ended in a wide circle. It was a popular spot for seasoned hikers to the head up into the mountain. At the moment, Rush just wanted to use it as a

U-turn. He'd circle back around, catch sight of whoever was at the wheel of the hatchback, memorize the details of their face, then head back into town so he could place a call to Garibaldi. His boss would be unimpressed that he hadn't shown up, but it was better than the alternative, and Rush would come up with a good excuse. He was a smooth liar. A natural by-product of spending his entire career in undercover roles.

He tapped his finger on the steering wheel as he reached the wide crescent-shaped end of the road and used it to turn the Lada around. He pushed his foot to the gas again—more gently this time—and got the vehicle up to cruising speed. His hands tightened a little on the wheel, but other than that, he kept his body perfectly relaxed, betraying no hint of apprehension at the encounter that he knew was coming any second.

"C'mon, you little silver weasel," he said under his breath. "Give me a good, five-second look."

When the other vehicle didn't immediately appear, Rush frowned. He was sure—*so sure*—that it had been tailing him. He would've bet his badge on it.

"So where the hell are you, buddy?" he muttered, slowing to a near crawl.

Maybe the driver's trying to avoid a confrontation, he reasoned.

Lord knew he wouldn't want to get in a fight alone in the woods with one of Garibaldi's thugs if he could avoid it. And he was supposed to *be* one of thugs, so that was really saying something.

It wouldn't be an easy feat to get away unnoticed, though. Aside from coming up the way he'd done himself—or maybe being pulled up in a spaceship's tractor beam—there was no other way to simply turn and go.

Rush dragged his gaze back and forth, considering it. What would he have done if the roles were reversed? There were thick shrubs on either side of the narrow road, and deep ditches, too. He wondered if a smaller car could've managed a complicated turn. Or if the driver might've backed all the way out. He thought the latter would take too long, and the former would require both confidence and skill.

Or...you could just be wrong about being followed. He sighed and eased his foot off the brake pedal. *Maybe the flash of silver was in your head. Or it was an animal. A gray wolf. Or a—*

His thoughts cut off as he reached the end of the dirt road. There, hanging half in and half out of the ditch, was proof that his imagination hadn't run wild. A silver Prius. And something unexpected. *Someone* unexpected. A woman, standing beside it.

Without meaning to, Rush ran his gaze over her. Toe to head instead of the other way around. Unconsciously drinking in her eclectic appearance.

On her feet, she wore a pair of flip-flops—dark brown and made of some kind of woven fabric. Her pants were loose, wide-legged, cinched at the waist with a string, and a color that reminded Rush of the beach. She had on a plain white T-shirt, which was far too large. She'd tied it in a knot just above her hip, and the collar hung off her shoulder, revealing a tantalizing expanse of skin.

As Rush lifted his eyes to her face, his throat went a little dry. He was close enough to see the frustrated look on her face. Close enough to note her perfectly arched brows and full lips. Her cheekbones were high and honey-kissed. Touched by a few loose tendrils of the darkest auburn hair, the rest of which was piled up in a loose bun. There was no denying her allure. So Rush didn't bother to try. Especially since staring at her nearly made him lose control of his vehicle.

It was actually the jarring bounce as he hit a bump that made him come to his senses.

The woman wasn't someone he'd met over the cantaloupe section in the grocery store. She wasn't someone he'd locked eyes with from across the room in a bar. She was the person who'd *stalked* him. Followed him from who knew how many miles, for who knew what reason.

Maybe you should stop and ask?

The question pricked at him as he coasted by. It nagged at his conscience as he looked in the side-view mirror and saw her jaw drop open as though she was stunned by the fact that he wasn't stopping. Her arms came up in a frantic wave. For a second, he wavered. He found himself fighting for a reason to stay. Then he forcefully reminded himself that as attractive as she was, and as helpless as she seemed, it was that very thing that made her all the more dangerous. Cynics like him knew that pretty packages didn't always have pretty contents. And he stepped on the gas.

Alessandra Rivers watched, stupefied, as the man in the truck sped up, then kept going. She spun slowly to stare at the back end as it rumbled away.

Is he seriously just going to leave?

She stood still, certain he was going to turn around. He *had* to, didn't he? Even if chivalry was out of fashion—and really, Alessandra wasn't all that interested in being a damsel in distress, anyway—there was still some human decency to speak of, wasn't there? What kind of person left someone visibly stranded on the side of the road like that?

And she was 100 percent sure he'd seen her. Even his mirrored sunglasses and his curved brim hat couldn't hide the fact that his gaze had slid over her.

But the truck didn't show any sign of coming back. No approaching engine. No renewed cloud of dust. And now Alessandra could feel a thick ball forming in her throat. Dread and worry. And threatening tears.

She drew in a breath and closed her eyes, trying to ward it all off. It was a hard sell.

She'd been lost on the back roads of Whispering Woods for a good fifteen minutes before even spotting the rusted-out hunk of junk and the stranger who'd just abandoned her. At first, she'd been so glad to see him that she actually forgot to react. By the time she'd stuck her arm out the window, he was gone. And she'd tried— hard—to catch up. But her Prius wasn't much good on anything that wasn't smooth, and every few feet she seemed to hit a deep pothole that inevitably made the car bounce, her heart pound and her teeth knock together. It didn't help at all that the guy in the truck seemed to be on some crazy mission to take as many weird turns as possible. Alessandra had been *relieved* when he turned up the dirt path with the no-exit sign at the front.

But the relief was short-lived. It went straight down into the ditch along with the front end of her stupid little car. And hope followed it. Or maybe not followed *it*. Maybe the hope disappeared up the road along with Mr. Blue Truck.

With a frustrated exhale, Alessandra turned back toward her vehicle. She had a sudden overwhelming urge to kick the door. Multiple times. It was an unusual sensation, and not just because it was such an aggressive thing to want to do. Alessandra prided herself on having a very even temper. On channeling inner calmness and on projecting an outer peace. She wasn't much into relaxing candles, meditation or yoga. Those had been her mom's things. But when life went wrong, a few deep breaths and a reminder than she had a million things to be grateful for was usually enough. And even when *that* didn't work, she always had her own inner strength to draw on.

Except today, she thought. *And maybe every moment of the last two weeks.*

Or to be more exact, the last thirteen days. Not that Alessandra was particularly superstitious, but that did seem a little coincidentally unlucky.

Thirteen days ago, she'd found the letter in an old box of her mom's stuff. Tucked in between a box of incense, a bundle of sage and a pile of tarot cards. She'd only opened it because she'd recognized her father's handwriting on the outside of the envelope, and she'd known exactly what it was. A love note.

Throughout her childhood, her father had left them scattered in secret places for her mother to find. Her mother had requested that the notes be buried with her, lovingly explaining to Alessandra that they were far too private to leave out in the world.

But when Alessandra had found this one, she'd felt no guilt at opening it. Not an ounce. She saw things like that as kismet. Meant to be. And really, she'd just been hoping to hear her dad's voice in her head. Her mother had only been gone for two years, but he'd passed fifteen years earlier, and sometimes it was hard to remember him.

As Alessandra had unsealed the envelope, she'd been excited. But a first glance had changed the excitement. She'd been unsettled. Then surprised. And finally, stunned beyond all reason.

The paper was like a patchwork quilt. A hundred tiny pieces, torn up, then painstakingly taped together.

For a minute, she'd just stared at it without reading it, wondering why it had been destroyed, then considering the amount of effort required to reassemble it. When at last she did read it, squinting through the Scotch tape at the faded ink to make out the words, her breath had stuck in her throat. The content was a shock.

> *Dear Mary,*
> *I can't imagine what my death did.*
> *I'd undo it if I could.*
> *Do you remember our honeymoon?*
> *I'll live there. Always*
> *Love you forever,*
> *Randall*

As she recalled the words again, a renewed trickle of fear made Alessandra shiver, and anxiety sent her heart rate spiking.

She questioned once more if the note held any underlying meaning. A secret message of some kind. It seemed like such an odd thing to write, then destroy. Had father done it himself because he never intended her mother to see the letter? Or had her mother been the one to do it? And if so…why?

From the moment Alessandra read the letter, things had only gone downhill. There was a police report that resulted in a friend's supposedly accidental death. Then a fire at the surf shop Alessandra called home. And finally, an unexpected invitation to meet with an old family friend. Jesse Garibaldi. Who'd informed her that he now called the small tourist town of Whispering Woods home. The very place her dad referred to in his letter. Where her parents had spent the weeks after their private ceremony, and where they'd joked that Alessandra had been conceived. What were that chances that it was a coincidence?

She shivered yet again, a chill running through her in spite of the sun overhead.

"Don't think about any of that," she ordered aloud to herself. "Focus on getting out of *this* moment, then think about the rest."

But it was a little hard to maintain a cheerful outlook with her car hanging half in a ditch. She couldn't even tell herself that it was half *out*, and somehow put a good spin on it. Especially when she was unable to call for help. The first thing she'd done when she realized she was lost was to go for cell phone. But at the exact moment she pulled it from her purse, she'd hit a bump. The phone went flying. As she'd tried to grab it, she'd knocked over her coffee. And of course, the coffee spilled directly onto the phone. By the time Alessandra pulled off the road—which she should've done in the first place—the phone was nothing but a dismal black screen of death. And it still showed no sign of magically self-repairing.

Okay. Deep breath. Then make a list. What are the positives?

For a second, she couldn't think of a single one.

"Well," she finally said. "I'm not dead. So there's that."

But the thought was a little too dark to be truly humorous.

Alessandra looked down at her car again. She vaguely recalled things about ropes and pulleys and levers from high school science. But she had a feeling that trying to hoist a car out of a ditch was slightly more complicated than moving a paper airplane with a drinking straw and elastic band. A bit of a different scale.

"Okay, then," she muttered. "I guess the only thing to do is to walk until I find some help."

Wincing at the generally sorry state of her car, she climbed back into the ditch and leaned through the driver's side door to grab her oversize patchwork bag from the front seat. She eyed her suitcase in the back seat, but decided to leave it. There was no way of knowing exactly how long she'd have to walk, and she didn't want to weigh herself down too badly.

And besides that, she told herself, *you're going to be able to get help, and you're going to get back here just fine. It's not like a wild animal's likely to come along and steal your clothes and toothbrush.*

Feeling slightly more positive, she made her way out of the ditch back to the dirt road. She lifted her hand to shield eyes, glanced in the general direction of the sun and tried to gauge the time. Noon, maybe? And she *thought* she could tell which way was west. With a determined spin, she took a few steps. Then stopped almost immediately as a growl filled the air. Her eyes widened. She swallowed nervously and started to turn back to her car, half expecting to see that a bear or a wolf *had* taken an interest in her belongings. But aside from her familiar car, the ditch was as empty as it had been a moment earlier.

Then she clued in.

She closed her eyes and listened. The growl became

a rumble, which grew louder and closer. And more familiar.

Slowly—not wanting to let herself give in to false hope—Alessandra opened her eyes and focused her attention toward the end of the road. Not really aware that she was doing it, she squeezed her fingers into fists and bounced a little on the balls of her feet.

Please, please, let it be him.

And suddenly, there he was. Or there his truck was, anyway. Barreling toward her at full, furious speed. Almost as if the fact that he was headed her way made the driver angry.

For a second, Alessandra's feet stayed rooted to the spot, puzzlement outweighing worry. *Why* would he come back if it was just going to make him mad? As the truck got closer, dirt flying up hard, Alessandra's brain gave her a little tap, and she realized that if she didn't move, there was a good chance she might be mowed down. But she no sooner started to jump out of the way than the blue truck came to a grinding halt, and the driver's-side door came flying open with a force that matched the speed at which the vehicle had approached. Quick and fired up. It was enough to freeze her again. It was also enough to send a sharp zap of curiosity through her. And the curiosity only deepened as the driver jumped out.

Alessandra watched as he planted his steel-toe boots firmly in the dirt and spread his dark-denim-clad legs hip distance apart, then just stood there, unmoving. She had the impression that he was assessing the situation. And maybe her, too. It was disconcerting, and an inexplicable sweat broke out on her upper lip. But she couldn't seem to speak. So she just took advantage of the silent, still moment to look him over as thoroughly as he was looking over her.

He was lean, but not skinny. In fact, he had corded muscles on the lower half of his inked arms—just visible because he had his long-sleeved charcoal-gray T-shirt pushed halfway to his elbows. As she stared at the bit of exposed ink, a prickling heat built just under the surface of Alessandra's skin. For a moment, the warmth threw her off. But it didn't take long to realize the source. She—or her body, anyway—found him attractive.

She sucked in a breath, tried to calm her suddenly racing heart and forced her eyes to his face. He still wore the dark reflective glasses, and he had a ball cap emblazoned with a truck logo pulled down over his forehead. Even though his cheeks and chin were dusted with a salt-and-pepper beard, what she could see of his skin was smooth and at least as young as her own. The contrast, which created a slightly enigmatic look, did nothing to ease the quick thrum of her Alessandra's pulse.

But then she spotted something that flew straight at her like a bucket of icy water.

One of the truck driver's hands hung loosely at his thigh, fingers flexing. The other hand was poised over—but not quite touching—a shiny metal gun.

Chapter 2

Rush saw the pretty redhead catch sight of his weapon. He noted the way her eyes widened nervously, and how—when she tipped her gaze back up—they stayed that way. Not like a deer in headlights. She was startled, but there was no hint in naivete in her gaze. There was intelligence. Some kind of understanding. And an undercurrent of fear, which made Rush feel surprisingly guilty. Though even acknowledging all of that still didn't prepare him for what happened next.

She *jumped* at him. So quickly and so unexpectedly that he didn't have a chance to react the way he should have. The way he was trained to. Instead, he kind of stumbled backward, flailing his arms a little. He actually had to catch himself on the still-open door of his Lada.

The whole thing only stunned him more. No one ever got the drop on him. Not the police coming up against him when he was undercover, and not the guys he turned in at the end of each case. For the sun-kissed redhead to do it now…it was almost unfathomable.

He expected her to continue with her leap. To knock him to the ground and disarm him. So it was another surprise when she simply used her advantage to turn and run. Her flip-flops smacked against the ground in an almost comical way. She cast a final, heartbeat-long look over her shoulder, then *leaped* over the ditch and darted into the woods.

"What the *hell* just happened?" Rush growled, staring at the space where the redhead had just disappeared.

Before he could come up with a logical explanation for the way she'd run off rather than taking the clear advantage, a distinctly feminine, distinctly terrified scream carried out of the foliage. The scream did for Rush what seeing the woman waving at him from the side the road hadn't; it sent his protective instincts into overdrive.

Without a second thought, he set off at a run. His long legs brought him to the ditch, then over it. They carried him through the low brush, then into the trees. There, just inside the first patch of shade, he paused and whipped his head back and forth.

"Hey!" he called, then paused as he realized he didn't have a name to call. "Uh. Red? You out here?"

He wasn't sure if he wanted her to scream again, or not. On the one hand, it would sure as hell help him locate her. Let him know she was alive as well. On the other hand, he didn't have much desire to hear the ear-piercing shriek a second time, and he didn't want her to have to go through whatever it was that caused it again, either.

"Red!" he yelled a little louder.

A faint reply—words, but not ones he could hear

enough to understand—floated up from somewhere just ahead. They had a strange, echoey quality he couldn't quite place. So he took a few steps forward, then paused again.

"You there, Red?"

There was a few seconds of silence before he heard her voice again, a mutter that made Rush wonder if she was really answering him at all.

"I don't know if—" She cut herself off, then added another string of incomplete sentences. "God. What if… no. I just—no."

"Red?" he replied, puzzled this time. "You okay?"

"You know…" said her disembodied voice. "*Some* of us gingers find that nickname offensive."

For no good reason at all, Rush felt the need to ask, "Are *you* one of those gingers?"

She didn't reply immediately, and he could perfectly picture her face—a face he didn't even *know*, for crying out loud—puckering up as she thought about what to say. He could easily imagine her arched brows buckling together in a frown. Even though it was completely impossible in reality, he swore he could practically hear a sigh escaping from her full lips.

"No," she finally called.

"Okay, then, Red," Rush replied. "Keep talking so I can get to you."

The request was met with more silence.

"Now would be good," he prodded.

She did answer this time, but her tone was somehow muted. "Are you going to shoot me?"

"Shoot you?" he echoed before recalling the reason he was chasing her in the first place.

He nearly laughed. Just a few minutes earlier, he'd

been furious at himself for leaving her on the side of the road. Then *more* furious at himself for being weak enough to go back. He knew damned well it wasn't because he needed to know why she followed him. Although *that* would've made perfect sense. The real reason was far more basic. Far more *base*.

From the moment he pulled away, Rush couldn't stop seeing flashes of her tanned skin. Her throat. Her shoulder. The thin line between her tied-up T-shirt and the waistband of her pants.

If she'd been a sixty-five-year-old man with a bushy beard and dirty old jogging pants, he wouldn't have turned around. Or maybe he would've just stuck around in the first place. At the very least, he would've saved himself the trouble of the ridiculous inner argument. Yet there he was, standing in the middle of the woods, searching for his stalker and worrying more about her well-being than he was worrying about his own.

And you forgot *all of that?*

"Um. Mr…Sunglasses?" The redhead's voice—a little clearer but still hesitant—dragged him back to the fact that he was supposed to be doing something.

"Mr. Sunglasses?" he repeated, tipping his head to listen for her reply.

"Well," she said, "it was a toss-up between that and Mr. Blue Truck."

"It's a Lada," he corrected as he took a few steps in what he thought was the right direction.

"A what?"

"The 'truck' is actually a Lada."

"Oh. Does that matter?"

"Well, it's not really a truck. It's more of an off-road vehicle."

"It looks like a truck." The statement had a stubborn note that made Rush smile.

"It's not, though," he said. "Technically."

"Technicalities are *that* important?" she asked.

Rush's smile slipped away. The flippant way she said it made him sure it wasn't a dig of some kind. She wasn't aware of his past. She couldn't possibly have a clue about just how much weight a technicality could have in someone's life. In *his* life. But it was still a damned good reminder that he wasn't in Whispering Woods to make friends. He was there to right a decade-and-a-half-old wrong.

"Is there a particular reason you were following me?" he asked. "Or is stalking something you do for fun on Wednesdays?"

"I wasn't following you," she replied.

Her voice sounded impossibly close. Like she should be standing just in front of him.

Rush stopped walking, his eyes narrowing as he searched the dense trees for a sign of her. "You expect me to believe it was a coincidence that you made every turn I made while keeping a few hundred feet behind me?"

"That's…well. Okay. Yeah. I can see how that could seem like stalking," she said. "I mean. I *was* following you. But I wasn't following *you*. If that makes sense."

Weirdly…it did.

"Are you telling me all of this is because you took a damned wrong turn?" he asked.

"I was lost. It happens." She said it like a shrug.

He considered it. He supposed she could be telling a story to cover up her true intentions. He had plenty of experience with liars, though, and if the redhead *was* one, she had to be damned near perfect at it. The thing that really tipped him in favor of believing her was her scream. He was damned sure it'd been genuine.

"Are you still there?" she called.

"Yeah. I'm still here. And I'm pretty sure *you're* still lost." He took two more steps.

"I'm not lost," she told him. "I'm right down—"

Whatever else she said was swept away as Rush took another step, then *fell*.

Not over.

Not in a tumble or a trip.

Down.

An undignified holler and a stream of curses escaped his mouth. His back bumped painfully over dirt and roots and God knew what else and he scraped his way—down, down, down—into what appeared to be a *pit* in the middle of the forest floor. At the bottom, he hit the ground hard enough to rattle his teeth and cut away his breath. Remarkably, he was sure he wasn't otherwise hurt.

He tried to inhale. To regain some sense of control. Instead, when he opened his eyes, the oxygen whipped out of his lungs again. The redhead sat in front of him, and her hair had ripped out of its bun, her lips were parted in surprise, and her gaze—the biggest, bluest one he'd ever seen—was fixed on him. Drawing him in. Holding him there. It gave Rush the strangest conflict of emotion he'd ever experienced.

Part of him was angry all over again. This woman, whose name he didn't even know, had ruined his whole day. More than ruined it. She'd sent him barreling needlessly through the back roads that surrounded Whispering Woods. Then somehow got him to set aside reason and self-preservation in the name of coming back for her. Both of which stopped him from meeting with Jesse

Garibaldi and pared down his chances of making the headway he'd been hoping to make. As if that wasn't bad enough, she now had him stuck in a literal hole. Probably eight feet down.

But in spite of it all, another, surprisingly forceful part of him wondered if being lost in her eyes might actually be worth it.

The small space was suddenly much smaller. And for a several moments, the forced intimacy was almost overwhelming. Crouched down the way they were, there was only room for a few scant inches between Alessandra and the man who'd slid to a stop just in front of her. In fact, the space between their knees was nearly nonexistent. Alessandra could feel the heat of his body, the air a conduit from the denim of his jeans to the cotton of her pants. She was sure that the slightest shift would result in a touch. And for some reason, the idea sent her heart thumping.

You should be scared, a small voice in her head pointed out. *The man has a gun. And he's probably even less impressed now than he was when he pulled up in the truck.*

Unconsciously, she dropped her gaze to the holster at his hip. The weapon was still there. But it didn't worry her. Mostly because she spied something that was a greater concern. Something that should probably have been the *first* thing she realized. Something that seemed impossible to have missed, even in the wild, dirt-flying moment.

The man's fall had caused an automatic reaction on her part. She'd shot out a hand, maybe to steady him, maybe to reassure him, it was hard to say. Either way, the result was the same. Her fingers were wrapped around his wrist. And for the life of her, Alessandra couldn't get her brain to make them unfurl to release him.

She drew in a sharp breath as she tried to make her hand cooperate. The inhale was a mistake. Her nose immediately filled with a woodsy, masculine scent. It mingled with the smell of damp, loose dirt. And even though Alessandra had been an ocean girl her whole life—raised on the beaches of the Washington coast—and loved the salt-tinged ocean air, the pleasant, earthy aroma struck a chord somewhere inside her.

Startled by the sensation, she jerked her head up, which earned her the first full view of the truck driver's face. He was no less attractive up close, either. And there was something about his appearance that perfectly matched his scent.

In the somewhat muted light—filtered and cooled by the trees overhead—she could see that his eyes were deep, deep brown. The color of freshly brewed coffee. Alessandra's favorite indulgence. A steaming cup on a cool morning. They were just as warm and inviting, too. She'd also been right about his age. In spite of the sweep of gray across his temple and the matching smattering of white in his beard, he definitely wasn't much over thirty, if at all.

Alessandra's stare fell to the slash of pink that cut through his thick stubble. *His lips.* Not excessively full, but somehow appealing. She could easily picture them curling up in a smile. Parting as he laughed at some piece of dry wit. And—in a surprising turn of her mind—she could imagine the feel of them, too. Soft but firm. Warm like his skin under her fingers.

Embarrassed, Alessandra jerked her eyes away from

his mouth. But when her gaze found his eyes again, she saw that the warmth she'd spied before was gone. In its place was careful neutrality.

A mask, she thought, even though she had no reason to assume a single thing about the stranger's state of mind. *Or maybe a shield.*

But when he spoke, it was with just enough antagonism that she suspected she was right.

"Why in God's name didn't you *warn* me?" he growled.

"I did scream," she reminded him, at last able to drop her hand from his wrist.

"Yeah. In a way that made me think you'd been attacked. Not in a way that made me think, 'Hey, I fell into a hole, so be careful.' Which might've been more prudent."

"Prudence wasn't foremost on my mind."

"No?"

"No. I was a little preoccupied with not wanting to get shot."

"Is there some reason why someone you've never met might want to shoot you?"

Try as she might, Alessandra couldn't stop her mind from slipping to the note and to everything that she'd experienced since finding it. And it made the question strike a nerve.

"Is there a reason why you might *pull* a gun on someone you've never met?" she countered.

He didn't react, except to divert the conversation from the question by tipping his face toward the opening above them and muttering, "I need to get out of here."

"I think you mean *we* need to get out of here," Alessandra corrected, inching back so she could push herself to her feet and look up. "Because it's definitely going to take two of us."

He grunted an acknowledgment, then stood up as well. And even though the opposite should've been true, it made the space between them smaller. Or maybe it was just an illusion, created by the fact that now, instead of sitting across from him, she was standing nearly flush against him. They weren't touching, but she could still feel his strength. He was compact but solid. Probably just barely topping six feet—not that much taller than her own five-foot-nine height. But his body had a palpable denseness. Like every bit of him packed a muscle-bound punch. It was impossible not to be aware of it.

Alessandra tried anyway. She stared up for a second more, and a solution popped to mind. What she needed was a good old-fashioned boost. Of course, getting one would involve deliberately being in physical contact with the gruff stranger. Being near enough to know just how deep that woodsy scent of his ran, and to confirm that he was as solid as she presumed him to be. But it was still the easiest and most logical answer. So she cleared her throat, preparing to suggest it.

But when she spoke, something entirely unplanned came out instead. "I feel like I need to tell you something. In the name of transparency. Because it's my fault you're down here. And if I *don't* say something, then I feel like I'm doing you a disservice."

His brown eyes were unreadable when he looked down at her, but he was near enough that she could feel the slight increase in tension in his body.

"All right," he said evenly. "Tell me."

"It was kind of a lie," Alessandra replied.

"What was?"

"I've never met a ginger who minded being called Red."

He stared at her. "Why'd you lie about it?"

She drew in a breath. "I was trying to make a personal connection."

"I'm afraid you're going to have to back it up and explain that."

"You know…so you'd have to ask my name. And if you asked my name, then you might feel less inclined to…uh…kill me."

"Kill you?"

"If you happened to be some kind of hired killer."

His eyebrows lifted marginally, and she swore his lips twitched with a hint of amusement. "If I *was* a hired killer, and I was hired to kill *you*, wouldn't I already know your name?"

Alessandra sagged a little. "I didn't say I thought it through very well."

Now one of his eyebrows went even higher, and his response was flat. "Unless I was hired to kill someone else, and you're a witness. And therefore collateral damage."

She stood up straighter, her mouth going dry as her eyes dropped to his weapon once more. Why hadn't that occurred to her?

Maybe because everything you think you know about killers is based on questionable late-night crime dramas on TV?

"Thinking about trying to wrestle it away from me?" he asked in a low voice.

Her eyes jerked up, and she knew her answer was both too quick and too emphatic. "No!"

"Good. Because you wouldn't be successful. And I'd hate to accidentally get shot in the foot."

"I wouldn't…" She trailed off as she caught another twitch of his lips. "You're just making fun of me, aren't you?"

His face stayed straight. "I'm actually more concerned for your safety now than I was when I thought you might've been eaten by a bear."

"You *are* mocking me. But I don't care. It's more normal to not know how contract killing works."

"Hmm."

"What?"

"You have to admit. It's not really normal at all to assume someone *is* a contract killer."

Alessandra pressed her lips together, forced her mind not to dwell, then sighed and said, "Normal's relative, isn't it?"

"So I hear."

There was a grimace in his words, but he didn't elaborate on what he meant. And before Alessandra could inquire about it—and she *was* strangely curious about him and about what his normal was—he turned his attention away from her and back to the opening above.

"What do you think?" he asked.

She craned her neck up to follow his gaze. "I think you should give me a boost so I can climb out."

"Then what? You find a branch, hang it down and pull me up?"

"It works in the movies."

His eyes found hers again. "So it's safe to assume you believe everything you see on TV or in the theater?"

Alessandra's face warmed. "Are you always this antagonistic?"

"Only when I'm not out shooting strangers."

"Funny."

"Good to know that you think so." His voice was dry. "I've been told my humor's too macabre for most."

He brought his gaze back to her. His eyes were cool. Assessing. It made her wonder if she'd just imagined that glimpse of heat in them before. She started to shift from one foot to the other, then stopped abruptly as her knee brushed his.

"Sorry," she mumbled.

Up went one of those eyebrows of his. "You're going to have to do more than bump into me if you want a hand getting up there."

Even though there was no possible way he meant the words to have the dark, sexy edge that they did, Alessandra couldn't help but hear some innuendo. And truthfully, it gave her a little thrill.

She forced out a breath and made herself speak in a neutral voice. "Does this mean you're buying into my idea?"

"It means I'm wondering if I can trust you to stick around long enough to make sure I get out, too."

"I wouldn't leave you here."

"No?"

"Even if I wanted to, I couldn't. My car's in the ditch, remember?"

"That's true. But I've got some rope in the Lada. Keys are in there, too, so…" He shrugged.

She rolled her eyes. "Right. I'll just steal your not-really-a-truck truck, and I'll be on my way."

"You assumed I was an assassin. I don't think suggesting you might commit a crime of opportunity is on the same level."

"You're not going to let that go, are you?"

"Probably not," he admitted. "Come closer."

She started to tell him she didn't think she *could* get closer—there was barely breathing room as it was—but he made the first move anyway. He dropped to a crouch, threaded his fingers together at knee level, then cleared his throat and looked up expectantly.

"Step up, bend a bit, put your hand on my shoulder, and let me know when you're stable," he told her.

Alessandra only hesitated for a second before lifting a foot and pressing it into his hands. She took another moment to put her hand on his back, though. It seemed more personal. More intimate. And unsurprisingly, when she *did* touch finally touch him, he was rock solid.

And warm.

She shook off the too-pleased voice in her head and pushed up from the ground. She expected at least some give, but his palms didn't move.

"You good?" he asked with no sign of strain in his voice.

"I'm up," she confirmed.

"Okay," he replied. "Move your other hand to the side of hole. Make sure it's firm, but keep your hand loose enough that you can let your fingers crawl up as I hoist you."

"You're going to hoist me?" She didn't know why she sounded so surprised.

"That's generally what happens when someone gives someone else a boost," he said drily.

"Right," she muttered. "Okay. I'm ready."

"I think I can get you high enough that you should be able to rest your elbows on the ground above us. Put a knee or a foot on my shoulder if you have to."

"All right."

"Here we go." He pushed her up, slowly but easily. "Hey, Red?"

"Yes?"

"I forgot to ask you…what's your real name?"

She started to answer him, but a familiar, masculine voice from overhead beat her to it.

"Alessandra," it announced.

And it startled her so badly that she wobbled, then tumbled straight back down into the truck driver's arms.

Chapter 3

Hearing his boss answer the question from above nearly made Rush drop the redhead—*Alessandra,* he told himself—straight to the ground. At the last second, he managed to stick his arms out to snatch her from the air. Her body hit his hard enough that he stumbled back and let out an "Oof!" and the noise earned an echoing chuckle from Jesse Garibaldi.

Rush was just glad that the other man was too far up to see his expression. He was sure the wave of displeasure and unease that hit him at the man's unexpected appearance had slipped past his usual mask. As he worked to get the carefully indifferent look back in place, he realized a little belatedly that while Garibaldi might not have spied the look, the woman in his arms definitely had. Her expression told him as much. It was easy to see the curiosity in her baby blues. Easy to read the question on her partially parted lips. She was looking right at him, far too interested for comfort's sake.

And she knows Jesse Garibaldi.

That changed everything. Even if Rush couldn't really say what "everything" meant to start out with. It was enough to make his mouth set into a thin line, and he eased her to ground, then directed his attention up, speaking in the gruff, slightly angry voice he knew Garibaldi would expect.

"You just gonna stand up there and laugh at me, boss?" he called without looking up. "Or send down some help?"

"What?" Jesse replied. "Looked like you were doing fine without me."

"Then why the hell are you here?"

"Hmm. Now that's a damned fine question."

Garibaldi stepped back and issued an order to someone while Rush mentally gritted his teeth. It really was a damned fine question. How the hell had Garibaldi tracked him there? And why? Who was Alessandra to the other man? Rush didn't get a chance to come up with any answers before a pair of thick arms appeared overhead.

"Send my friend Al up again," Garibaldi ordered. "Ernest here will tug her out without breaking one of her nails. Or one of his own, for that matter."

Rush forced out a dry laugh. "I'm sure that's foremost on Ernest's mind."

He turned back to Alessandra—for some reason it grated on him that Garibaldi had a nickname for her—and unceremoniously dropped down, slid his arms around her calves, then lifted her straight up. She let out a little squeak. She wobbled, too, and her hands slammed to his shoulders to steady herself. The effect was imme-diate. Overwhelming.

Her summery smell—light sweat, a kiss of salt and something else entirely—wafted up to him. *Through* him, somehow. Like he could taste it and absorb it. He almost wished he could do both for real.

Then her hands released his shoulders to stretch up to the man who waited above, and things grew even worse. With the motion, her shirt lifted, exposing her stomach. And just like that, it—*she*—was pressed to Rush's face.

The smell of her had permeated his senses, but her skin…it seemed to permeate his very existence. Soft. Buttery. He couldn't escape it. Hell. He didn't want to. He wanted to turn his face so that his lips would meet her bared flesh instead of his cheek. He wished—like a crazy man, he was sure—that he didn't have the beard so there was no barrier between them.

Then she was gone. Yanked up by Ernest and his meaty paws. Like an even crazier man, Rush felt a rush of resentment. Not quite jealousy. Not that he was going to admit, anyway. There was definite, undeniable annoy-ance at the loss of contact, though.

Been too long since you went out with a woman, eh, Atkinson?

He answered the silent, self-directed question in a mutter. "Clearly."

"Did you say something to me?" Alessandra's voice carried down, and when Rush looked up, he saw that she was hanging over the hole.

"Nope," he lied. "Just eager to get the hell out."

Garibaldi appeared beside the redhead, a sly smile visible on his face. And just as Rush did nearly every time he saw the man, he fought a bubbling fury. Garibaldi looked just like anyone else. Nondescript, even. Brown hair, tidily cut. Smooth face. Casual but expensive clothes.

It only made Rush resent him more. The man who was responsible for his father's death ought to stick out. He didn't deserve the exterior normalcy. Or even the smooth voice he directed Rush's way now.

"You want Ernest to try to pull you up, too?" he asked.

"I think I'd rather dig my way own way out," Rush said, covering his distaste by bending over to snag his hat and sunglasses from the dirt.

When he'd shoved both items back on, he looked up and saw that Garibaldi and Alessandra had slipped out of sight. A moment later, though, a thick piece of rope dropped over the edge. Rush gave it a tug, found it secure, and started to pull himself up. It reminded him unpleasantly of high school PE. Hand over hand, he climbed to the top, waving off Ernest's offer of help.

"Well," said Garibaldi. "Now I know that sitting at the bottom of a pit doesn't help your mood any."

Rush didn't even have to try to curl his lip. "Think it would improve yours?"

His boss didn't react. It was the kind of relationship they'd built over the last few weeks. Rush playing up the role of bad-tempered, slightly resentful underling— which barely scraped the surface of how he really felt about being near the other man—who always pushed the envelope. His tough-guy act was supposed to be a way into Garibaldi's good graces without the need for brownnosing. Some men were insecure in their power and appreciated a suck-up, but it'd taken only a few days to figure out that wasn't the case with Jesse Garibaldi. The man wanted people he could trust not to fold under pressure, and he was secure enough in his own hold over his shady business that he didn't worry about being personally challenged.

It was all a game. Rush knew it. He was sure the other man thought of it that way, too.

But the difference between his awareness and mine is that I actually know what the object of the game is. He just thinks he does.

Rush adjusted his ball cap and met his boss's eyes, deliberately avoiding a glance in Alessandra's direction. No need to make an overt acknowledgment of her presence. If Jesse Garibaldi had something to say about her, he would.

"So. I missed our meeting," Rush stated instead.

Garibaldi chuckled, then nodded toward the redhead. "Actually, it looks like you brought the meeting to me."

Rush flicked a quick, indifferent glance in the woman's direction. "I always thought you preferred brunettes."

"Hey!" Alessandra protested. "I know what you're implying, and I don't—"

Garibaldi cut her off with another laugh. "Relax, Al. I'm afraid Rush's manners are a little lacking, and his humor's off-color."

"You mean he's a giant jerk?" the redhead snapped.

Now Rush did turn to face her, raising an eyebrow and speaking before he could think to stop himself. "A giant jerk who followed you into a hole in the ground just to save you."

He tensed and waited for her to point out that he'd *fallen* in. Maybe to point out his somewhat foolish assumption that he'd thought she was tailing him through the woods. Instead, she scrunched up her face a little and turned to Garibaldi. Which irked Rush in the same way her nickname had. The two obviously knew each other well.

"I'm sorry, Jesse," she said. "I wasn't trying to insult your friend. Even though *he* insulted *me*."

"Did he really jump in there to save you?" Garibaldi replied. "Sure doesn't seem like his style. In fact, I don't know that I've ever seen this man do something that wasn't to his own direct benefit."

Rush snorted. "How am I supposed to get ahead if I'm always thinking about someone else?"

"True enough," his boss said easily, then smiled at Alessandra. "Want to explain how you wound up in the hole in the first place?"

Rush stood back and waited—again—for the redhead to tell Garibaldi what had happened. Instead, she more or less left out his part in the events. She explained that she'd been lost, and that the final wrong turn had resulted in disaster.

Rush wanted to narrow his eyes. He had a feeling she was deliberately leaving out any mention of unintentional stalking and accusations of hit man status. He just didn't know *why*. She sure as hell didn't seem like the type who'd be interested in saving him a bit of embarrassment. Not that he couldn't or wouldn't play it off if she brought it up.

But still...

His gut told him she was hedging around the exact circumstances for some other reason. It made him more than curious, and he was so busy musing over it that he all but tuned out what Garibaldi was saying. It was only a very specific sentence that drew him back out of his own head and into the conversation.

"…so the two of you should be nice and cozy in the cabin," his boss was saying. "It's not going to be a problem, is it?"

Rush felt his forehead crease. "What?"

"You hit your head on the way down, Atkinson, or what?" the other man asked.

"Feel like I must've," Rush muttered.

He glanced at Alessandra. She had a strange mix of emotions on her face. She looked nervous and apologetic, and both of those were laced with a hint of defiance. It only made Rush frown harder.

He sighed. "Sorry, boss. Back it up. Who's staying in a cabin? And why?"

Garibaldi gave him a truly speculative look, and Rush straightened his shoulders a little, cursing the fact that he was giving the other man a reason to question even a single aspect of his cover. He couldn't afford doubt. He needed his so-called boss to trust him. To rely on him. To give him access to whatever the hell he was working on, so that Rush could catch him in the act and promptly throw him in jail.

It was Alessandra who broke the silence by clearing her throat and speaking up. "Jesse was explaining that things are pretty busy in town now that tourist season is in full swing. He's got some business associates staying at *his* place. Which he forgot when he invited me up for the week."

"Total brain lapse," Garibaldi confirmed. "Anyway. I feel terrible, but Al drove five hours from up near Seattle, and I didn't want her to turn around and drive home, which is why I texted—or tried to, anyway—directions to one of my private mountainside cabins instead."

Rush said nothing. His mind was momentarily overloaded with more questions and concerns. There was pretty much zero possibility that Garibaldi had "forgotten" the hordes of people in town. The man had his fingers in every piece of tourism pie in all of Whispering Woods. From the five-star lodge to the seasonal rentals throughout the town to the companies that ran off-road tours in the summer and taught ski lessons in the winter, there wasn't a single damned thing that didn't have his name attached to it somewhere. He even owned 90 percent of the real estate along Main Street. It was all a front. A clever way to hide the money he brought in through his drug smuggling business. But he was far, far too smart to be genuinely unaware of the things that allowed him to do what he wanted. So why would Garibaldi invite a "friend" into town, only to not be able to offer her a place to stay? Who was she to his boss? Who was she, in regard to his boss's business?

A shadowy lick of wrongness crept in, and Rush had an urge to roll his shoulders to rid himself of it. He forced himself to stay still, though, and spoke in a dismissive voice. "Still not seeing what this has to do with me."

Alessandra's cheeks were a bit pink. "Jesse thought I might be more comfortable with a tour guide."

Rush went silent again. The lick of wrongness became a roar of malcontent that demanded attention. Every other oddity aside...why would his boss invite this woman here only to immediately pass her off? Rush kept his lips pressed together until Garibaldi clapped him companionably on the back.

"Told you I had a special assignment for you, didn't I?" said the other man.

This time, Rush didn't hide his grimace of dissatisfaction. "Not in the slightest what I had in mind."

Garibaldi's eyes turned sharp. "Maybe not. But it might be just the leg up you *are* after."

Rush didn't like the dirty tingle down his spine. He'd made no secret of his desire to move up in Garibaldi's world, but he couldn't think of a good or pleasant reason for this particular assignment to help that along.

He turned to Alessandra, expecting her to be an ally in the protest. After all, she'd come a fair distance only to be handed over to a stranger by the very man she'd come to visit. But if she had objections, she didn't voice them. The oddity of it struck Rush almost as hard as the feeling that something was very wrong. He tapped his thumb against his knee. Just once. Then nodded.

"All right," he said slowly. For show. Like he was doing everyone a favor. "I'll do it. I'll play tour guide. But it damned well better be worth my while."

He spun on his heel, grinding his teeth together with very real frustration. Dirt kicked up around him, but he didn't let the need to cough take over. He didn't look to see how closely Garibaldi, Alessandra and Ernest followed him, either. Though he wished he could.

He wanted to spin, wipe the speckles of dirt from his face and demand to know what the hell was going on. He knew too well that any kind of reaction would've been out of place with his projected persona. If Garibaldi was testing him, he wanted to pass. So he just kept going, shoving his way through the woods with vigor.

When he'd almost reached his Lada, though, he realized his trek had been uselessly vicious. A quick turn sideways told him that the two other men and the redhead had matched his pace. They were just coming out of the trees. Alessandra even smiled as Garibaldi said something and lifted a branch for her to step under.

Yet another spasm of irritation hit Rush.

He strode the rest of the way toward his truck, and made it as far as putting his fingers on the door handle before Garibaldi's voice stopped him.

"Hang on, Atkinson," said his boss. "Need to get you something from my car. Meet me over there in a sec."

Wary—but not willing to take a chance on arguing—Rush dropped his arm and turned to the nondescript sedan on the other side of the road. As he walked toward it, he pretended not to hear the pleasant chatting that carried to his ears as Ernest retrieved Alessandra's bags from her car. He ignored the big man when he came to the car and climbed into the driver's seat, too. He also didn't look over as Garibaldi promised the pretty redhead a tow truck ASAP, then excused himself. In fact, he didn't move at all until his boss took a position beside him and cleared his throat.

"I know you're not thrilled about this," said the other man.

Rush grunted. "Nope. But you're the boss. I'm just here to do as I'm told."

"We both know that's not how you work."

"We both know I *work,* period."

"True enough. You're an exemplary employee."

Internally, Rush snorted at the use of the word *employee*.

Aloud, he said, "An exemplary tour guide, you mean?"

"I need someone I can really trust here, Atkinson," Garibaldi said.

Rush decided some skepticism was in order. "Gotta say that I honestly don't get it, boss. You said she's a friend and that you invited her up. If you're too busy to show her around, that's fine. I'm on board. And you know I'm not in the habit of questioning the stuff you want done…but I'm just not seeing why this is so significant."

Wordlessly, Garibaldi cast a nearly blank look toward the Lada. Rush followed his gaze. Alessandra sat inside the vehicle now. Her eyes were forward, but it was easy to see that she was nervous, even from as many feet away as they were. She had her plump bottom lip sucked in, and her fingers twirled a piece of hair, then released it, then twirled it again.

An unusual twist of worry pricked at Rush.

"You sure this isn't something you want to do yourself, boss?" he asked.

The other man reached out and opened the car door before he replied, "I'm sure. I really prefer to keep my hands clean."

Rush's throat constricted. "What do you mean?"

Garibaldi smiled a dark smile, then leaned a little closer. "Take her to the cabin where you were supposed to meet me. Find out what she knows about my operation. Then take care of her."

Chapter 4

Alessandra breathed out, watching as Rush and Jesse continued their conversation. She was sure her instincts should be screaming at her to argue with what was about to happen. To protest against being carted away by a stranger. But something in her gut told her that Rush was the safer bet. It was strange. She'd known Jesse Garibaldi since they were kids. Their fathers had been buddies. Yet seeing him today—hearing him call her the old nickname—made her want to walk very quickly in the other direction. And that feeling that his invitation wasn't a coincidence solidified even more.

Are you sure that's not just a bias created by Dad's letter? she asked herself.

As she thought about it, she bit her bottom lip so hard it hurt. Truthfully, it was a possibility. The last thirteen days definitely had her on edge. Suspicious of everyone and everything.

Except for a certain not-a-truck truck driver.

It was true. As uneasy as she'd been about the first sight of his weapon, her crazy run into the woods had been a knee-jerk reaction more than anything else.

She sneaked another quick look in his direction. In *their* direction. Then quickly looked away as she realized both men were looking at her, too. Jesse with a smile that didn't quite touch his eyes, and the brown-eyed stranger—whose first name Alessandra still didn't know—from behind his sunglasses. She assumed his look was displeased. Brooding, even. Because as much as he'd tried to be dismissive about being ordered to be her own personal tour guide, she was 100 percent sure that he hadn't been happy about it.

And why is Jesse ordering anyone around, anyway? she wondered.

She fought an urge to look yet again. The last time she'd seen him was at her mom's funeral, and the interaction had been brief and specific to the situation. Words of condolence and a promise of getting together more often than they had in the past. But nothing had ever come of it. In fact, until now, Alessandra hadn't even known where Jesse was living. And if it hadn't been for the circumstances driving her forward, she was sure she would've found some excuse not to come at all. Aside from the friendship their fathers shared, she wasn't sure they had enough in common to make maintaining the connection a priority.

Jesse was a few years older than she was, and even when they were younger—she a kid and he a teen—she'd regarded him with a strange kind of awe. Jesse had always been clean-cut. Mild-mannered and average-looking. Ready with a smile. A go-with-the-flow guy.

But she'd seen him manipulate his own father so easily that no one in the room noticed. She'd been sure he could tell someone—anyone, maybe—that black was red and red was white and that they would just buy it. He that was slick. That smart. Always determined to get his way. And rarely *didn't* get it.

She, on the other hand, was anything but slick. She spoke her mind when she shouldn't. Her mom had told her ad nauseam that her middle name ought to have been "stubborn," and Alessandra couldn't deny it. She'd turn down a deal if it didn't sit right, and would probably do so to the detriment of her own livelihood. That wasn't to say that she was over-the-top altruistic. It was just that she let her emotions lead it all—her heart, her head and her mouth on far too many occasions. It was even how she ran her surf shop. On gut instinct rather than savvy.

Used to run.

She flinched at the mental reminder. Eventually, the insurance would kick in. Eventually, she would get her home and her shop and her life back. She'd rebuild.

"But that's not the point," she said out loud to herself. *But what* is *the point?*

She wasn't really sure. Her eyes flicked to the rear-view mirror. The men were focused on each other now, instead of her, thank goodness. Discussing something intently.

She breathed out. Maybe the point was just that she didn't feel comfortable with Jesse. That slight bit of awe she'd felt as a kid had morphed into something else. Intimidation, maybe? He still had that same easygoing demeanor. It was clear that he'd put his wits to good use, and his business in Whispering Woods was thriving. The welcome sign on the way into town even had his company logo on it. But something felt off. The gut that Alessandra used for her business transactions was screaming it. Jesse had *lackeys*, for crying out loud. Like Ernest, the terrifyingly burly man who seemed to communicate in grunts. And Mr. Sunglasses, who she realized was currently striding toward the not-truck with a scowl.

"Crap," she muttered, quickly turning her gaze to her lap.

But her concern over being caught staring was unfounded. As the sour-faced man flung open the door and climbed in, he didn't even glance her way. He didn't speak as he started the truck, either. And the negativity was rolling off him like a dark cloud. If Alessandra hadn't been so worried about his reaction, she might've tried to roll down the window in an attempt to cleanse the air.

She knew she should probably be asking for some more details about their destination. How far away was it? Would there be a phone? Other amenities? Would anyone else be staying there, too, or was she stuck with the stone-faced—but undeniably attractive—driver? But her usually overexcited tongue stuck to the roof of her mouth. And after a few more moments of weighted silence, she settled for closing her eyes and performing one of her mom's favorite breathing exercise instead.

In-in-out. In-in-out.

Deep in.

Out-out-in. Out-out-in.

It was almost enough to distract her. Or it might've been, if the man called Atkinson hadn't chosen to cut through her moment with a throat-clear. At the sound, Alessandra's eyes flew open, and her head swiveled toward her reluctant tour guide. He was staring straight ahead, his hands tight on the steering wheel.

"So which is it?" he said, his abruptly gruff tone making her blink.

"Which is what?" she replied.

"Al, or Alessandra?" He sounded annoyed by his own question.

Alessandra frowned. "What?"

"Your name. Which do you prefer?"

"No. I mean. I know what you're asking, but—" She cut herself off and shook her head. "Never mind. A lot of people call me Al."

"Like Jesse."

"Yes."

He went silent again. Brooding again.

The moments ticked by, the air thickening with some unnameable tension.

Alessandra breathed out and started to close her eyes once more. But her companion spoke again, his tone just as irritated as it had been a minute earlier.

"Think I'll just stick with calling you Red," he told her.

"Fine by me," she replied curtly.

She tried again to shut her eyes, but then narrowed them at him instead.

"What about you?" she asked.

"What *about* me?"

"What do you prefer to be called? Mr. Sunglasses or Surly Stranger?"

"I'm not surly," he said.

"You are," she argued. "But that wasn't an answer to my question."

"It's Rush."

"What's a rush?"

He tipped his head in her direction for the briefest second, and she could swear his lips were twitching with amusement. "My name."

Her face warmed. "Oh. That's…"

"Unusual," he filled in.

"Yes."

She noticed that his hands had relaxed a little.

"My dad named me," he explained. "He said my mom was always in a hurry. Couldn't even wait until she got to the hospital to have me. I was born in a convenience store parking lot."

Alessandra surprised herself by laughing. "That can't possibly be true."

"I'm afraid it is." His tone was rueful now, rather than resentful. "Probably the source of my surliness."

"I thought you *weren't* surly."

"Yeah, well…maybe just today. It hasn't exactly been ideal for me."

"Me neither. Falling into a hole then being pawned off on a stranger wasn't exactly on my to-do list for the day."

He paused, one thumb moving restlessly on the wheel. "What *was* on your list?"

The question was casual, and the paranoid part of Alessandra's brain asked if it might be a little *too* off-hand.

Relax, she said to herself. *It's just small talk.*

She let out a silent exhale. "Well. I guess I assumed that Jesse would show me the town. Maybe take me for a bite to eat so we could catch up."

His thumb stopped its movement, and his hands squeezed tighter. "You're old friends?"

Alessandra frowned. She was starting to think his fingers were his tell.

"Our parents were," she said. "What about you? How long have you known Jesse?"

The fingers held their knuckle-whitening position. "Just a few weeks. I was looking for work, and a mutual acquaintance referred me."

"So you're in property development, too?"

"Hardly." His hands relaxed, just marginally.

"What do you do, then?" Alessandra asked.

Tight fingers. "Anything your friend asks me to, apparently."

The words had an undeniably ominous ring to them, and Alessandra couldn't suppress a shiver. What instructions had Jesse left him with? And just how far would he take "anything"?

She swallowed nervously and tried to push down the need to open the door and jump out. "Sorry."

Rush turned his head her way, and she sensed some heavy scrutiny behind those mirrored sunglasses of his.

"Sorry?" he repeated.

"I'm sure you've got better things to do," she replied. "So if you want to just leave me at the cabin or whatever, I get it."

"And risk getting fired?" He said it lightly, but his hands gave him away—they were so tense that it looked painful.

She forced a laugh. "I'm sure Jesse wouldn't fire you for not wanting babysit me."

"Oh, yeah? When was the last time you told him he couldn't have what he wanted?"

Alessandra couldn't help but notice that the question reflected her own earlier thoughts on Jesse. But she didn't comment on her wholehearted agreement.

"Honestly," she said instead, "if I'd known he was going to be too busy to have me here, I wouldn't have come."

As soon as the words were out, she realized they weren't true. Her reason for accepting Jesse's invitation had nothing to do with the man himself, and everything to do with her need for answers about her father's note. Nothing would've kept her away. It occurred to her—a little belatedly—that Rush might be able to give her a clue. Or at the very least, help her decide whether or not Jesse, the note and her father's death really were connected. The way she was starting to dread they might be.

She tried to think of a way to steer the conversation in a direction that would flow naturally in the direction she'd need it to take. But for some reason, she couldn't think of a subtle segue into, *Hey. Does your boss's business include anything shady? You know...like the untimely death of an old friend and a creepy, postmortem note that led me here?* Thankfully, though, she didn't have to. Rush kind of the led things there himself.

"So you were saying that your parents and Jesse's parents were friends?" he said, picking up the previous thread with that the same too-casual tone.

She nodded; there was nothing to hide about their shared pasts. "Our dads were, anyway. Before they each died."

Rush's jaw ticked, and a quick look at his hands told Alessandra that the topic was far from comfortable for him. It made her curious, and for an odd second, knowing why seemed more important than anything else.

"My dad was killed in an accident," she added, carefully gauging his reaction. "Jesse's was killed in a police incident a little while before that. Less than a month apart, actually."

Now Rush's profile was as rigid as his grip. "Sorry to hear."

"It was a long time ago now. But it was definitely a hard time in both our lives."

"It made you close?"

The question sounded almost like an accusation, and Alessandra frowned, but shook her head and answered honestly anyway. "No. I was only eleven—almost twelve—at the time. Jesse was fifteen or sixteen. So not a ton of common ground."

Rush persisted. "Still. A loss like that could create a bond in spite of an age gap."

"I guess it could. But I had my mom, and we leaned on each other a lot. And Jesse…" She trailed off, thinking about it.

What *had* happened to him after his dad died? Alessandra had fuzzy memories of the senior Garibaldi's funeral. She knew Jesse had been there. She recalled specifically that he was a pallbearer, and that he'd given a brief eulogy. And after that, she couldn't remember much of anything. It seemed funny, now, that she hadn't really put much thought into what he'd gotten up to. Her own father's passing had happened so quickly after, and her plate had been full of her own problems. The only thing she *really* had a clear memory of was a phone conversation she'd overheard about a year after the fact. Right that second, she could actually recall it quite vividly. She'd walked into the kitchen to grab an apple from the bowl on the counter. Her mom, dressed in her typical flowing skirt and embroidered blouse, had been standing with her back to Alessandra.

"I don't know," her mom said into the phone. *"Jesse always seemed like a good kid. But my client was utterly sure that she saw him."*

There was a pause while the person on the other end said something Alessandra couldn't hear.

Then her mom shook her head. "No. She saw an old photo of the kids and us on my desk. I think she commented by accident."

Another pause. Another headshake.

"No," her mom said. *"A court stenographer."*

At that moment, Alessandra had accidentally dropped her apple to the floor, and her mom had turned, then quickly diverted the phone conversation to a new topic. At the time, it had piqued Alessandra's interest only mildly. She'd had other things going on. A new, cute boy at school who she and her best friend both liked. A dismal grade in PE. And all the other general drama of being thirteen.

Maybe you should've paid a little more attention.

"Hey, Red? You still with me?" Rush prodded, and Alessandra realized she'd been sitting in silence for a little too long.

"I'm here," she replied quickly.

"You didn't finish your sentence," he told her. "Jesse what?"

"I don't know," she admitted. "With his dad gone, it couldn't have been easy. I think he was in a bit of trouble of some kind."

"Trouble." It was a flat statement rather than a question, and it was followed by silence, which made Alessandra turn her head sharply toward him.

Is it just me, she thought, *or did this conversation get a little more intense than the average bit of small talk?*

She waited for him to say something else. Maybe another question that would confirm her thought. But he was quiet, his eyes focused out the windshield. His jaw was still, his firm-looking lips pressed together. He didn't even seem to notice the prolonged look she was giving him.

Her eyes drifted to his hands. They were moving in a pulsing squeeze. Rush was tense—brooding and surly again—no doubt about it.

Alessandra worried at her lower lip with her teeth. What was it that made him like that, over and over? As she stared at his fingers, she realized she'd been subconsciously leaning toward that idea that it was something to do with *her.* Maybe it didn't make a lot of sense. They didn't know each other in the slightest. But he'd seemed extra strained when asking about her nickname. And again when she'd suggested just leaving her at the cabin and told him what she'd thought her plans might be. And a third time when talking about her father's death.

Alessandra had no clue why the details of her life would bother Rush Atkinson. But the evidence seemed to be pointing that way.

But not a second ago, she reminded herself.

His last bit of tension was definitely centered on the idea that Jesse had been in trouble fifteen years earlier.

Why? Then her mind suddenly seized on a different explanation for his repeated little tell, and she wondered why she hadn't seen it before. *It's not me. It's Jesse.*

Jesse's nickname for her. What *Jesse* was going to do with her while she was in town. And *Jesse's* father's death.

It was Rush's boss that made him so tense. But why? What did it mean? And was it in any way helpful to Alessandra's own search for answers?

She opened her mouth—though she wasn't sure exactly what she was going to say because no way could she just come out and ask—but snapped it shut quickly as Rush pulled off the main road and onto a gravel one. It wasn't the change in scenery that gave her pause. After all, she was expecting to be taken to a cabin, and had assumed it wouldn't be right along the street that led into Whispering Woods. What did make her stare was that fact that she *recognized* the scenery. The trees overhead that arched into each other. The wide patches of oddly white rocks on either side of the gravel. And of course, the cabin itself, which flashed into view between the trees.

It was small and made of natural cedar. It sat up on the hills, nestled against the rock, and Alessandra knew for a fact that the veranda in the front was bigger than the building itself, and that there were exactly forty-seven stairs leading up to it. Just like she knew—even though she supposed a lot had probably changed in three decades—that the windows had once held cream-colored curtains, flecked with tiny bluebells, and that the double bed inside had once had a matching duvet. She recalled it perfectly. Because her parents had an entire collage of photos dedicated to the place. It was their honeymoon spot. The same one mentioned in the torn-up, patched-together note.

Chapter 5

As Rush slowed the truck and guided it up the slightly winding road toward the cabin, he stole a quick glance at Alessandra. The expression on her face was enough to make him momentarily forget the frustrated tumble of thoughts related to his pseudo-boss.

The redhead's full lips were parted a little, her body leaned forward. Her baby-blue gaze was intent on the parted trees, and there was definitely recognition in her eyes. He followed her stare and after just a moment, he realized she was staring at the cabin, which peeked through the foliage every few seconds. He sought her face again, confirming that she did look like she knew exactly what to expect.

She's been here before, Rush thought, his mind taking a different turn. *When? With who? Garibaldi?* He paused, irritation heating his neck. *And why the hell does the idea bother me?*

Under the cover of his glasses, he narrowed his eyes, then jerked his attention back to last stretch of road in front of them. He really had no reason to care where Alessandra had been in the past, or whom she'd been with. But that didn't seem to be stopping him from wondering. If he was being honest, it pricked at him, also, that she called the other man by his first name, when everyone under the sun seemed to call him by *Mr. Garibaldi* instead.

Rush gritted his teeth, annoyed at himself for even being annoyed in the first place. He had an urge to step on the gas and floor it until he had no choice but to either slam on the brakes or drive into the hillside.

Yeah, Atkinson. Really mature means of dealing with things.

He gritted his teeth even harder and eased his foot up a little, just to prove that he was perfectly capable of controlling his temper. The Lada slowed to a crawl. Alessandra didn't comment, and another quick look at her told Rush she was still focused on their nearing destination. Which was a good thing. It gave him an extra minute to try to sort through his thoughts in a calm manner.

He'd been steering the conversation toward Garibaldi under the pretense of finding out what she knew about the man's enterprises in Whispering Woods, illegal or otherwise. After all, it *was* what his boss had asked him to do.

Now you're taking Garibaldi's orders to heart? Are you going to kill her, too?

He shoved off the dark sarcasm. Obviously, he had no intention of following through on that particular request. He did, however, need a means around it. A convincing argument. An irrefutable one. If she knew a single damned thing about Garibaldi's opiate business, it was going to be impossible. So Rush had a valid excuse for questioning her. One that lined up with his job and his current mission. If those reasons coincided with Garibaldi's request, then so be it. Hell. It might even buy him a little time, if he could string his boss along with any of what Alessandra said.

Except so far... Rush wasn't sure what to make of the tidbits of information she'd given out. He considered himself more than capable of getting a good, quick read on people. He was pretty damned sure every word out of Alessandra's mouth was the truth, but something felt off. Like her words were true, but her motivation for sharing them was less than straightforward. It made him want to scratch his head.

What was she hiding? He was truly curious.

As they rounded the final piece of road and came up to the flat, packed-dirt driveway in front of the cabin and its tall stairs, he flicked a third glance her way. This time, she was looking right back at him, her baby blues flooded with emotion. It was impossible to say which was most dominant. Worry? Sadness? Fear? He didn't know for sure.

What *wasn't* impossible, though, was to say how her mixed expression affected him. Rush's chest compressed, and before he could stop to think if it was the right thing to do or not, her put the Lada into Park and reached a hand over the console. He clasped her fingers and gave them a squeeze.

She didn't try to pull away. In fact, she clung to his hand. Her skin was soft and warm, and her hand fit just right in his. A jolt of electric attraction shot up from the space where their palms met. The feeling startled Rush so badly that it took him a moment to recall that his touch had a purpose. It got worse when he accidentally drew in a sharp breath. Her sweet, pleasant scent filled his nose in a way that bordered on mouthwatering.

Dammit.

He had to clear his throat of a sudden dryness, and he had to force an impassive tone, too. "You all right over there, Red?"

She offered him a nod that immediately became a headshake.

"I know this cabin," she said, confirming his belief about her honesty.

"You've been here before?" he replied.

"No. But I've seen a dozen pictures of it." Her eyelids sank down, her long red lashes brushing her face as she inhaled. She held on to him even tighter, then murmured something that didn't make any sense. "Glad I put that in storage."

Rush frowned, puzzled. Before he could ask for clarification, though, she opened her eyes again, their blue catching the light and holding him captive as her irises turned the same color as the sky.

"My parents had their honeymoon here," she told him.

Surprised, Rush looked from her to the cabin, then back again. "Here? You're sure?"

"One hundred percent. They talked about it all the time when I was a kid. The way the cabin was built into the hill. The big porch." She paused. "Have you been inside?"

He nodded. "A few times. The boss likes it because it's private."

"I think that's the same reason my parents liked it so

much." A smiled tipped up Alessandra's lips, and she added, "Well. Maybe not *quite* the same."

Rush was distracted by the curve of her mouth. She had an unusual dimple. It wasn't in her cheek. More in the groove beside her smile. He had a nearly unstoppable urge to reach out and caress it. His free hand itched to do it, and he had to order himself not to make the move. When he spoke, though, his words were almost as bad as a touch.

"It *is* a pretty romantic setting," he said.

Alessandra lifted one of her already arched eyebrows and shot a speculative look his way. "It is, isn't it?"

Rush knew he should pull his fingers free. Hell. He shouldn't have been holding her hand in the first place. Damn if he could do it. Instead, he gave her yet another squeeze, then eyed the cabin.

"It's held up well for thirty years," he said.

"Is it nice inside?" she asked. "Does it still have that window in the back that doesn't look at anything except the rock face?"

Rush noted that her expression had changed again. It was wistful and a little hesitant, and he had a need to accommodate her feelings. Maybe it was a random moment of rare softness, or maybe it was brought on by the fact that he'd be equally torn by being allowed a glimpse into his parents' past. There were things he'd like to know, but also plenty he'd rather not be privy to. It actually made his chest ache with a peculiar sense of loss. So he understood her hesitation, and he didn't push Alessandra to jump out and explore the area right away. He could give her a moment and resume his soft interrogation later.

He offered her a nod. "The window's still there. But

it has a little crack up in one corner, and someone fixed it with some kind of epoxy, so there's a jagged yellow line covering that spot."

"Is it ugly? Or does it add character?"

"Definitely character."

"Does the woodstove work?"

"Hope so. Gets cold up here at night."

A long, silent moment hung in the air after Rush said it. He wondered if she felt the same trickle of realization. They were going to be alone in the cabin. Overnight was a strong possibility. It *did* get cold. And there was only one bed inside.

That's not *where you need your mind to be,* Rush told himself.

It was impossible, though, to rid himself of the awareness of the impending circumstances. He could swear that the heat in the Lada rose a few degrees just thinking about it. The fact that Alessandra's thumb started to move back and forth over his hand didn't help things, either.

Stifling a groan—and a true reluctance to let go—Rush pulled his hand free and said, "Think you're ready to go check it out?"

Alessandra's gaze dropped to their separated hands, then lifted to his face, and the flash of heat he saw just before she nodded made him think he was heading straight into trouble. Which was saying something. Because Rush was a man who'd spent his entire adult life mingling with hardened criminals.

Alessandra climbed from the truck and watched as Rush wordlessly grabbed her bag from the back and started toward the staircase that led to the unusual cabin.

It took her a moment to follow. Not because of the mix of emotions swirling through her. Though they definitely factored in. She was excited to see the place that had seemed like a piece of lore throughout her childhood. She was worried that she might find something connected to her father's note, and equally afraid that she might not. The fact that Jesse owned the cabin filled her with unease and reinforced the thought that his invitation to join him in the small town was anything but a coincidence. But none of that was really what slowed her feet as she finally took a step forward. What made her hesitate was the idea that had occurred to her as she'd held hands with the man who was now effortlessly carrying her things up the stairs. The thought that wormed its way in when he mentioned how romantic the setting was, and when she agreed.

That *maybe*…the best way to get information from Rush Atkinson might be to employ a bit of good old-fashioned flirtation.

But the idea was so base that it was almost embarrassing.

Almost? she asked herself with a mental headshake. *It's stooping to the lowest of the low. Feminine wiles. What is this…the 1800s?*

But she couldn't shake the thought that it might work.

He was attracted to her, she was sure. She caught the way his gaze lingered on her lips for a second too long. Felt the quickening of his pulse when their palms were pressed together. If she could distract him with flirting, it might make it easier to slip in a more significant question or two. An extra touch here. A little query there.

Of course, a seduction on any level would mean actually having a set of eyelash-fluttering, giggle-giving, suggestive-comment-delivering skills. And Alessandra wasn't convinced she did. She'd always been too straight-forward to play games.

"I like you…do you like me…" she muttered under breath. "What's so wrong with that?"

Rush stopped so abruptly that she nearly crashed into him. He turned his head. "Did you say something?"

Alessandra's whole face heated. "No. Well. Uh. Yes. But it was nothing. Talking to myself."

She couldn't see his eyes or his forehead, but she got the feeling he was frowning at her. Thankfully, he didn't push it. After a second, he just swiveled forward and resumed his trek up the stairs. And Alessandra waited until he was almost at the top before continuing behind him. Just in case.

Yeah… said her reasonable, internal self. *So. About that flirting in order to extract information thing…how's it going so far?*

She rolled her eyes, brushed off the thought and focused on the moment. Rush was on the porch now, and showed no sign of exertion as he set down her bag. Alessandra recalled his easy strength when he'd boosted her out of the hole in the woods. Clearly, he was in good shape.

Well, she thought. *Two can play at that game.*

Channeling her inner fitness guru, she took the stairs quickly, pleased that she didn't break a sweat. But when she reached the last step, she turned just enough to catch sight of the panoramic view, and all thought of cardio-vascular superiority and botched seductions completely slipped away. Even the torn-up letter took a back seat. Awe took everything else's place.

She couldn't help but step forward to lean on the railing and take it all in. They weren't all that high up, but the visibility was still incredible. On one side, it was trees as far as the eye could see, broken only by the narrow strips of road that cut through the mountains. On the other side, there was just a hint of the town. Alessandra imagined that at night, that hint would be made up of warm lights. And she bet that overhead, there'd be a million stars. She inhaled deeply. Fresh air and the scent of pine filled her nose and made her toes tingle. She exhaled, then breathed in again, wanting more. But this time, a muskier scent came in with the woodsy one, and she knew before he even spoke that Rush had moved in closer.

"Hell of a view," he murmured.

His voice was right beside her ear and full of genuine pleasure. And Alessandra's toes tingled for a different reason. Smiling, she started to turn. But he was even closer than she thought, and when she spun, she bumped right into him.

"Whoops!" Her face tipped up with the exclamation, and her breath caught.

Rush was inches away. He'd taken off his sunglasses and stuck them on top of his hat, and his chocolate gaze was trained her face. Warm. Caring. Lacking the resentment she would've assumed would be there. Like the mountain air had washed it away.

Then his eyes dropped down, and she realized it wasn't just *them* that was inches apart. It was their *lips*. So close that she could feel the heat of them. And he didn't move away.

"It'd be nice at night," he said, echoing her own silent sentiment.

"Yes," she agreed, her voice breathier than she would've liked.

Flirtation, a voice in her head reminded her.

Maybe it wouldn't be quite so hard after all.

She leaned forward a little more and put her hand on his forearm. "I can see why my parents liked it here so much."

He didn't pull away. "You know what's kind of funny…"

"What?"

"I've never appreciated it quite so much before."

That, she thought. *That right there is what you need. Smoooooooth talking. Flirtatious words. Dammit. He's not supposed to be saying them,* you *are. Get it together, Aless—*

Her thoughts cut off abruptly. They had no choice. Because Rush's lips came down, stopping any and all reason from working through her brain. Instead it did a Goldilocks routine.

His mouth warm, but not overpoweringly hot. Soft, but not too yielding. Not so big as to overwhelm her, but just big enough to encompass her. In other words, everything about his lips—everything about his kiss— fit her just right.

She actually felt a small moan building in her chest. It was a primal reaction. Her body liked kissing Rush and wanted to tell him. To show him, too, if her hands' movement was any indication. They came up to Rush's forearms, dancing over the tattoos she couldn't see but knew were there. They slid over his pushed-up sleeves, then paused on his biceps. She could feel the thick muscle there, and her mind filled with an image of it. Of *him.* Bare from the waist up. Lean and tanned. Pressed against her. The thought of it brought the moan up higher.

It slipped from her diaphragm to her trachea. It hung there for a moment, making the back of her throat ache. Then Rush's tongue came out to touch—just barely—her bottom lip, and there was zero chance of Alessandra being able to hold in the sound any longer. It pushed free, vibrating between them. And it made Rush pull abruptly back.

He blinked down at Alessandra for a second, his brown eyes full of undisguisable want. Then he gave his head a visible shake, and he stepped away, his expression turning stony as he extricated himself from their brief embrace. When he spoke, his tone was equally stiff.

"Alessandra," he said. "I'm sorry."

"Sorry?" Her voice was as puzzled as her body, which was anything but apologetic.

"That was incredibly unprofessional of me."

This is it, said the little voice in her head. *Time for the flirting. Time for reaching out and telling him that you're not sorry. That you wanted him to kiss you.*

But she hesitated. It was something in the way he said "unprofessional" that gave her pause. Maybe it wasn't in his best interest to kiss the woman he'd been tasked with babysitting. Alessandra could see that. But his emphasis made her think what he said had a little more meaning than that. He didn't exactly give off a suit-and-tie, all-aboveboard vibe. And he definitely wasn't afraid to argue with his boss. So stealing a kiss—one she was willing to give—hardly seemed like a serious offense. It piqued her curiosity, and as Rush snapped her bag up from the ground and moved toward the cabin door, Alessandra couldn't help but wonder what she was missing.

Chapter 6

Rush jammed the key into the lock and cursed his own stupid impulsivity.

He'd never considered himself to be a cautious man, and he was also a big fan of the whole action-over-words adage. But he was still perfectly capable of being patient. He knew damned well that sometimes, timing was everything. That waiting was just a prelude to doing. None of that meant a lack of self-control. Not usually.

He pushed open the door and stepped into the cabin. In spite of the temperate air outside, the interior of the small building was chilly enough to necessitate a fire in the pellet-burning stove. Which was actually a relief. Rush needed the reprieve. The required prep work was a perfect excuse to avoid talking to Alessandra. Unfortunately, the busyness couldn't shut off his brain. His mind insisted on turning things over, demanding to know what the hell he'd been thinking.

The problem was that when he'd leaned down and brushed his lips to Alessandra's, it had felt like *that* moment. The one at the end of the wait. He'd been swept away. By the warmish mountain breeze. The amazing view. The way Alessandra leaned into him a little when he spoke to her. Her scent and the way her hair caught strands of sunlight and became living fire.

What the hell, Atkinson? You're a sucky poet now, too?

With a self-directed growl, he slammed the stove shut and spun toward Alessandra, determined to shift things back to the task at hand—finding out what she knew about Garibaldi. Except whatever he'd been about to say died on his lips. When he'd started with the fire, he'd caught her sitting on the couch from the corner of his eye. He'd assumed she'd still be there. She wasn't. Instead, she was standing in the opposite corner of the room, her fingers running over an exposed beam, a look of wonder on her face. Then she turned his way, and the smile she directed at him made him want to kiss her all over again.

Dammit.

He needed to find a way to get a hold of his libido. At least Alessandra seemed unaware of the way his need roiled under the surface.

"Look at this!" she said excitedly.

"At what?" he replied.

She didn't wait for him to figure out what she meant. She walked quickly across the cabin, grabbed his hand and tugged him back to the spot where she'd been standing. Without letting him go, she pulled his fingers up to a beam and pressed them to a groove in the wood.

"Feel that?" she asked.

He could feel something under his fingertips, but he

was far more aware of *her* than he was of anything else. Her shoulder brushed his chest, and her hip bumped his thigh. It was more interesting than whatever she was making him touch, but he shifted his feet anyway, trying to focus.

"All I feel are some dips in the wood," he admitted after a moment.

"Here," she said. "I'll show you."

Her hand dragged his over the grooves, slowly this time. The she spoke, her voice dropping low, like whispering would help him feel whatever it was she wanted him to feel.

"See?" she said softly. "That first one…it's an *M*. Then there's a little plus sign. And an *R* at the end. Mary plus Randall. My parents carved that there. My mom felt so guilty about the vandalism that she tried to sand it off. But my dad stopped her and left a hundred-dollar bill with a note instead."

Her fingers finally left his, but Rush kept his hand up for a moment longer, tracing the thirty-year-old carving once more.

"Sounds like they were really in love," he said.

"They were *embarrassing* with it," she told him with a laugh. "It drove me nuts when I was kid. All that mushiness. But when my dad passed…"

"You missed it," he filled in.

She nodded. "A lot. I had no idea how much I'd wish he'd walk into a room and give my mom an over-the-top kiss, or make some lovingly suggestive comment that I never should've heard. For a long time after, it felt like my mom was half a person. I was just so used to them being a unit."

She eyed the carved letters one more time, then

brushed past him to sink into the couch. Rush only hesitated for a second before following suit. He was careful to leave a space between them, but he felt a compulsion to be near enough to reach out if she wanted him to. He could see that she might, and if it was a little odd to feel so compelled to offer a stranger any comfort she might need, he simply brushed it aside.

She wrinkled her nose a little. "Too much information, right? I'm sure the last thing you want is to hear a woman you don't know rambling on about her dead parents and their honeymoon. I'm just feeling overwhelmed."

Rush shook his head, then said something that surprised himself—something true, and which had nothing to do with his undercover backstory, and which he rarely brought up voluntarily. "Unload all you like. I lost my dad, too, fifteen years ago, so I get it."

Alessandra's eyes immediately sought his, their brilliant blue muted with empathy. "I'm sorry."

Rush leaned back, his mind dancing around the part of his past he kept roped off. "S'okay, Red. Like you said about your dad…it was a long time ago."

"It's still hard sometimes, though, isn't it?"

Deflect, he ordered silently.

But for no good reason at all, he answered honestly. "It's not just hard. It's hell. My parents weren't happy like yours. They fought constantly. My dad was a good man. A *really* good one. My mom was a bit…messy. And when my dad was alive, she always tried to play us off against each other. It worked a lot of the time. Made me a rough and pretty troubled kid."

When he paused, he saw that Alessandra was studying him intently. Listening, for sure. Maybe trying to figure out if he was still rough and troubled now.

Deflect, his subconscious repeated.

Instead, he went on, and the spilled words were strangely therapeutic. "I've gotta admit that my dad's death changed me for the better."

"How so?" Alessandra asked, her voice infused with just the right balance of curiosity and sympathy.

"Things went steadily downhill after he died. My mom never held it together all that well. But without my dad…all the already-frayed edges came loose. She was even angrier at him after he died than when he was alive. I was no help. I was too angry, too. Mad at the whole world. Typical teenager with a big giant chip on my shoulder. A year went by of us only talking to scream at each other. Then something happened that made things worse. But it was a wake-up call for me. I needed to be a man like my dad."

When he finished, he braced himself for a question about the "something." He knew he'd have to lie, and that he'd more or less set himself up for failure by even mentioning it. Telling her the truth—that fifteen years ago, Jesse Garibaldi, then a minor with a protected identity, had gotten away with murder—wasn't an option. Alluding to the situation was bad enough. It risked his life. The lives of his three partners. Alessandra's life, too.

So why did *you bring it up, then?* he wondered.

He honestly wasn't sure. What he *was* sure of was that he didn't want to lie to the pretty woman sitting beside him. What the hell would he say to her, if—when—she asked?

Deflect. The voice in his head was an insistent whisper now.

Except when she spoke, it wasn't to say what he'd been expecting.

"Did you succeed?" she asked.

"Succeed?" he echoed.

"In becoming a man like your dad."

"I'm closer, I think. But still a work in progress."

"I think that applies to all of us, don't you? I know I'm far from perfect."

"*I* think perfection is relative."

Without meaning to, Rush swept his gaze over her. When he finished his quick head-to-toe look and brought his eyes back to her face, he found her stare hanging on his lips. He knew she had to be thinking of the brief kiss. *He* sure was, and he couldn't quite recall why he'd stopped it. Being professional seemed awfully unimportant.

As the moment dragged on, the heat in the one-room cabin spiked, and it had nothing to do with the toasty woodstove in the corner. Her knee bumped his, and he realized he'd unconsciously slid closer to her.

Alessandra looked down at their touching legs, then back up at him again. He saw uncertainty in her eyes, and it was enough to bring him to his senses. He wasn't supposed to be thinking about how her lips felt; he was supposed to be trying find a way get her out of Whispering Woods. If he kissed her again, he'd not only jeopardize everything he'd been working for, he'd jeopardize her chances of staying alive for another two days.

Trying to look like he wasn't jerking back too suddenly, and pretending not to feel a stab of disappointment, he pulled away, cleared his throat, and smiled. "So…after all that…which one of us is doing the whole too-much-information thing?"

She smiled back, but it looked as strained as his own felt. "It's good, actually. It makes you seem a little more…"

"What?"

"Nothing."

"No, seriously."

Her cheeks were pink. "A little more human."

He lifted an eyebrow. "What was I before? A robot?"

"No."

"Worse?"

She frowned. "What's worse than a robot?"

His mouth twitched. "I dunno. *Two* robots? Or maybe a single evil, sentient robot, hell-bent on world domination?"

She stared at him for a moment before a laugh burst out of her mouth, the sound filling the cabin. It made Rush glad he'd opted for a bit of humor.

"So not a robot, then," he said. "Alien?"

Her pretty blue eyes rolled in spite of her blush. "No, not an alien."

"Now I'm extra curious."

"It doesn't matter."

"You saying that makes it matter even more."

"Okay. Look. Don't take this the wrong way…" Her cheeks went even brighter. "But you give off a bit of a thug vibe."

Rush would've laughed it off—it was the appearance he was aiming for, after all—but it provided a perfect segue back into the discussion he was *supposed* to be having with her.

He still made sure to keep his reply light. "I don't know if I should feel insulted, or just be concerned that you think your old friend employs thugs."

"I'm starting to think I don't know very much about him at all, actually. Maybe it's been too long. Or maybe I never knew him that well to start out with." She sighed. "Until now, I didn't even know where he was living, let alone that he owned this cabin."

"All this…" He swept his hand over the room. "It's not the reason you came up to Whispering Woods?"

She shook her head. "No. I mean, I'm glad to see the cabin. But I kind of thought it wouldn't be here anymore, and it didn't even occur to me to look for it."

"So you came all this way just for a visit with a man you don't really know?"

"When you say it like that, it just sounds weird."

He didn't buy her joking tone. "Isn't it weird?"

Alessandra sucked in a breath and looked down at her lap. "It's complicated."

He wanted to reach out and tip her chin up so he could read what was in her eyes, but he refrained, and instead echoed her earlier sentiment. "Doesn't that apply to all of us?"

"I think my situation is a little different."

"You wanna talk about it?"

Now she did lift her eyes, and Rush was disappointed to see that her expression had become guarded. She looked a little tired, too—just a slight droop around the corners of her eyes—and he realized the morning had probably been exhausting for her. Driving five hours, first thing in the morning. Getting lost and her car getting wrecked. Not to mention the fall into the hole and the fact that her plans for sightseeing with Garibaldi were completely askew.

Rush decided to rein in his soft interrogation.

"You hungry?" he asked.

Alessandra blinked at him in surprise. "Starved. I haven't had anything to eat since five this morning."

"Lunch?"

"Um. Okay?"

"Good. I can either scrounge up something here— Garibaldi keeps things stocked—or we can eat in town. Whispering Woods Lodge has a buffet. I can show—"

"Here," she said quickly.

"All right. Let's see what I can find." He pushed to his feet and made his way to the tiny kitchen area, pretending he wasn't pleased that she'd opted to stay in rather than head to town.

Alessandra watched Rush dig through the cupboards, wondering if she'd lost her mind. Maybe the stress of the circumstances had finally caught up to her. Because she was literally biting down on her lip to keep from spilling everything to this stranger.

The stranger who kissed you once already, and looked like he was about to kiss you again? She answered her own silent question. *Yes, him.*

She bit her lip a little harder, and nodded as Rush showed her a can of chicken noodle soup and a package of crackers. At least if she was stuffing her face, she wouldn't be able to tell him anything she really shouldn't.

But that doesn't answer the question of why you even want to.

She stared at Rush's back, trying to pinpoint the urge. But he chose that exact moment to reach up to grab a pot from a high shelf above the sink. The motion pulled his long-sleeved T-shirt tight along his shoulder blades, and she could see both the ridges of his muscles and the outline of another tattoo. And it was distracting enough that it made Alessandra momentarily forget everything. She squinted, trying to get a better look at the ink, but he sank down and turned his attention to rummaging through a drawer, and the cotton of his shirt relaxed back into opaqueness. But Alessandra's mind hung on his tattoos for a little while longer anyway.

Owning and running the surf shop meant she'd seen more than her fair share of tattoos. Plenty of exposed bodies in her business, and lots of chances to talk about the why behind the ink. She'd met lots of people who went for traditional markings. Hearts. Flowers. Some other image they liked and wanted to make permanent. There were many who had just a small meaningful picture or two. Maybe a song lyric or a name. And there were others who felt compelled to mark their skin with all the moments of their lives. Like their bodies were both an outlet and a canvas at the same time. Alessandra had a feeling that Rush fell into the latter category. He seemed like the kind of man who'd rather express himself with a tattoo needle and ink than in words.

Because you've known him for a couple of hours, and now have access to his every thought and motivation?

Alessandra shook her head to herself. Obviously she knew little about him. But that was kind of the thing. In spite of how little she knew, she could read enough.

He was tense, with a bristly temper. But he wasn't what she'd describe as quick to anger, and she wasn't worried he'd lash out at her. It was more like some permanent tightness just under the surface. It was what gave him that brooding quality. And he'd *apologized* for kissing her. For *barely* kissing her. She was sure that translated into a strong sense of right and wrong.

But that doesn't mean you can trust him. He works for

Jesse. A man you do *know. Or did, anyway. And if you don't trust* him, *why would you trust Rush?*

"You know that saying?" His voice made her jump a little, and she was glad that he didn't turn around to see her sudden awkwardness.

She exhaled. "What saying?"

"Eyes burning holes in your back."

"What? I don't think there's a saying about that."

"There definitely is. And I can feel you staring at me."

"I'm not staring at—" She cut herself off with a sigh. "Okay, fine. I am. But don't read too much into it. I was just thinking about tattoos."

He pulled out a drawer, grabbed a couple of bowls and set them on the coffee table. Then he turned back to the stove to grab the already-steaming pot and a ladle, and brought both over.

"So. Thinking about tattoos…mine, or yours?" he asked as he filled the bowls.

"Just in general," she replied, heat creeping up her cheeks. "And *I* don't have any."

"Not one?"

"No."

"Why not?"

"It's always seemed too big of a commitment."

He put the pot back on the stove, and pulled off his hat and set it on the edge of the armchair at the end of the table before seating himself and lifting an eyebrow. Alessandra's blush deepened even before Rush spoke.

"Commitment issues, huh?" he asked teasingly.

"Only when it comes to permanently marking my body," she replied.

He handed her a stack of crackers, then crumbled a

bunch into his own bowl and waved his spoon at her. "You should try it."

"I own a surf shop," she told him. "Trust me when I say I've seen enough ink-related regret to know it's not for me."

He grinned, the smile making his eyes crinkle pleasantly in the corners. "Good to know. But I meant the soup."

Alessandra was sure her face was going from pink to crimson. "Oh."

He laughed. "But if you ever change your mind about the tattoo, I know a guy."

"I'm sure you do."

"He's only on his second prison strike, too."

She made a face. "I take back the human bit. You're definitely a thug."

Some unreadable emotion passed over is features, and he turned his attention back to his soup. "Tell me about the surf shop."

Her embarrassment immediately slipped away, and she shook her head as sadness filled her. "That's part of the complication."

"The complication that you don't want to talk about."

"What do you really do for Jesse?" she countered, more to make a point than because she actually thought he'd change his story.

"I run errands," he told her.

"You can make a living running errands?"

"Plenty of full-time assistants out there."

"Sure. In an office setting."

"Are you saying I'm not office material?"

"I can't even imagine you in a suit, let alone behind a desk."

He set down his spoon. "I feel like we're gearing up to play a strange version of 'you show me yours, I'll show you mine.'"

She met his eyes. The need to trust him rolled over her, and she had to forcibly remind herself that she didn't know him at all. He was just her tour guide.

"I have nothing to show," she lied.

"I think you do," he replied easily. "But if you don't want to share, that's fine. We can pretend. I'll take you into Whispering Woods and show you the sights. Take an off-road adventure or go on a hike."

"That's why I'm here."

"So you say. But if there happens to be a bigger reason... I might be the one guy you can trust."

Then he shrugged, picked up his spoon again, asked her about the Seattle weather, then took a casual slurp of his soup.

Chapter 7

By the time they finished their lunch, Rush was 100 percent sure of three things.

The first was that Alessandra wasn't in Whispering Woods because she knew anything about Garibaldi's business.

The second was that she was definitely there for something more than a casual visit.

The third was that her reason for not sharing it with him was that she didn't trust her old friend in the slightest.

Can you blame her? he thought, stealing a quick glance her way as he dumped kettle-boiled water into the sink.

He'd waved off her offer to help wash up with the excuse that six dishes was hardly a two-person job, so she sat on the couch, her legs tucked up under her body and a book in her hand. She looked relaxed enough, but Rush wasn't convinced. Every few seconds, he could feel her gaze shift his way. Assessing him. He waited, knowing this was one of those need-to-be-patient moments.

He was glad she didn't trust his boss. Partly because it meant she was smart enough to recognize that the man was far slimier than his exterior indicated. Partly because it meant she was on the right side of the law. Mostly, though, it was because he didn't want her to be involved with the other man on any level.

He scrubbed at the saucepan a little harder. His little twinge of possessiveness wasn't just unreasonable. It wasn't just dumb. Or more ridiculous than anything he'd felt in as long as he could remember. It was also selfish. After all, he'd already admitted that he had nothing to offer her. Less than nothing, really. Except a threat to her life. On top of that, he'd resigned himself not to kiss her again, no matter how great the temptation. There was also the fact that he'd known her for all of five seconds and had zero romantic claim on her.

Acknowledging all of that and following through on it are two different things, though, aren't they?

His finger ached from how roughly he was scrubbing the pot. Irritated at himself, he dipped the metal into the bucket of cool water for rinsing, then hazarded yet another look at Alessandra. Her book was in her lap now, her eyes closed.

"Red?" he called softly.

She shifted a little, but only so that she slumped sideways. Apparently, her relaxed position wasn't a fake; she was definitely asleep.

Rush quickly finished with the other dishes, fully expecting her to wake by the time he was done. She didn't. Not even when he'd dried his hands and made his way to the spot beside her, or when he sat down beside her and put a hand on her calf.

"Red," he said again.

She let out a sigh, but didn't wake.

"Alessandra," Rush murmured, moving his fingers off her leg and up to her shoulder.

The gentle nudge did nothing.

"Tired as all hell, aren't you?" he asked, just above a whisper.

The question earned him a wordless mutter that made him smile.

"All right, then, Red," he said. "Don't take this the wrong way, but I'm going to put you to bed."

He stood up, then knelt down. He slid one arm under her knees and the other under her back. Then he lifted. She muttered something else, and he waited again for her to wake and maybe issue a vehement protest to being manhandled. She still didn't. Instead, she settled her head against his chest and pressed an open palm against his ribs.

"Dammit, Red," Rush said as a lick of desire coursed through him.

She wiggled a little, and he rolled his eyes at himself as his pulse jumped again. He clearly had zero control. Which was ironic, considering that she was out cold and he was the one with all the power. He cast a look down at her peaceful face, and something else struck him. As distrusting as she was, she'd still felt comfortable enough to fall asleep in front of him. He knew her ability was compounded by her exhaustion, but that didn't stop a warm, pleased feeling from forming in his chest. Because he also knew that no matter how tired *he* was, he'd never be able to let down his guard like that with a person he didn't fully trust. Hell. He slept with one eye open half the time no matter what.

He studied the line of Alessandra's profile. From her arched brow to the reddish-brown of her lashes to her high cheekbone and soft, slightly parted lips, she was truly one of the most beautiful women he'd seen. Makeup-free. Messy hair. It didn't matter. He had to admit that everything about her appealed to him.

"Good sign that you need to put her down," he muttered.

He let himself stare for a second more before he carried her to the double bed. The mattress and box spring rested on an old metal frame, which was positioned under the strange window with the view of the rocky face behind the cabin. It was an odd setup, and Rush had wondered a few times why Garibaldi even bothered leaving it there. The meetings he held in the cabin weren't exactly of the need-a-bed type. But right then, he was grateful for it.

He laid Alessandra down carefully, then pulled up the fuzzy throw from the bottom of the bed and tucked it around her shoulders. As he stepped away, she sighed contentedly, then promptly flopped over into a starfish position. She let out a snore, and Rush couldn't help but chuckle. In spite of his amusement, though, he still reached down and adjusted the blanket so that she was partially covered. The woodstove gave off a fair amount of heat, but the air was still cool, and he didn't want her to wake up cold. She'd probably be displeased enough at having been carted from the couch to the bed.

"Sorry, Red," he said to her sleeping form. "Need a bit of space, too, and the seating options are limited."

He gave her a final look, shaking his head at her

splayed-out form, then stepped back toward the couch with the intention of firing off a few coded texts to his partners. Though he preferred to stay tight-lipped and liked working solo, he'd grudgingly agreed to keep the three men in the loop. This was as much their case as it was his, after all, and they'd want to hear about a delay like this. Each of them had come into Whispering Woods to gather information on Jesse Garibaldi so they could put him behind bars.

Brayden Maxwell had confirmed that the man running the town was the same one they'd been searching for, and he got the ball rolling for their investigation.

Anderson Somers had protected their informant and figured out that there was a lot more going on than they initially thought and connected Garibaldi to the drug smuggling business.

Harley Maxwell—Brayden's younger brother—had put the pieces together and figured out that Garibaldi was using an art shop to run the drugs.

Rush was there to finish it all off. To catch Garibaldi in the act and finally do what should've been done at his trial fifteen years earlier—put the man behind bars for good. To get justice for their fathers.

Rush's stomach rolled unpleasantly as he thought about it. Dwelling on the past wasn't a favorite activity, but he wanted peace as much as his brothers-in-arms did, and he'd be glad when it was finally over.

Action, he said to himself. *That's what I need to focus on.*

Except it was hard to act when he was paralyzed by the current task. He glanced regretfully over at Alessandra, then down at his phone, deciding that updating his partners could wait a few more minutes. He might rather keep the pretty redhead close, but what he *needed* to do was check in with Garibaldi first. He had to try to convince the other man that letting Alessandra go would be in his best interest. For all of their sakes.

Sighing, Rush decided to step outside to place the call. He forced himself not to look at Alessandra again, then slipped out to the deck and dialed. Garibaldi picked up in the second ring.

"How's my favorite tour guide?" the other man greeted.

Rush gritted his teeth. "The sights aren't exactly what I've been told they might be."

"My old friend giving you trouble?"

"None at all."

There was a pause. "You having second thoughts about the assignment?"

"Made it pretty clear I didn't have *first* thoughts about the assignment, didn't I?" Rush said, making sure he sounded extra snarly.

"She's a risk."

"She doesn't know a damned thing."

"Al tell you that?"

"Yeah, boss…right between me asking her if she knew anything about what you were *really* doing here in Whispering Woods and her offering to perform a striptease."

Garibaldi chuckled. "Point taken."

Rush ran a hand over his head and exhaled an extra-loud sigh. "I just don't see the *point*. The cleanup will be more work than the cleanup, if you get what I'm saying."

"Her pretty face is getting to you, huh?"

"I'm not gonna deny her good looks, boss. I'd be a liar and an idiot if I did. But it's not that. She knows nothing. All she's talked about is her childhood and her parents. Seems like a needless expenditure of energy to—"

"Stop right there," the other man ordered curtly. "Did she tell you why she agreed to come up here?"

"I assumed it was to see you."

"In all the years I've known her, she's never once made a social call. Or any call at all. And I've never trusted her, because *my* father couldn't trust *her* father. I took that to heart, Atkinson, and I've kept an eye on Al for the last fifteen years. Waiting. And two weeks ago, I got a call from a connection I've got with the Seattle PD. My old friend came in with a query about something that ties directly to me. Something that could destroy everything I've built here."

Rush bit back an urge to remind Garibaldi that the illegal nature of his business left him at permanent risk of losing both his life and his livelihood, and turned back to face the cabin. He knew he should be trying to appease the man by agreeing to do what he wanted done, even though it wasn't ever going to come even close to being true. For some reason, he couldn't quite do it.

Was it possible that he'd misread Alessandra? His gut rarely steered him wrong.

Something's off.

The thought no sooner came than Rush was sure that it was right. He just didn't know what he was right about. Yet.

"Atkinson, you there?" Garibaldi sounded annoyed.

"I'm here," Rush replied.

"Can I count on you?"

He cleared his throat and tried to make his reply sincere. "Always, boss."

"Good." There was a pause. "Just a suggestion, Atkinson. It might be easier for all of us if you took care of her before she woke up."

"Right."

"Tell me when it's done."

The line went dead, and Rush frowned down at his phone, his unease growing.

Then it hit him.

How the hell had the man on the other end known Alessandra was asleep?

"Crap," he said under his breath, resisting the urge to look around for a visible camera and cursing himself for not considering the possibility.

Had Garibaldi revealed the fact that he could see them on purpose? Had he assumed Rush knew already? Or was it a genuine slip?

Rush's fingers tightened on the slim device in his hand, and he mentally flipped through everything he'd done since they arrived. Aside from the kiss, almost everything else was suitably neutral. He was damned glad he'd managed to keep from saying anything incriminating.

If I'd called the guys first...

He shook off the thought. His secret was still safe, and there was no sense dwelling on what might've gone wrong but hadn't. Besides that, his need to call his partners only increased with the knowledge that Garibaldi was watching him more closely than he'd thought. Maybe he'd try Harley first, to see if the computer genius could figure out what his pseudo-boss was using to spy on the cabin.

Not here, though.

"Good time to get some air," Rush said aloud, just in case the watching extended to listening.

Then he took the stairs, two at a time, and strode good and far into the woods before dialing one of the only numbers he knew by heart.

Alessandra woke slowly, the memory of a dream hanging just under the surface and warming her from the inside out. She wiggled a little deeper under the covers, trying to get the dream back. What had she been doing? Had she been curled up in some tall, dark and handsome stranger's arms? Staring into a pair of chocolate-brown eyes?

Yes. That sounds about right. He smelled good, too. Musky with a hint of woodsmoke. His hands were warm and—

She sat bolt upright as she realized it wasn't just a memory of a *dream*. It was an actual memory.

Rush Atkinson. The cabin.

Her gaze flicked around the room, searching for him. When she didn't see him right away, she started to slide her leg off the couch. Then realized she wasn't *on* the couch. She was on a bed. The awareness startled her so badly that she nearly fell straight to the ground, and she just barely managed to stick out a hand in time to grab a hold of the mattress and hang on.

The mattress.

Just the word made her cringe. She was sure that when she'd closed her eyes—just for a second—she'd been on the couch. Which meant she had to have had help getting where she was now.

Embarrassing.

She slid back up the bed and took another useless look around. The few hundred square feet didn't exactly lend itself to a dozen hiding places.

"Rush?" she called, then rolled her eyes at herself and muttered, "Oh. Because you can't see him but he might *hear* you, right?"

But as Alessandra pushed to her feet, worry tickled at her. A quick glance toward the window—the one that actually had a view of outside rather than of the mountainside—told her there was still plenty of light in the sky. She hadn't been asleep long. So where was Rush?

She crept toward the door and told herself it was unreasonable to assume the worst. Especially when she wasn't even sure what the worst was in this situation. But her feet still dragged. Swallowing a nervous lump in her throat, Alessandra put her hand on the doorknob and turned. She inched the door open. Very slowly. She peeked out, her heart hanging somewhere in her throat.

"Rush?" Her voice was a whisper.

You're being ridiculous.

She took a breath and forced herself to step the rest of the way out onto the deck. A glance back and forth told her nothing had changed. The sun was on the other side of noon, but aside from that, there was no discernible difference. Rush's worse-for-wear Lada sat in the same spot. The temperature was warmer outside than inside. And the woods were peaceful.

"Rush?" Alessandra called, managing to make her voice carry this time.

She still got no answer. Puzzlement and worry made her move cautiously, but she still covered the full length of each side of the deck, her eyes flitting around in search of the gruff man.

"Rush!" Now she wasn't able to prevent a hint of fear from creeping into her tone. "Ru—"

She cut herself off as the tiniest flash of light caught

her eye. It came from somewhere up on the wooded hill. She stared, willing it to come again. And just a moment later, it did. Only this time, Alessandra was able to home in on it, and she realized it wasn't actually a *flash* of light; it was a reflection of it. Something glass? Or something metallic, maybe? She wasn't sure. Then it moved. Not away, but in the same spot. Up and down, then back and forth.

Like someone's holding something, she thought. *Is it Rush?*

She stepped forward and pressed herself to the chest-high fence, trying to get a better view. It was a useless endeavor. The foliage was too thick to let her see much of anything.

"But it *has* to be Rush out there," she muttered.

There was no sign that anyone else had come into the small yard. Aside from hiking in, there was no way to approach without being detected, and nowhere to stash a vehicle.

Alessandra stared at the spot where the flash had come from, torn. On the one hand, she felt compelled to go investigate. On the other, she felt an increased need for prudence. She shifted from foot to foot. The seconds ticked by, and she finally decided to satisfy both desires. She'd head for the source of the flash. But she'd do it slowly and carefully, just in case.

She made her way down the stairs, mindful of how hard her feet hit the wood and vigilant of her surroundings. At the bottom, she took a deep breath, then started another ascent, this one over rocks and dirt and the occasional wayward root. It was a steep climb, and by the time she reached the tree line, Alessandra was slightly out of breath. So she paused to pull in a few gulps of oxygen. And when she did, she realized she could hear a masculine voice. Low enough that she couldn't discern the words. But audible enough that she recognized it.

Rush. Thank God.

Her mind quickly connected the dots. The flash she'd seen was likely his phone, and he'd probably just sneaked off to have a quiet conversation. But the relief at having an explanation was short-lived. Because as Alessandra lifted her foot to move closer again, and opened her mouth to call his name, a light bit of wind kicked up and carried his voice to her. Clearly now, so she could completely make out his words.

"I've really got no choice," he growled. "I have to get rid of her."

The two statements were rough, angry and ominous. And they made Alessandra stumble. She hit the ground, one knee smashing to a rock so hard that it took all of her mental strength to keep from crying out. For a few seconds after her miniature crash landing, she didn't move. She didn't know if she *could*. Or if she should.

Do I run? How far would I even get on foot? Not very. He'd come looking. So do I pretend I never heard any of it and go for a more subtle escape? Or do I confront him? Or—

Her tumble of frightened thoughts stopped short as a new sound carried to her ears. It was the crash of a man pushing through the bushes. Rush was headed her way. For another moment, fear held her captive. Then survival instinct kicked in. Moving swiftly and far more silently than her unwitting pursuer, Alessandra turned and fled.

She skidded down the hill and prayed that he wouldn't hear the small rocks that followed her descent. He didn't need a heads-up, but she was sure *she* needed a head start. Thankfully, she made it to the bottom without detection. And she didn't stop. Her feet hit the packed dirt with muted thump after muted thump. She started to speed past the Lada, then stopped as she spied something jutting out of the center console.

Rush's gun.

Alessandra didn't know when he'd taken it off or why he'd left it there. She didn't care. The weapon was a gift horse, and no way was she looking the damned thing in the mouth.

She grabbed a hold of the door handle, yanked it open and snapped up the gun. The fact that she had almost zero shooting experience didn't deter her in the least. With steady hands, she spun. She waited. And the moment Rush's strong shoulders parted the brush, she raised her voice.

"Stop!" she ordered.

He kept moving.

"Stop!" she repeated, hoping there was no hint of hysteria in her voice.

Rush slowed, then halted. He'd slung a plaid jacket over his long-sleeved shirt, and was missing his hat and sunglasses. He was also close enough that Alessandra could see his face. And instead of looking worried, or even defensive, his features just crinkled with confusion. She stared at him, willing him to have at least a little concern.

I will protect myself, she thought firmly.

"Do. Not. Move."

He lifted a booted foot. "Red, I don't know what—"

"Put your hands on your head. And if I see you take one more step…" She trailed off, hoping she sounded more menacing than tremulous.

"You're not seriously considering shooting me. What the hell happened in the last hour?"

"You tell me. Who were you talking to?"

"A friend."

His face didn't change, but Alessandra knew better than to look at his eyes. Her gaze dropped to his hands. They flexed. Once. Twice. And a third time. Then they finally came up to rest on top of his head, and Alessandra breathed out.

She kept her voice cool. "What friend? Jesse? His buddy Ernest?"

"No."

"Who?"

Rush's attention flickered—just barely—toward the cabin. "A personal one."

"Your girlfriend?" Alessandra blurted, then blushed as she realized how ridiculous the question sounded.

Now the bearded man's expression *did* change. Back to confused. Only *more* confused.

"My... No. Hell, no," he said. "Could you just..."

"Could I *what*?" Alessandra's embarrassment made her reply more snappish than she wanted it to be.

"Maybe stop pointing my gun at me?"

"To quote you...hell, no. I want some answers."

"This isn't the way to get them."

Something in the set of his jaw made her sure he wasn't going to tell her anything no matter what. She lifted the gun a little higher. But she knew she'd only fire as a last resort.

She cleared her throat and decided to try something else. "Actually. I take that back, anyway. I don't want answers, I want your keys."

For a second, he looked like he might argue, but then

he nodded instead. "I'm going to have to move my hands to make that happen. They're in my pocket."

Alessandra bit her lip. Her gut churned a warning. She shoved it off. What did her gut know, anyway? It'd been telling her to trust him. It'd let him kiss her without suggesting a punch in return. And gut aside, it wasn't like she had a ton of options at the moment. If she wanted to get away without being gotten "rid of," she needed transportation. She fought a shiver. For now, saving her own life was the most pressing issue. Everything else—her questions, whatever Jesse knew or didn't know about her father's note or his death—it could all come after.

"Keys," she said firmly.

"All right," Rush agreed.

He moved slowly. As if she were the one who couldn't be trusted. It made her want to roll her eyes, but she managed to refrain, watching carefully as he freed one hand from his head and dipped it into his front pocket. He dragged the keys free, then dangled them out in front of his body. For a moment, she thought he expected her to step toward him. But he just tossed them, underhand, to a spot near her feet.

"Hands back up," she ordered.

He lifted an eyebrow, but did as he was told.

Alessandra drew a breath. She bent, her eyes locked on him. Her fingers closed on the key ring. She was tense with waiting for him to do something reactive. But he just watched, his gaze holding its typically implacable state.

Alessandra exhaled. Then stood. She took a few slow steps toward the Lada, gun still up and speaking as she moved.

"I know I can't control you once I'm gone," she said.

"But I'd prefer it if you stayed right there until I'm all the way out of sight."

"I think we both know I can't do that," he replied, his voice flat and quiet—almost gentle, really.

For whatever reason it made Alessandra pause. Maybe it was even his intention. Because the heartbeat of an interval was all Rush needed. And before she could react, his compactly muscular body was hurling toward her.

Chapter 8

As Rush knocked Alessandra to the ground, he pulled a move that was really more stuntman than undercover cop. He slid a hand under her head to protect it, and he angled himself to take most of the impact. He had no clue if she noticed or not, but for a moment after landing, she stayed still. It gave him too much of an advantage.

He tried to silently convey the need to tread lightly. He had no idea what had changed her mild distrust to outright fear, but damned if he could ask. He needed to get her alone. Out sight and out of electronic earshot.

He bent toward her ear and growled, "Fight me."

His words earned him a surprised gasp. Not the reaction he was hoping for. The widening of her eyes didn't help, either.

Then she spoke, and her voice far too damned loud. "Why wouldn't I—"

"Sorry about this," he muttered, swiping his free forearm lightly over her mouth to muffle her words.

Her head whipped back and forth under his arm, and though he exerted almost no pressure, he hoped that her panic would make it look like she was struggling.

He dipped his head again. "Fight *harder*."

Irritation flashed through her baby blues, and at last the fight reflex seemed to kick in. Her teeth sank into his skin, hard enough to make his eyes water.

Thank God.

Brushing off the pain in his arm, Rush reached out for the weapon she still clasped. She bucked a protest, then took her free hand and whacked him in the back. It hurt, but not enough make him let go. He pretended that it did anyway, releasing her wrist and cursing. She immediately tried to raise the weapon. He knocked her hand out of the way, and the gun went flying. It landed a few feet away, and Rush lunged for it. As he moved, Alessandra rolled over and tried to slide to the gun faster than he could.

Once again, he let her have the upper hand. He pressed his booted toe to the ground and allowed her an extra moment. The second her fingers were on the weapon, he pushed forward and overpowered her. He rolled her to her back again, straddling her. He opened his mouth, trying to think of a way to communicate his true intentions. But then her knee drove up between his legs, and he had to jerk sideways to avoid some more serious damage. He still narrowly missed losing control for real.

"That's fighting dirty," he snarled, adjusting so that both her legs were more firmly pinned down.

"I'm smaller than you are. Physically weaker, too. And unlike you, I'm not a natural-born thug, so if I see an advantage, I'm going to take it." She punctuated the end of her furious little speech with a head butt.

Her maneuver was a little futile—her forehead smacked his throat rather than any part of his face—but Rush had to admire her grit. He'd wrestled with experienced criminals who gave up more easily.

Hoping to God it looked as real as it felt, he grabbed each of her wrists, pressed them to ground, and dipped his head down once more. "I want you to punch me. Then run."

"What?" Her reply was a gasp.

He didn't offer any further explanation. He just loosened his grip on her right wrist. Thankfully, she took action without any more prompting. Her hand ripped free, balled into a fist, then drove straight into his gut with enough force to make him grunt and fall back for real. As he did, Alessandra gave him a violent shove. He rolled off, doubling over for just long enough that she could get to her feet.

Run, he ordered silently, and a heartbeat later, the sound of her feet hitting the ground slammed through the air.

Rush lifted his head and pushed to his feet, then gave chase. She was fast. Almost unexpectedly so. She reached the tree line well ahead of him, and he had to really push to close the gap between them. Even then, her lithe form gave her an advantage—she was able to easily slip between the dense bits of foliage. His own movements were more like a wild boar, crashing through with no subtlety whatsoever, and he couldn't quite catch up.

"Red!" he hollered. "Stop!"

"Like hell!" she called over her shoulder, and kept going.

Rush crashed through a few more patches of trees. He was getting winded.

"I'm not going to hurt you!" he almost wheezed.

"Says every villain in every movie *ever*!" she yelled, sounding not in the slightest bit bothered by the mad flight.

"I'm trying to help you!"

"Help someone else!"

Any second, she was going to pull ahead. God knew where she'd take off to, and once she was out of sight and out of reach, Rush wouldn't stand a chance of being able to protect her from Garibaldi.

Then luck finally threw him a bone. Alessandra let out an abrupt shriek, flailed her arms, and fell forward.

One part grateful for the break in his favor and one part worried whether or not she'd hurt herself, Rush pushed on. He at last caught up. Just as she rolled from her back to her front, spitting dirt from her mouth as she aimed his gun at him yet again.

Rush stared down at her, his ragged breathing forgotten as he caught sight of her. Her too-big T-shirt had come untied at the side, and the loose collar was torn halfway down one sleeve. Her chest rose and fell quickly, as distracting as her wild, tangled mess of hair. Dirt streaked her clothes and her face. But in spite of it all, there was nothing vulnerable about her appearance. She was tough and defiant. Determined to best him despite everything.

Might have something to do with the fact that she's got that thing pointed at you, he thought wryly, his eyes flicking to the gun.

"Go ahead," he said calmly. "Fire."

Her eyes narrowed suspiciously. "You're saying that because you think I won't."

"I think *most* people prefer not to shoot others," he replied. "And if you weren't at least a little bit hesitant, then you would've shot me already. As you so nicely pointed out…you're not a natural-born thug."

"Maybe I'll aim for your knee."

"Like I said…go ahead."

She grumbled something unintelligible, then sat up, swung the gun to the side and pulled the trigger. It clicked uselessly. Alessandra's eyes widened. Then they moved from him to the weapon. She tried again with no difference.

"Play with it all you want," Rush said. "You'll get the same result. I'm not quite inept enough to leave a loaded weapon just lying around."

Alessandra dropped the gun and started to scramble backward. She almost immediately slammed into a tree.

Rush stepped forward and held out his hand. "Want some help? Maybe have a bit of a nonviolent conversation?"

"There's something seriously wrong with you," she told him angrily.

"Wrong with *me*? I still don't know exactly what's going on here. When I left you, you were sound asleep. Snoring."

"I don't snore!"

"You do. But that wasn't my point."

"You told your 'friend' you were going to get rid of me. If you're just going to toy with me…"

He missed the last part of whatever she was saying as he finally clued in. She'd asked about his phone conversation because she'd overheard it. Or the last bit of it, anyway. No wonder she was ready to shoot him. Hell. He was probably lucky she *hadn't* found a way to seriously hurt him. She was pretty calm, all things considered.

Calm? She's about to bolt. Again.

It took him a second to realize the thought wasn't a generic one. Alessandra was literally crouched down like an Olympic sprinter, just a heartbeat away from running.

With a frustrated grunt, Rush sprang forward and tackled her. This time, he didn't mess around with a pretend struggle. He knocked her to the forest floor, pinned her arms to her ground on either side of her body and used his own weight to hold her lower half in place.

"Let me go!" Her demand was forceful, but softened by the tears forming in her eyes.

Guilt hit Rush, but he knew better than to ease up, and instead, he spoke in a soft voice. "Back it up, Red. Don't you think if I was going take care of you, gangster-style, I would've done it by now?"

She blinked. "How would *I* know what the protocol for offing someone is?"

In spite of the circumstances, he had to fight a chuckle. "Well. I can assure you, it's not letting someone with an unloaded gun get the better of me. Think about it for a second, Red. I've got you alone at a cabin. You have a known habit of getting lost, and a broken cell phone. And on top of that, you're wearing flip-flops. You have no viable means of escape. If I were going to off you, it'd be over already."

She relaxed—just enough that he could see the tension go out of her shoulders—and persisted. "Maybe you needed to extract information from me, first."

Now he fought a sigh instead of a laugh, because it was at least a partly true suggestion. "What information could I possibly extract from you? Have you got secrets I should know about?"

"No," she said quickly.

"You sure? You don't want to think about that for a second or something?"

"See? Now you *sound* like you're interrogating me. And holding me captive hardly breeds trust."

"If I let you go, you'll hit me, kick me or run away."

"To be fair, you *told* me to fight you." She paused, her face screwing up in a frown. "Wait. Why *did* you tell me to fight you?"

"Because, Red…" He trailed off, mentally calculating how much he'd have to tell her to convince her he was once of the good guys. "The truth is, I needed it look like we were struggling so I could get you away from the cabin."

"What? Why?"

"If I sit up to explain, are you going to attack me?"

She offered him a horizontal, poorly executed shrug. "Possibly."

He let the chuckle out this time. "All right. I'll go halfway, then."

"Halfway?"

"Yep. Handcuffs. But no leg shackles."

"Um…"

He slid back with the intention of sitting up while still maintaining his hold on her. Instead, he somehow managed to pull her into his lap. The effect was immediate. Thoughts of why they were there slipped away as Rush tried his damnedest to hold on to them. Why the hell did she fit against him so well? And why did he suddenly feel like instead of giving her an explanation, he was going to give her another kiss?

* * *

Alessandra's body was having an utterly unreasonable reaction to their new position. And it was winning out over the reminders her brain tried to issue.

Thirty seconds ago, you thought he was going to kill you. Now you're snuggling up to him because he said that's not his plan? He hasn't even told what the real issue is! Stop staring into his pretty brown eyes. Stop thinking about how nice his hands feel, too. And don't you even start *to notice his...er...appreciation of you.*

But Alessandra knew she was already a goner. In spite of logic and reason and adrenaline, the pheromones were going to win. One soft touch of his lips to hers would be all it would take.

If he leans down...

But instead, his hand came up to touch her cheek. His knuckles brushed her skin and made her shiver.

"Red," he said, his voice thick. "I promise you... I would *never* hurt you, or let you get hurt."

His words should've been farcical. But Alessandra just wanted them to be true.

"How can you say that?" she replied, hearing the need in her own question. "You don't know me at all. You don't know my situation."

"No. I don't. But I don't *have* to know you to make that promise. I'm one of the good guys, Red." He stroked her cheek again, then smiled the most stupidly sexy smile she'd ever seen, and added, "For the record, I'd *like* to know you. And not because I'm trying to extract information from you, either."

More unreasonableness licked through Alessandra, and she leaned into his touch. Her gut was nudging her, reminding her that her initial instinct was to trust him.

Her brain lost even more ground in its fight against the attraction.

Never mind that she still didn't have an explanation for his strange behavior. Never mind that they were on the cool, dirty forest floor, or that Alessandra still had more questions than answers. Her heart was thrumming and her body was buzzing. She tipped her face up and leaned forward, but kept her eyes open, waiting to see if Rush would stop before he started. Or if he would hesitate, another apology on his mind. But he didn't. He just stared right back at her, want the only thing in his gaze. Then his wrist twisted so that instead of running his knuckles over her cheek, he was cupping it with his palm. He was so close that she could feel the heat of his mouth.

You might regret this, warned one last voice in Alessandra's head.

But she was already sure any hint of regret would be worth it. As Rush's lids sank shut, hers did, too, and her whole body lit up with anticipation. Then his mouth came down and coherent thought fled to the deepest corners of her mind. Everything else was in the moment. Feeling and doing.

Rush tasted like heaven. Somehow, the earthy, musky scent that he exuded had managed to make its way into his mouth. It was a flavor that begged to be consumed. Alessandra parted her lips, hoping for more. And he gave it to her. His tongue dipped into her mouth in a firm exploration. She moaned against the attention, then dragged her hands to the back of his head to deepen the kiss even more.

Rush seemed happy to oblige. He kissed her harder, tasting every corner of her mouth, and his arms snaked around her waist to pull her closer. The motion unbalanced them, and they toppled over.

Alessandra's eyes flew open. Rush was flat on the ground, and she was on top of him. Her breasts were pushed against his chest, and her legs were tucked around one of his thighs. It was an undeniably intimate position. A little embarrassed, Alessandra started to pull away. But Rush stopped her. His hands landed on her hips, holding them firmly in place, and his head lifted from the ground to plant another kiss—this one light— on her mouth.

Embarrassment slipped away, and enthusiasm took its place.

She pushed her lips harder against his, and his head dropped back. His hands stayed on her hips, but they loosened enough to circle around in a maddening caress. And Alessandra wanted more of him. She shifted so that she was straddling his hips instead of his thigh, and the new position made her desire that much more specific. She wanted *all* of him. All of Rush. The man she barely knew and whom she was crazy to trust. None of the rationalities made even a slip of difference. The physical need outweighed it all.

"Alessandra." The groan of her full name against her mouth made her quiver.

She was wanting. Needing. *Vibrating.*

Her eyes opened as she realized the last bit was more physical than metaphorical. She could see from Rush's expression that he felt a real-life buzz, too.

"My damned phone," he said.

"Should you get it?" Alessandra breathed.

"Trust me when I say that I'd rather not."

"But you should?"

"Pretty sure it's my friend, calling me back. And if I don't answer, he'll just keep trying," he told her regretfully.

"Damn him," she said as she sat up and moved back a bit to give him some space. "Whoever he is."

Rush chuckled, leaned over to give her a soft, swoon-worthy kiss, then reached into a pocket on the side of his plaid jacket and shot a smoldering look her way as he answered. "Atkinson here."

In spite of the two feet between then, Alessandra could still clearly hear the response.

"Damn, man," said the man other the other end. "I was getting a bit worried there for a second."

"What are you now, Harley? My mother?" Rush said the teasing words with true affection, and it made Alessandra curious. But not quite as curious as the reply.

"All right then," the other man—Harley—said. "I'll just hang up without telling you what I found out about the surveillance system."

"Now, see? You should've *led* with that threat."

An audible snort carried through the line. "Right. Forgot who I was dealing with."

Rush smiled. "Yeah. I've always been the smart one."

"Oh. So *you're* the one who figured out exactly how Garibaldi's been spying on the cabin, then devised a way to jam it?" Harley asked.

Alessandra sucked in a sharp breath. *Spying?* It explained Rush's need to get out of sight. And it reassured her about where he stood in regard to Jesse. But it also filled her with renewed disquiet. Why was her old friend spying on them? Was it about her or about Rush? She was so distracted by her own unease that she almost completely missed Rush's friend's explanation for what he was doing about the situation. Something about relays and interference and being fine for at least a little while.

She shook her head, trying to bring her attention back to the conversation, sure it would reveal a few more clues as to what was going on. Instead, she got distracted again, because Rush had slightly adjusted his position, and his coat had flapped open. And what Alessandra saw made her have to hold in a gasp. Strapped to his side was a gun.

He'd been armed the entire time she'd pointed her useless weapon at him. And maybe it should've embarrassed her that she didn't notice it before, even when lying on top of him, but it just flooded her with relief. He truly didn't mean her any harm. If he did, he could've just pulled out his own gun.

So maybe kissing him wasn't so unreasonable after all, she thought.

She flushed as her mind went to just how wantonly she'd engaged in that particular activity. And she could feel her cheeks grow even hotter when she met Rush's eyes. His gaze was as heated as her face, and Alessandra knew instinctively that he was thinking about their kissing, too. Then he sent her slow wink, and her insides flip-flopped.

Dammit, Al, she said to herself. *Focus!*

"So…" Rush was saying into the phone. "We have a few hours before he even notices that there's an issue, then?"

"I'm not going to give you a hundred percent guarantee," his friend replied, "but I'd eat one of my own sculptures if he caught on that quickly."

Alessandra had no idea what the other man meant, but Rush laughed.

"All right, buddy," he said. "You go back to your girl and your extended vacation. I'll pick up the slack."

"You know what? I won't even argue with that. It's about time you did something on the case. You just call me when you need a technological bailout."

Alessandra missed the sign-off. She was too lost in the conclusion that had just popped into her head.

The gun. The good guy. And the case.

She brought her gaze up, and she blurted out the idea before she could stop herself. "You're a cop."

Chapter 9

Rush's biggest—often only—fear was getting caught in his deception. He rarely worried for his own life in a general sense. Even though the tough, dangerous assignments he took on always posed an explicit threat, he hardly ever thought about it. A stray bullet was a part of the job. Same went for bumping elbows with murderers. Rush had no desire to die in the line of duty, but worrying about it was a rarity. Being made, however, was a different story.

It'd almost happened once, his second year on the job. He'd been working his way up through a crew, getting in good with the boss. The situation had been harmless enough. He and another lackey were grabbing coffees for the senior guys. A banal task, at best. He'd snagged the latte of the counter, laughed at something his crime buddy said, then turned toward the door, and smacked straight into a dude from high school. A dude who recognized Rush. Called him by name. Then asked if the "thing" with his father ever got sorted out.

The moment he'd heard the question, sweat-inducing fear had made Rush's blood run cold, then hot. He'd seen the curiosity on his fellow thug's face. He'd spied a glimpse into the near future, too. The old classmate wouldn't take a simple reply. Rush's new buddy would sense something was amiss, and would push the matter. He'd bring it up in front of their mutual boss. By the end of the week, Rush would be dead. So would the innocent man standing in front of him.

So he did the only thing he could think to do. He drew back a fist and slammed the other man straight in the face. He'd felt sick about it. *Still* felt sick about it. It'd had the right effect, though. His old classmate had collapsed. A nearby cop came running in before someone could even dial 911. In minutes, Rush was in the back of a squad car. In under an hour, he was back on the street, his credibility doubled, his boss impressed, his cover story perfectly in place, and a lingering, unsettling fear that it might happen all over again with far less favorable results. The doubt never went away.

In spite of all that, though, Rush felt nothing but relief at hearing Alessandra connect the dots and call him out. But he still answered carefully, assessing her reaction to his words. Watching for a hint that being a cop wasn't a good thing.

"What makes you say that?" he asked, his voice neutral.

"You're not denying it?" she replied.

"Seems to me that a flat-out denial would be an obvious attempt at a cover-up."

"You're not exactly an obvious guy, though, are you?"

He felt one side of his mouth tip up in a smirk. "I wouldn't call myself subtle."

She studied his face, her blue eyes probing and intelligent, and he expected a question about the nature of his investigation. Or maybe an insistence to know her conclusion was correct. He didn't get either.

"Do you still want to know why I'm really here?" she asked.

He nodded. "I do."

She took a breath. "Okay, then. Here's my story."

Rush listened intently as Alessandra explained the frightening things she'd been through over the last two weeks. She told him about the note she'd found from her father, her voice quavering slightly before she quickly went on to talking about how she'd gone to someone she knew at the Seattle PD for advice. She explained how that same someone *did* think the note warranted a bit of an inquiry, and how she'd waited to hear back, only to find out that it would never happen. The officer was dead. An accidental overdose that Alessandra swore was impossible. Her friend was very open about the fact that she'd grown up in an addict's home, and was proud to have risen above it all to become a well-decorated officer.

"There's no way she was doing drugs," Alessandra told him, her voice full of conviction and sadness. "We had lunch just the week before all this happened. She was hoping to get moved onto a narcotics task force. Rush... I'm not naive enough to believe you can know everything about another person, and we weren't all that close, but this... I'd have *known*."

He reached over and squeezed her hand. "I believe you, Red."

It was true. He'd spent enough time around liars and

cheats to know the difference between someone who was sure about something and someone who just wanted to be. He might've said there was a chance she was mistaken, but coupling her story with the fact that Garibaldi admitted to having a source inside the Seattle PD... Rush was just as sure as Alessandra.

Her fingers tightened around his, and she shot him a look so grateful that it was almost heartbreaking. An uncomfortable thickness formed in Rush's throat, and he had to clear it before he could speak again.

"So after all that happened," he said, "Jesse Garibaldi invited you up here, and you came because of the correlation to your father's note?"

Her mouth curved a little. "Now you actually *sound* like a cop."

He lifted an eyebrow. "I can honestly say that's something I've never been accused of before."

She smiled for a second longer, then shook her head and went back to his question. "It *is* why I came. But there's more."

She told him about the surf shop she owned. Even though he was puzzled as to why she was giving him so many details, he listened intently anyway, enjoying her enthusiastic description. The store was right on a beach, so close that Alessandra sometimes got wayward sea life right on her doorstep. She said that there were other stores nearby, but that hers stood alone. Independent, she called it with an affectionate laugh. She talked about the sunrises and the sunsets, and about the crazy customers, and the way the store rattled when it stormed. Rush could tell she truly loved it. So when her words tapered off and her face fell, he could feel the pain rolling off her, and he knew something bad was coming. She paused, her hand holding his hard enough to hurt.

Then she blew out a breath and said, "It burned."

"It burned?" he repeated.

"To the ground."

"Suspicious circumstances?"

"Arson, for sure. But they said it was probably accidental. Some drunk kids who got carried away." She swallowed. "I'm sorry. I need a second."

"Take all the time you need."

She stared at him for a moment, then dropped her eyes to her hands and shifted a little closer, seemingly unaware of the movement. Rush immediately pulled her in, enfolding her into an embrace and rubbing his hands up and down her arms. Her skin was cool now—much cooler than when their bodies had been pressed together—and when Alessandra shivered, Rush realized the temperature had dropped several degrees. He held her even closer, trying to stave off the chill while still giving her the mental space she needed.

After a few moments, she spoke softly, her voice a little muffled by the fact that her face was buried in his shirt. "It's kind of catching up to me, and it feels like it's my fault."

"It's not," he said quickly.

"I think I did things the right way. Or I hope I did. But it didn't help, did it?"

"You can't hold yourself responsible for the bad actions of others, Red."

Her fingers plucked at the fabric of his jeans. "I know. Or I'm currently *telling* myself I know, anyway. But it's hard not to wonder what would've happened if I'd just held on to the note instead of taking it in, and—"

She cut herself off, and it took Rush a second to realize

that she was crying. He slid his hands from her arms to
her head, and he smoothed back her hair. It was strange,
to feel so much concern for a woman he barely knew.
Stranger still, to be holding her close and murmuring re-
assuring words that he truly meant. And strangest of all to
find himself opening his mouth to tell her his own secrets.

In fact, he was sure he would've spilled them all if it
weren't for the sudden rumble in the sky and the splash
of an oversize raindrop hitting Alessandra straight in the
nose. Rush brought up his thumb to swipe it away, then
kissed the same spot.

"Should we head back to the cabin?" he asked as he
pulled back.

"Are you sure it's safe?" she replied.

"Harley said so."

"And you believe him?"

"Of course. He's like a brother to me. Hell. He *is* my
brother as far as I'm concerned. He wouldn't steer me
wrong."

As soon as the words were out of his mouth, Rush realized something. The impending storm didn't make a
difference. He wanted to tell Alessandra everything anyway. He stared down at her for a second, trying to figure
out what it was about her. But damn if he could. It was
more than the way her blue eyes seemed to see into him.
More than the physical attraction that coursed through
him, and more than the very recent memory of her warm
lips. Whatever it was, he had a strange feeling it was only
going to get stronger.

"C'mon. I'll explain it when we're warm and dry,"
he said, then pushed to his feet, pulling her with him,
marveling again at just how right her hand felt pressed
into his palm.

* * *

By the time they reached the top of the cabin's stairs, the rain was coming down full force. But in spite of that—and in spite of the heaviness that had been in her chest just moments earlier—Alessandra was warm all over. She was even smiling. It felt good to trust Rush. It felt *right*. Which really made her realize that over the last two weeks, she'd been walking around with a deep worry permeating every corner of her existence. Understandable. Justifiable. And while coming to Whispering Woods had been her attempt to deal with it all, it was the kind of thing that could benefit from a professional. And if that professional happened to have soft lips, a tough-but-tender demeanor, and the world's sexiest sleeve of tattoos…then so be it.

Alessandra warmed even more and told herself the reason she trusted him wasn't just that he was nice to look at. It didn't hurt. But her faith in him was based on her instincts, on evidence, and on the fact that he was on the right side of the law.

Although…

She eyed Rush's back as he stepped to the cabin door and put his hand on the knob. He hadn't actually *admitted* that he was a cop, but she knew it was true anyway. The clues were there. And Harley's comment about "the case" kind of slammed the theory into place.

Alessandra stopped and frowned, and Rush turned to look at her.

"You coming in?" he asked teasingly. "Or would you prefer to stand out in the rain?"

She didn't answer right away. Instead, she studied his face, her brain working at something. He was currently smiling, but she knew the gruffness was under the surface, ready to be called at will. In fact, she'd truly believed that gruffness was the real him. And even though she'd *wanted* to trust him, she'd bought into the idea the he was a thug.

Because he's good at it, she thought. *Utterly convincing.*

"Red?" he prodded, the smile slipping a little.

"You *let* me figure it out," she blurted.

His smile came back, widening to a Cheshire cat grin. "Hmm."

"What?"

"That doesn't sound like the work of a good undercover cop."

"But you did do it," she insisted. "You *let* me hear that conversation with your friend."

"Why would I do that?" His tone was far too innocent.

Alessandra rolled her eyes. "Because you couldn't tell me the truth without breaking some law or rule or code and you needed a way around it."

"Well. At least that'd make me pretty clever."

"Pleased with yourself, aren't you?"

Whatever he was about to say was swept away by a sudden gust of wind that blew the door back and seemed to make the entire structure rattle. The rain kicked it up a notch, too, flying sideways in stinging drops. Clearly deciding enough was enough, Rush reached out, grabbed Alessandra by the wrist and yanked her into the cabin. Inside, he released her to pull the protesting door shut. Then he turned to face her, and as he kicked off his boots, Alessandra's breath caught in her throat.

In the warm firelight, Rush was the epitome of handsome ruggedness. His salt-and-pepper beard was just the right thickness—scruffy without being unkempt. The rain had dampened his hair and the wind had mussed it up just right, and it practically begged to have fingers run through it. His clothes were wet, too. The plaid jacket was open, revealing his long-sleeved shirt, which clung to his sculpted chest in a way that made Alessandra's knees weak. And his jeans were no drier or any less clingy. The denim was darkened with rain, and it hugged his thighs and showed off his thick, all-muscle quads. He looked strong and capable. Indestructible and sexy.

Yeah, she thought. *Like a lumberjack who moonlights as an underwear model.*

Alessandra's cheeks heated, and she forced her eyes up to Rush's face. It did nothing to quell the rush of her pulse. His stare was on her body as much as hers had been on his. His gaze moved over her slowly. Deliberately. It rested on her curves. She could feel the way he drank in her soaked body, and every inch of exposed skin rose up in tingling goose bumps. When at last his eyes found hers, they sent a thrum of need through her, so hard that it made her gasp.

She couldn't have said who made the first move. Or maybe it was neither of them; maybe they stepped at the same time. Either way, they went from undressing each other with their eyes to tearing at each other's clothes for real. Lips and arms. Ripping cotton, laughter, breathy apologies. Rush's jacket and weapon tossed aside. Shirts up and off. More lips. Moans and gasped endearments.

At last, Rush's hands found Alessandra's hips, and he lifted her from the ground. For a second, she stared down at him, basking in the rampant desire on his face. Reveling in the way they fit together, even like this. But when she bent to kiss his perfectly firm, perfectly delectable lips, a terrible thought occurred to her. And she couldn't help but voice it aloud.

"Rush?" she said against his mouth.

"Alessandra."

"Are you sure Jesse can't see us?"

He pulled back, his mouth twisting with amusement. "Should I comment on how much I don't love that you're talking about another man right now, or just leave that alone?"

She blushed. "Sorry, I'd just prefer it if he didn't see me naked."

The heat in Rush's eyes became an inferno. "I'd prefer that, too."

"So you're sure?"

"What can I do to prove it?"

"I don't know."

"How about this?"

He punctuated the question with movement, carrying her over to the bed on the other side of the room. There, he laid her down. He kissed her once, hard and sweet at the same time. Then he let her go, stepped back, and brought his hands to his waistband. Alessandra couldn't do anything but sit up and watch.

The belt slid out.

The metal button popped free.

The zipper slid down.

The jeans lowered.

And with each new thing, Alessandra's breathing quickened a little more. Her worries about being seen by some invisible camera were seeming less and less important. By the time Rush had shimmied free, Jesse Garibaldi was ridiculously far from her thoughts. The man standing in front of her commanded her complete attention. From his broad shoulders to his well-muscled chest. From his beautiful abs to the sexy vee that was just visible above the waistband of his boxer shorts. Every bit of him begged to be stared at. So she *did* stare. So hard that it startled her when he spoke.

"Convinced yet?" he asked, his voice low and thick.

"Convinced?" It took her second to recall what he meant. "Oh. Um."

She sucked in her lower lip, considering the question. On the one hand, she was sure that Rush wouldn't be standing around in his underwear if he thought there was a chance they were being watched. But on the other hand, if she admitted as much, he might not feel compelled to the remove the boxers. And she really, really wanted to see him finish the striptease.

Her eyes started to drift back to the underwear—and what was underneath them—and she jerked her attention back to Rush's face. He wore a sly half smile that made Alessandra sure he knew where her mind had headed. She refused to give in to the embarrassment.

"No," she said firmly. "I'm not convinced. At all."

"Okay. How about this instead?" He paused, looked around, then yelled, "Hey! Garibaldi! You self-serving son of a you-know-what… Wanna hear my badge number?"

Alessandra laughed. "That's not what I had in mind."

"Care to share what you were thinking?"

"How about you come here and I'll show you?"

"Twist my rubber arm."

Rush stepped closer. Then closer again. Then again. He finally stopped and pressed his knees to hers. He lifted a salacious eyebrow, then used his legs to part her thighs. And stepped closer still.

Alessandra's face was at eye level with his stomach, and her heart was racing so hard it almost hurt. She leaned forward and placed a small, soft kiss just below his belly button. Rush inhaled sharply. The sound made Alessandra ache all the way down to her toes. She kissed his abdomen again, brought her hands to his cotton-covered hips, then leaned back and dragged him down on top of her.

His mouth sought hers, and his hands began an exploration of her body. She met the attention eagerly, arching into his hand as it dragged across her ribs, then over the lacy fabric of her bra. Her skin was on fire. And her mind raced with mixed needs. She wanted him to continue slowly, to make it all last. But she also wanted to hurry up, because she craved skin-to-skin contact. But she didn't have to worry. Rush's timing was impeccable. He touched her thoroughly. He removed the rest of her clothes quickly. But just when she thought the torment was over, he angled his body so that he was beside her instead of on her, and propped himself up on his elbow and sent her an ultraserious look.

"I've never been the kind of man who plays it safe, Red," he said. "But with something like this…with someone like you…"

His words hit her like a brick to the gut. A dozen "unsafe" scenarios played through her head, and each made her as unhappy as the last. And for no good reason, all of them made her want to cry.

Rush stared at her, concern filling his face as he read her expression. "Crap. No. Not like *that,* Red. I meant that I have a habit of putting action before everything else. Measurable results. But I've literally known you for hours, and I don't want you to think I'm just…or that this is…" He trailed off, scrubbed his free hand over his beard, then muttered, "I'm screwing this up."

Alessandra smiled a watery smile. "If it makes you feel any better… I have no idea what I'm doing."

He raised a doubtful eyebrow. "I'd argue against that."

"That's not what I meant. I meant I don't usually hop into bed with a man whose middle name I don't know."

"Yeah. Me, neither."

"Shut up. You know what I'm saying."

"I do. So in the interest of confession, I feel like I should tell you that it's been two years since I kissed a woman. In the past six years, I haven't had a relationship that wasn't a part of an undercover operation."

"Oh."

"Oh?" he repeated.

"I don't know what the right reaction is," she told him. "Sorry?"

He chuckled, then leaned over to kiss her mouth. "It's easy. You confess that all of your relationships over the last six years were also fake, and that you've been waiting for me to come into your life, chase you into a hole in the woods, then sweep you off your feet and make you forget about everything else that's been going on. Oh. Then you tell me that you've got a condom in your purse, because I seem to be fresh out."

Alessandra couldn't help but laugh, and she traced her fingers down Rush's bare chest as she replied, "All of my relationships over the past six years haven't been fake. But they *have* been nonexistent. A few casual dates, and I did have a two-month fling with a surfer who came to Seattle for the summer a few years back. And if you want to go back *seven* years instead, I had a boyfriend through college. We were both in business admin, but I chose the more entrepreneurial route, and he went after some corporate job in New York, so we amicably went our separate ways."

"That's good news."

"It is?"

"Mmm-hmm. I'm glad to hear that you're not otherwise attached. And equally glad to hear I've got the corner on the feet-sweeping." He reached up and grabbed her fingers, then kissed the tips.

Alessandra could swear that her whole body was sighing with pleasure. "And about that other thing...you might actually be in luck. There's a little bag inside my big bag, and if I remember correctly..."

"Say no more." Rush jumped up and padded across the floor in his underwear to grab her bag, which he lifted and held out. "You want to look?"

"Go ahead," she replied. "The other bag's purple. It should be easy to spot."

Alessandra watched him dig through, wondering if the mood should've been dampened by the conversation and the delay. If maybe admitting that she had condoms stuck down in the recesses of her bathroom bag should've embarrassed her. But it didn't. And if anything, the syncopated sharing of their histories heightened her desire. She was glad to know a little more about him. She *liked* what he'd told her. She liked watching his big, strong hands paw through her things in his search, too. It was strangely intimate.

It's also taking too long, she thought after a few seconds.

Anticipation made her squirm a little impatiently. And just when she was about to suggest he either dump the entire bag or bring it to her, he yanked out the purple pouch. He quickly unzipped the smaller bag, freed the small strip of foil packages, then turned her way.

"It's Aaron," he said.

"What?"

"My middle name."

"Oh. Good to know." And then he stepped toward her, and Alessandra forgot everything but the rush of need that roared through her.

Rush woke up colder than he expected to be, and his
mind drifted sleepily to the fact that he'd been a little

Chapter 10

Rush woke up colder than he expected to be, and his
mind drifted sleepily to the fact that he'd been a little
negligent in keeping the woodstove going. It was late
spring, but with the storm and the higher elevation, it still
managed to cool down overnight. If he'd been thinking,
he would've fed the fire a little more before crashing.
But he'd been a little...distracted. Twice. And the distraction was followed by dinner. Then a third distraction.
Which led to the tangle of bedsheets where he was now.

With the intention of fueling the woodstove, he started
to push off the mess of blankets, then abruptly realized
he had a far better source of heat right beside him. Not
bothering to curb his eagerness, he reached out for Alessandra. His hands found nothing but air. His eyes flew
open. The bed was disappointingly empty, and seeing
it actually sent a strange sense of worry into his gut. He

sat up and realized belatedly that the cabin was almost pitch-black.

"Red?" he called softly.

When he didn't get a response right away, the worry spiraled a little higher.

Cautious and on alert, Rush swung his legs over the edge of the bed and scanned the room the best he could. The curtains were drawn, the stove barely offered a glow, and the sound of rain still raged outside. It'd been a perfect backdrop to the night before. Now it was eerier than Rush cared to admit. Years of experience kept him outwardly calm and utterly silent as he pressed his feet to the floor and stood up. Now that his vision was adjusting the dark, he took another quick sweep of the cabin. Nothing looked out of place.

Except Alessandra...who should be in *place,* he thought as he snagged his pants from the ground and slipped them on.

It was true, though. Aside from the missing redhead, nothing appeared to have been disturbed. It wasn't like Rush believed someone could've come in and whisked Alessandra away without him knowing about it, but he still took inventory anyway. The dishes were where they'd left them. Their clothes were in a heap on the floor. His gun hung from the hook beside the door. His eyes rested on the weapon for a second. He didn't think he needed it right then, but as he stared in its general direction, he realized something else. The door was unlocked. The slide chain dangled against the wood, and the dead bolt was in the open position.

Rush exhaled and stepped quickly toward the door. Out of habit, he grabbed his gun and jammed it into the rear of his waistband before putting his hand on the knob.

He eased the door open slowly, unsure what to prepare for. But whatever might've been in his head, it sure as hell wasn't what he found.

Alessandra sat on one of the oversize patio chairs, her feet tucked up under her body, her eyes on the horizon. Her hair was loose, whipping wildly with the still-churning wind. She'd tossed on a shirt—one of his own white ones, he noted absently—but it was already wet.

How long has she been sitting out here?

The thought spurred him to action. Forgetting his own state of undress, he strode forward and bent down. Every protective instinct he had was alive and buzzing in a way he'd never experienced before.

"Red," he said, the urgency clear in his voice. "It's cold and rainy and you're sitting out here without a coat."

Her face jerked in his direction, and her cheeks were lined with streaks he was sure were more than rain. She made no move to get up, either. Instead, she held out a soggy white envelope. Rush's eyes dropped to the object, and it was then that he noticed her legs were bare. It was all he could stand. He didn't know what had woken her or why she'd come outside. All he wanted was to fix it. So he slid one hand under her knees and the other around her back, and he lifted her up. She didn't protest. If anything, she tucked hers head against him a little tighter as he carried her over the deck and back into the house.

Inside, he adjusted so that he could drag a chair to the woodstove. He set her down and wrapped her in a blanket. He added an excessive number of pellets to the fire before he finally pulled up his own chair, then pressed his denim-clad knees to her microfiber-covered ones and at last reached out to take the envelope from her now-clenched hands. She said nothing—just watched him stare it down. He recognized the logo in the right-hand corner of the envelope right away. It made him frown.

"Where did you get this, Red?" he asked.

She drew in a shaky breath, then nodded across the room. "That box."

Rush swiveled to follow her gaze. He immediately spied what she meant. In the firelight, he could see it just fine. A small wood box. Carved with an indecipherable pattern of some kind, and resting on a windowsill. He frowned a little harder. Had it been there all along? He wasn't sure. He supposed it didn't matter if had been, or if she'd dragged it out from somewhere else.

He turned his attention back to Alessandra. "Do you know what this is?"

Her head bobbed down, then up, and when she answered, her voice wobbled. "A note from my dad to my mom."

It wasn't the reply he was expecting. "I—what? This is sealed and there's no name on it."

"I know. The other one I found—the one I told you about—it was in an envelope just like that one." She reached out and tapped the logo. "It had the same mark."

Rush stroked his thumb over the same spot. "*This* mark?"

Alessandra nodded, then started to tear up again. "I'd show you, but the note got burned in the fire at my surf shop."

Rush balanced the envelope on their touching knees and brought his hands up to cup her cheeks. He didn't know why it made him ache so hard to see her cry, but it did. In fact, it pushed other thoughts—important ones, like things about his case or why her father had access to these particular envelopes—to the back of his mind. He had to force them forward.

He dropped his hand and pointed to the paper in their laps. "Do you know where that logo's from?"

Alessandra looked down. "No."

"It belongs to the Freemont City Police Department," he told her. "Or I guess I should say *did* belong. It was their logo until twelve years ago. They retired it with the guy who designed it forty years before that."

Alessandra's expression grew puzzled. "It's a police envelope?"

"Definitely. Did your dad have a friend on the force, maybe? Or do some work with them?"

Unexpectedly, she laughed. "God, no. My dad was a 'fight the man' type, all the way to the end. He'd be so annoyed at me if he knew—" She cut herself off and blushed as he eyes drifted toward the bed. "Let's just say he'd be less than impressed. He wasn't exactly an up-standing citizen. Especially before I was born."

In spite of the situation, Rush couldn't fight a smile. "Rest assured. If things in my life hadn't been tilted in the right direction, I'd be on the other side of the bars myself right now."

"Really?"

"I'm surprised that you're surprised," he teased. "Aren't you the one who called me a thug?"

"I said you had a thug *vibe*," she corrected.

"That's different?"

"Yes. Because you're not actually a—ugh. Why are we having this conversation? My dad died a decade and a half ago, you're a cop, not a criminal, and—" Her eyes filled with tears again.

Rush leaned over and pulled her into an awkward embrace. "Hey, now. We don't have to talk about it."

She sighed against his chest, and the soft expel of air reminded him forcefully that he was still topless. Thinking he should do something about it before his body wanted to do something *else,* he started to pull back. Then she spoke, her words stopping his movement before it really got started.

"Tell me about the tilt," she said. "What made you become one of the good guys instead of the bad guys?"

Rush hesitated, but only for a moment. The need to tell her came flooding in. And he was *relieved* to feel it. Relieved to finally have an outlet for the things he kept bottled up.

He leaned away enough that he could look down and meet her eyes as he spoke. "It's funny. Every time I've been undercover—which is my whole career, really—I've never been able to pretend that he's alive. I've made up dozens of stories about his death over the last ten years. Cancer. Car accident. Heart attack. Jellyfish sting off the coast of Australia. You name it, my backstory dad has died from it." He paused, his fingers tracing the Freemont PD logo on the envelope while he tried to keep his voice as even as he could manage. "But the truth is, my dad was a cop, too. Back when this logo was still current, actually. Killed on the job."

"I'm so sorry, Rush." Alessandra's word were infused with understanding, and he was grateful for their sincerity.

He touched her cheek and went on. "About fifteen years ago, my dad was investigating a drug case. A big one that he and his buddies called a career-maker. The three of them were going over some evidence in a sealed room at the station when a pipe bomb went off. They all died."

Alessandra's hand came up to cover his, and she brought his palm to her lips and pressed a gentle kiss to the work-roughened center. It sent a jolt of longing through him. It mingled with the relief and made his chest expand in a nearly painful way. Telling her everything was like having a burden—one he didn't even consciously know he was carrying—lifted. Maybe it was unreasonable. Maybe it made no sense. But it was true nonetheless. He half wondered how the hell he'd managed to hold everything in all these years.

And he pushed on. "The other two men in that room with my father were my best friends' dads."

"Harley," Alessandra filled in.

"Him," Rush agreed. "Plus his brother, Brayden, and our other buddy, Anderson. We swore we'd get justice for our fathers. We made a pact. And that, Red, was the tilt."

"They didn't catch the guy who did it?"

"Oh, they did. But the courts didn't do what they should've. The kid got off."

"The kid?" Alessandra repeated, sounding startled.

Rush nodded curtly. "And the kid grew up and—"

He cut himself off abruptly as a faint sound from outside drew his attention. It only took a second to place it. The crunch of tires on gravel, carrying faintly over the rain.

"Crap," he muttered, disentangling himself from Alessandra, who shot a worried look his way as he stood up.

"What's wrong?" she asked.

"There's only one person who knows we're here, and I think he's on his way for a surprise visit." He grabbed his discarded shirt from the floor and slipped it over his head. "You might wanna put something else on, too."

Her gaze drifted down, then her eyes widened, and she jumped to her feet. As she scrambled to find her clothes, Rush moved through the cabin and attempted to erase any sign of their more-than-friendly encounter the night before. He cursed his own stupidity. He wasn't worried that Garibaldi had figured out what Harley had done to his surveillance system; his technophile friend was too good for that. But he should've considered the idea that his fake boss might physically check up on him.

Surprise inspection, he thought sardonically as he smoothed out the bed.

When he was done, he grabbed his gun and shrugged into his flannel jacket, then cast a quick glance around. Everything looked more or less normal. Except Alessandra, who looked a little too damned sexy for her own good. Even the hastily done, slightly severe bun did nothing to take away from her appeal.

You're only noticing because you spent the night looking at her naked, he assured himself.

He strode forward, gently grabbed her chin, planted a firm kiss on her lips, and said, "Forgive me in advance, okay?"

He let her go before she could ask for clarification, then moved to the door and flung it open just in time to see Garibaldi reach the top of the stairs.

If Alessandra hadn't already been anxious about Jesse's presence, then Rush's words would still have sent over the edge of worry.

Forgive you for what? she wanted to ask.

But Jesse no sooner swept into the room—his sharp eyes taking in every detail and making Alessandra feel like her father had just walked in and caught her mak-

ing out with her high school boyfriend—than she understood. Rush's whole demeanor changed. The unwinding
he'd done over the last twenty or so hours reversed itself
completely. The teasing warmth in his brown eyes had
disappeared. The quirk of a smile had vanished, too. He
looked rougher and meaner and more sullen even than
he had when he'd first fallen into the hole.

Alessandra actually caught herself lifting a hand up
to wipe her eyes, thinking maybe she was seeing things.
She definitely wasn't. It almost made her shiver. She
had to swallow against a sudden scratchy feeling in her
throat. Logically, she knew he was playing a role. But
that didn't stop her from wondering how he managed to
so quickly do away with the man who'd been cupping
her face in his hands just a few minutes earlier. Why was
it so easy to mask that version of himself?

But then Jesse turned his attention her directly, and
she had to pretend not be noticing any of it. She fixed a
look of surprised pleasure onto her face, unfolded her
legs and stood up to greet him.

"Hi!" she said. "You're up early."

Jesse smiled, but his gaze was still sharp. "What can
I say, Al? Early bird and all that."

Rush cut in, his voice as surly as the rest of him.
"Does this mean I'm off the hook? Because I gotta say…
some of us aren't so fond of the worm."

Alessandra caught his eye, and she saw a small plea
there. He wanted her to play along. She mentally exhaled.
At least being complicit in the deception would make her
feel like they were working together rather than feeling
like he'd just been able to turn off the last day.

She wrinkled her nose and narrowed her eyes. "If
you're calling *me* a worm…"

"Relax, Red." The nickname took on an insulting tone. "I meant that in all its metaphorical glory."

"Oh, look at that," Alessandra retorted. "A word with more than three syllables. Pleased with yourself?"

"Nothing pleasurable about this," he said back.

Jesse looked from Rush to Alessandra, his eyes finally losing their edge. "I actually just came by to make sure I hired the right man for the job. You want me to fire him, Al? I've got a few errands to run, but I can take care of you myself when I'm done."

Panic hit her harder than she dared let on. What if Jesse *did* take over the tour guide role? The thought scared her. And if she was being honest, it wasn't just because *Jesse* scared her all on his own. It wasn't even just that she was worried that she'd never find out what happened with her father. It was because she felt like things were just getting started with Rush. She wanted a chance to see where they would go. Alessandra had to bite her lip to keep from letting out a vehement protest. And thankfully, Rush jumped in anyway.

"Nah, boss," he said, his voice tinged with resentment. "I said I'd do this for you. I'll do it. Have some faith. Besides that, I've already got the day mapped out."

Alessandra let out the smallest breath possible. "Oh, yeah? Were you going to consult me about the plan?"

"Might've," Rush replied.

"Might've?" she repeated skeptically.

"Yeah. Might've. After a cup of coffee and some eggs."

"I didn't realize coffee and eggs were an option."

"Could be because you were up at the butt-crack of dawn."

Jesse sighed like the bickering was boring him, and

Alessandra tensed, wondering if he was going to intercede and insist on staying in Rush's stead.

Instead he asked, "Did he fight with you like this the whole night?"

Alessandra fought a blush and made herself answer in a grudging way. "No. We played cards, and he made soup."

"He made *soup*? Now that's something I'd like to have seen," Jesse said with a laugh.

"Stick around and you'll see me make toast, too," Rush told him. "Real exciting stuff."

The other man shook his head. "Love the idea of you all domesticated, Atkinson, but I've got Ernest waiting in the car. So as long as Al's not too mad about my abandonment..."

Alessandra shook her head. "I'm fine. I know you've got work, and I can handle Rush."

"Good to hear." Jesse reached out and gave her shoulder a squeeze that made her want to cringe, then added, "I'll be back in time for dinner. I promise."

The innocent-sounding words filled her with foreboding, and she had to force a nod. "Thanks, Jesse."

He turned to go, and she couldn't help but let out a relieved breath, glad he was satisfied. But he paused at the door, and when he swung his head in her direction once more, the hawk-like glint was back in his eyes. And Alessandra realized he hadn't been placated in the slightest.

"Hey, Al?" he said.

She resisted a nervous swallow and replied with as much casualness as she could muster. "Yes?"

"What card game did you play last night?" he asked.

For no good reason, the question made her tongue stick to the roof of her mouth. It was an easy lie. Rummy. Crazy eights. Anything would've done. But Alessandra's brain told her it was a trick of some kind, and it rendered her unable to come up with quick enough response. And then she clued in. It *was* a trick. But there wasn't a wrong answer. It was just intended to make her stumble—an attempt to catch her in a lie. And it was working. Jesse stared at her, waiting. It was only seconds, but it felt like hours.

Once again, Rush spoke up first. "Strip poker, boss. What else?"

It was enough to jolt Alessandra back to her senses. She shot Rush the dirtiest look she had, inwardly thanking him.

"We played *crib*," she told Jesse. "There was an old board in the cupboard. And I beat him three times. Just for the record."

"She cheats," Rush muttered.

Jesse stared for one second more, then shook his head. "She doesn't cheat, my friend. She's just very good. Always the smartest one in the room. Outplayed me a thousand times when we were kids."

"Maybe we can have a game when you get back?" Alessandra suggested.

"I'll add it to my schedule," Jesse said, then tossed a look toward Rush. "Take care of her."

Alessandra missed Rush's response. She was only vaguely aware of Jesse's exit. She was too busy forcing herself to breathe. Forcing herself not to panic.

Because her brain had just a made a terrifying leap.

Jesse Garibaldi—a man she'd known her whole life— was the one who'd killed Rush's father.

Chapter 11

In Alessandra's mind, it made perfect sense. Jesse was the right age to have been the kid Rush mentioned. It explained Rush's undercover mission and his obvious disdain for the other man. And on top of that, the time line matched with what Alessandra overheard her mom say all those years ago about her stenographer client seeing Jesse at the courthouse. She was right. She knew it. And the whole thing just about made her dizzy with thick fear. Because if Jesse had done that, all those years ago, what had he done since? And what were the chances that he knew nothing about her own father's death? And most pressing…what did it mean that he'd invited her to Whispering Woods?

Then the answer to the last question hit her like a brick to the gut.

Oh God.

She swayed on her feet, and only managed not to fall over because Rush's hands steadied her. And when she lifted her eyes to meet his, she saw the truth in his silent, apologetic stare.

"He wants you to kill me," she said, her voice a choked whisper.

"C'mon, Red," he replied gently. "Let's sit down."

"I don't *want* to sit down!" she snapped, anger flooding in to overtake the fear. "You knew what he wanted, and you just…we just… I can't believe we… You should've told me, Rush."

"What did you want me to say?"

"You could've started with a warning."

"Like what? 'Hey, Alessandra…your old friend would rather you not come out alive'? Would you have just stayed here?"

She started to say that of course she would have stayed, then realized it would be a lie. She dropped down onto the couch. She didn't know *what* she would've done. Freaked out, the way she was freaking out now? Most likely. Felt scared of staying in one spot, especially when Jesse not only knew exactly where that spot was, but also personally *owned* it? Definitely. And she still had no clue what was going on. But she wanted to. She exhaled and tried to calm her racing thoughts and heart.

"Explain it to me, Rush," she said. "Because right now I feel like I walked out of my life and into an action movie where I'm the target."

He ran a frustrated hand over his stubble. "What do you want to know?"

"Did Jesse kill your father?" She asked it as gently as she could, but he still winced like it stung.

"Yes," he said roughly. "Mine and my friends'."

She steeled herself against a wave of sympathy that made her want to stop questioning him. She understood his pain. But the man had slept with her, knowing full well her life was in direct danger. She deserved a few answers.

"Why?" she asked.

"Because *his* father was killed during a drug bust run by *our* fathers. That was the police incident, as you called it."

"And he got off on a technicality?"

"Yes," he said. "Something pretty damned close to that."

Alessandra took another breath. "Rush?"

"Yes?"

"Do you think he might've killed *my* father?" Her voice came out thicker than she would've like, and a heartbeat later, Rush was beside her on the couch, dragging her hands into his strong grip, and she didn't pull away as he spoke.

"I really don't know, sweetheart," he said earnestly, all traces of surliness disappearing. "I wish I could just tell you it wasn't possible. But I know what he's capable of."

Her heart leaped with renewed fear, and she met his eyes. "Things like ordering you to kill me."

"I've done a few questionable things in my time undercover. But I'm not a murderer. Even if I didn't like you the way that I do, and even if we hadn't spent the night together, I wouldn't hurt you." He released her hands to cup her face instead. "Hell. I'd do anything in my power to *stop* you from getting hurt."

Rush said it with such force that Alessandra had no trouble picturing him jumping in front of a speeding train to save her life. It was impossible not to lean into his touch. And it was even more impossible to ignore the solid tether of feeling it created. It was thickening around her heart in a way that scared her. Staying focused required more effort than she wanted to admit.

"And all this time…" she made herself say. "Fifteen years…you've been investigating Jesse?"

"To put it simply," he agreed.

"What if I asked you to put it *un*-simply?" she replied.

"When Garibaldi went free, we made the pact. It was Brayden's idea. He was always the good guy. Our fearless, well-principled leader." He smiled affectionately, taking the sting out of his words. "He made sure we did it right. The way our fathers would have."

Alessandra nodded her understanding. "You all became cops."

"We did. On slightly different paths, but we all got there. And we investigated Garibaldi on our own time. He's slippery as hell. Everything he owns goes through a series of companies before it finally trickles down to him. It took literal years to track him to Whispering Woods. But we've got almost enough to bring him in. I just need to catch him in the act."

As soon as Rush finished explaining, a realization dawned on Alessandra. She was in the way. An impediment to his whole investigation. But aside from the initial irritation at being stuck with her—which, judging by his interaction with Jesse, could've been exaggerated anyway—he hadn't complained a bit.

The warm feeling in Alessandra's chest grew, and she spoke without considering the absurdity of what she said. "What can I do to help?"

And to his credit, he didn't laugh at her offer. He

dragged her in and kissed her hard, then pulled back and pressed his forehead to hers.

"The first thing you can do is tell me anything else you think I should know about Garibaldi," he said. "And after that, you can help me find a way to make him think I've done what he asked."

Alessandra's eyes widened. "You want me to fake my own death?"

Rush grinned. "Well. When you say it like that, it sounds weird."

"But seriously..." she replied.

His face sobered. "Yes. Seriously. He's not going to let you walk away. That first note you found sealed the deal. He told me himself that he has a connection in the Seattle PD."

She felt the blood drain from her head, and she held on to Rush a little tighter. "So he killed my friend and burned down my shop."

Rush nodded. "I'm sorry, Red."

Even though somewhere in the back of her mind she already knew it was true, hearing it acknowledged still stirred something sorrowful deep inside her. Memories of childhood moments spent with Jesse made it even worse. Especially since they all seemed to be swimming right below the surface at the moment. A Thanksgiving here. A beach day there. Then came a swift, painful recollection—Jesse applying a bandage to a knee Alessandra had skinned when falling from her bike. In spite of the truth of what she'd told Rush about never really feeling a connection to Jesse, it was impossible to deny that her early years were intertwined with his. And the acknowledgment pained her. How could she have shared *any* time with a person who would grow up to be the kind of man Jesse had become? How did someone even become that way in the first place? No regard for human life, or the suffering inflicted on others?

She didn't realize she'd voiced any of it aloud until Rush answered her.

"You'd think with all the years I've spent in close quarters with the bad guys, I'd have a clear understanding," he said. "But the truth is, I just have theories. I think sometimes it's motivated by greed, and sometimes by a need to control everything around them. Maybe both, a lot of the time. And with guys like Garibaldi…" He shrugged. "I think they need to feel smarter than everyone else."

Alessandra nodded, her mind going to the comment he'd made about her and her intelligence. "So if he's so bad, and I'm such a threat, why isn't he just…you know… sniper-ing me, or whatever?"

Even though the question was darker than it was funny, Rush's mouth quirked up a little. "Aside from *sniper-ing* not being a word…he was looking for an assessment of just how much of a threat you are."

"Like…what do I know about what he really does, and have I told anyone else?"

"Exactly."

"And what did you tell him?"

"That you know nothing and have nothing to tell anyone."

"But he didn't care."

"Afraid not." Rush's voice was full of regret.

Alessandra straightened her shoulders and dug in for some resolve. "I'll do it, Rush. I'll help you pretend I'm dead. But I have a condition."

His lips twitched again. "A condition for saving your life?"

"I'm not kidding."

"Oh, I know. And it doesn't surprise me. What is it?"

"I want you to find out if Jesse was responsible for my father's death. Directly or indirectly."

"Done," he replied without hesitation.

Alessandra sagged with relief. "Thank you."

"You want to add to your list of demands, you just let me know," Rush said. "In the meantime, I think you should open that other note you found."

He stood up and crossed the room, then grabbed the envelope from the spot were Alessandra had stashed it. Seeing it made her nervous all over again. She lifted her gaze to Rush's face. She started to open her mouth to admit that she was scared. After all, the first note was the trigger for every frightening, heartrending event that followed. But she didn't get a chance to speak. As Rush held out the envelope, a *bang* and a *crack* echoed through the air.

For a stunned moment, Rush was puzzled by the noise, the flying glass and the sting in his hand.

"What the hell was—"

His brain caught up before the sentence was all the way out.

The *bang* was a gunshot.

The *crack* was the shattering window.

And the sting was the burn of a bullet that had hit the envelope in his hand, then lodged itself into the wood behind him.

Rush dived across the room. His arms wrapped around Alessandra, and he yanked her from the couch to the ground, shielding her with his body. His mind was already churning, trying to scheme a way out.

Front door? Out of the question.

A window? The shot had proven that wasn't a safe option.

He needed to look around.

"Stay down," he ordered in a low voice.

He started to push to his knees. Alessandra grabbed his arm before he got even halfway up, and Rush realized a little belatedly that her face was full of justifiable fear.

"It'll be okay," he said.

"Is someone *shooting* at us?" she asked, a tremor in her voice.

"Looks that way," he replied grimly. "I'm not a verified expert, but I'm thinking a long-range weapon of some kind."

"And you're going stand up? Are you insane?"

"I need to make sure the door's locked, then find us a way out."

"By making yourself a target?"

"I'll keep low."

"You're too tall to keep properly low!"

"You got a better idea?" He meant it half-sarcastically, but she nodded, and before he could stop her, she slid free. "What the hell are you doing, Red?"

"Helping," she replied.

"Don't—"

But she was already gone. With more agility than he could've managed himself, she crawled over to position herself under the window. Her hand snaked up, grabbed the edge of the curtain, and gave it a sideways flick. Rush tensed, expecting another shot. Nothing came. Alessandra maneuvered herself to the other side of the window and did the same with the other curtain. Then she moved across the floor again, this time toward the door. She reached up, snapped the dead bolt shut, then crawled back toward him.

"See?" she said. "I bought us a little security."

He thought about issuing her a lecture on endangering herself, then immediately rejected the idea. Both because he didn't have time for lectures and because Alessandra was right. The curtains were a light color, but they were thick. Designed to keep in the heat. And right that second, the heavy fabric was the only thing shielding them from the shooter's sights.

The shooter who's probably not *firing because he's on his way here right now to finish the job.*

Who knew how long they had until the gunman got there? Mere minutes, if he was efficient.

"All right," Rush muttered to himself. "Now we need a way out."

"What about the stove?" Alessandra said.

He looked from her to it, then back again, frowning. "The stove?"

She pointed up to the ceiling above it. "It's vented, and there's a panel there. Everywhere else is thick wood. But I think that part where it's attached is made of something else."

He followed her finger and saw what she meant. The metal piping ended in a flat round piece, which was mounted to a rectangular panel. The panel was set deep enough into the roof that Rush was sure it was a direct barrier to the outside. He could even see the bolts holding it in place. He had a utility knife in his jacket pocket with a tool he could use to pry the bolts free, too.

All we need to do is find a way up. Silently, and without being seen.

Like she could read his mind, Alessandra pointed again. "If we could somehow move the bookshelf over about four feet, and line it up with this side of the stove, it would give us some cover *and* a leg up."

He turned a raised eyebrow her way. "I thought you said you owned a surf shop."

"I did. And I do."

"And you moonlight as what? A spy? An escape artist?"

Pink crept up her cheeks. "No. I'm just a hands-on problem solver. It worked in my favor yesterday, didn't it?"

"You mean when you chased me down and wound up in the ditch?" he teased.

"Right. Because now's the time for jokes."

"It's always the right time for jokes. It makes dangerous situations seem less dangerous."

"Okay. But don't you think pointing out the purpose behind the levity kind of dilutes it?"

"Does it?"

She shot him a dirty look. "Are you going to help me move the shelf, or not?"

"You're the one talking. Just tell me what to do, and I'll do it," he replied.

She narrowed her eyes like she didn't quite believe him, then sighed and started quickly reeling off her ideas. "Okay. I think we can safely crawl over to the shelf without being seen. We can probably even stand up once we're there, because it'd be next to impossible to see that corner from outside. It'll be easier to move, too, so

I think we should take everything off the shelves. Then we just…push."

Rush deliberately flexed his biceps. "Pushing. That, I can do effectively."

"Ready?"

"One second."

"What?"

He leaned over, planted a kiss on her lips, then dropped nearly flat to the ground. "*Now* I'm ready."

She muttered something he couldn't quite understand—but that he was sure was the equivalent of a blush mixed with an eye roll—then joined him on the ground. And then immediately overtook him. He shook his head as she scooted past him to the shelf, somehow making the crawl look graceful.

"Fitness boot camp," she told him, jumping to her feet. "If we have a situation that requires me to swing some weighted ropes, I'll be all over that, too."

"Good to know," Rush replied drily.

"I'm practically a ninja."

She started sweeping the knickknacks and books off the shelf, and by the time he was at her side, she had most of the items deposited on the floor.

"You sure you need *me* to push that thing?" he said. "They don't cover that in boot camp?"

"Oh, they do," she assured him. "But I want to make sure you feel useful."

"Now who has the jokes?"

"Dangerous situation."

He couldn't fight a ridiculous grin as he put his hands on the shelf. It wasn't normal to have fun in a life-and-death scenario. He knew that. But damn if he could stop himself from enjoying it anyway. Still smiling, he gave the shelf a shove, and was glad to find that it actually slid really easily over the floor. In seconds, he had it positioned beside the stove, and he was ready to climb up. He stopped, though, when Alessandra's hand landed on his arm.

He turned his attention her way. "What's wrong?"

"You're not ready."

"I'm not?"

She pressed to her toes and kissed him—hard but quick—then pulled back. "Okay. Now you're good. I'll hold the shelf. You just try not to fall. Or get shot. Or die in any way, shape or form."

"I'll do my best." He kissed her again, just because he could, and started his ascent.

Alessandra's hold on the bottom was steady. The shelf barely moved as he climbed it, and in moments he was kneeling on the very top.

"Not dead yet," he told her as he positioned himself just below the four-foot-by-three-foot panel.

"Less talking, more doing," she replied.

He waved his hand over the metal—warm, but not hot, so he knew it was properly insulated and unlikely to burn him during the process—then dragged out his utility knife. "I'm thinking about having that tattooed on my lower back, actually."

"That would be a good look for you."

"Think so?" he said, grunting a little as he pried the first bolt free.

"Oh, I'm sure of it," she replied.

"Noted."

He moved on to the second bolt, then the third and fourth. On the fifth, he struggled a little with some rust, but the sixth and final one came off almost the moment he touched it. The panel dropped down and he was immediately assaulted by rain from above and by the chimney smoke that billowed into the cabin. Cursing and choking, Rush quickly repositioned the panel, angling it up and out. He made sure it was secure, then waved away the smoke in front of his face and started to climb down.

"What are you doing?" Alessandra asked.

He tipped his gaze her way. "Getting down so I can hold the shelf steady while you get up and out."

She shook her head. "No. That's a waste of time. Just climb out. I'll follow you."

"And take a chance that the shelf falls over and—"

A rhythmic *thump* from general direction of the door cut him off. The shooter was on his way up the stairs.

Chapter 12

At the distinct sound of feet hitting wood, Alessandra's head whipped toward the door, and true fear cut through her mask of joviality. The person on the other side had a gun. He had no qualms about using it. And he couldn't be more than twenty feet away.

She flicked her gaze back up to Rush, and whisper-yelled, "Hurry!"

Rush didn't argue. He didn't say a word. He just turned and climbed back up.

Alessandra tightened her grip on the shelf and worked to keep herself from scrambling after him before it was safe. It was the longest three seconds of her life. But she made it through. And once he'd pulled himself through the opening in the ceiling, she took a breath, said a silent thank-you to boot camp and all its sweaty, full-body-ache days, and started her own climb.

The shelf wobbled, but she was quick, and it held. By

the time she reached the top, Rush had already repositioned himself on the roof, and his arms hung through
the hole in an offer of assistance. She gripped his hands
gratefully. But her gratitude only lasted a moment. Because Alessandra no sooner slid the rest of the way onto
the roof than a creak sounded from below her feet. The
creak was followed by a resounding, shattering crash
that echoed up through the opening in the roof.

Alessandra didn't have to look down to know that
the shelf had just fallen over. She also didn't have to
check to see that the wood had splintered and that it lay
in pieces below. She knew it was exactly what had happened. And to top it off, there was no way the shooter
hadn't heard it, too. Automatically, she strained to listen
for some sign that their assailant had connected the dots.
There was no human sound, though. Just the rush of the
continuing storm.

But the reprieve could only last so long.

Alessandra lifted her eyes to meet Rush's gaze. His
expression said he knew it, too. The only hope was that
whoever the gunman was, he wouldn't think to search
the roof as an escape route. She was thankful that at least
they had the slope to protect them from sight.

*But we need to get out of here before things go even
more wrong.*

Rush nodded silently—agreeing with her unspoken
thought—then held out his hand. Alessandra took it,
praying for the best. With the rain beating down on them
and their fingers clasped, they slid down the slope of the
roof. They made it to the edge, where Rush freed his
hand and pressed his finger to his lips in a "keep quiet"
gesture, then eased forward. Alessandra held her breath
as he took a careful look, and she exhaled in relief as

he turned back and nodded again. And even though she knew what was coming, she drew in another lungful of air and held it again as Rush slid forward a little more, dangled his legs off the side, then jumped. A moment later, his voice came up in a whisper that barely carried over the sound of the pelting rain.

"All clear down here, Red," he said.

She copied his motions to bring her own body to the edge. But once she was there, she froze. How far down was it? What if she slipped on the rain-slick wood? On a scale of one to shattered femur…how likely was she to break her leg?

But you can't stay up here, a voice in her head reminded her. *And time is a luxury you don't have.*

"I know, I know," she muttered.

She inched forward and tried to look down. But a wave of dizziness made her vision swim, and she not only couldn't go any farther, she also couldn't see.

Then Rush's voice came again, filled with worry this time. "Red?"

"I'm here. But… I think I might be afraid of heights." Her own reply came out so low that she was kind of surprised he could hear her at all.

But he called up again right away, his tone a weird mix of amusement and urgency. "You scaled a shelving unit a minute ago."

"I know. But this is different."

"Okay. Not gonna pretend I understand, but listen to me. It's not as far as it seems. No more than eight feet from the low point to the ground. If you swing yourself around onto your stomach and hang your legs over the side, that cuts the distance in half. Four feet. Think you can do it?"

Four feet. That's not so bad.

But her voice still wavered as she replied in the affirmative. "I can try."

"I promise, Red. If you fall, I'll catch you."

For some reason, that last bit was exactly what she needed to hear. If she fell, Rush would catch her.

Literally.

Alessandra sucked in a breath and followed his instructions. It was surprisingly easy, and in moments, she was on the ground, her back pressed to Rush's reassuringly solid chest. He delivered a swift kiss to her cheek, then slid his hand to hers and pulled her so that they were both flush against the exterior of the cabin. Alessandra could see that they were on the back corner of the deck—out of viewing distance from whoever was in the front. A tall storage bin added further cover. They were momentarily safe.

Yeah. So long as the guy with the gun doesn't figure out you're trapped here between the cabin and the mountain behind it.

But the air around them remained devoid of any nonnaturally occurring noise. Oddly so. It would've raised the hairs on the back of Alessandra's neck if the rain hadn't been keeping it down.

Rush's agreement was obvious in his mutter. "Where *is* he?"

Several more seconds ticked by, and still the rain was the only sound. When at last a clatter of some kind came from inside the cabin, it was almost a relief. The gunman was far too close for comfort, but knowing his location was a lot better than *not* knowing.

"Okay," Rush whispered. "We probably have thirty seconds before he figures out what we did and comes out looking. We need to move fast and quiet. We'll make our way to the front, duck low and head for the stairs. If we're lucky, we'll get all the way down. Stay behind me until we're at the stairs, then stay in front of me instead, all right?"

Alessandra's mouth was too dry to answer, so she just nodded. Rush released her hand, freed his weapon from its holster, then moved in a crouched run along the cabin. Alessandra kept close behind him. When they reached the end of the exterior wall, Rush stopped, so she did as well. She waited tensely as he leaned the slightest bit forward, gun out. She exhaled as he took a step forward, then followed him as he took another. When he crouched even lower—almost to a crawling position—she did that, too. Together, they moved past the window.

Hope bubbled in Alessandra's heart. In just a few more steps, they'd be almost home free.

We're going to make it.

But the thought seemed to jinx the situation. Before they could turn toward the steps and switch positions so that she was leading, an ominous *click* echoed over the storm.

"Don't move," said a calm, gravelly voice.

It was a trick, Alessandra realized.

The armed man had baited them, and they'd fallen for it.

Rush's mind moved quickly.

He was well-versed in being on both sides of a gun— butt or barrel—and he was sure of at least one thing. People who issued orders to keep still weren't all that interested in shooting. The thoughtlessly violent didn't bother with words. Bullets were enough. So he took a risk, and he disobeyed the command. He turned. Slowly. And had to admit to himself that what he saw surprised him.

The gunman was…*off.*

The word popped into Rush's head and stuck there as he quickly inventoried the other man's appearance.

It wasn't that he didn't look rough and dangerous. He did. But in a strange way. He was bundled up, head to toe. He wore a black beanie, pulled low. He had an army-green scarf wrapped around his face, and only a few tufts of silver hair and a pair of piercing blue eyes were visible. The rest of him was equally covered. On top, he had on a camouflage jacket and gloves. On the bottom, he wore dirt-covered jeans and heavy work boots. He had a rifle slung over his shoulder, and in his hands he held what looked to be an antique revolver. The latter was pointed straight over Alessandra's shoulder and right at Rush.

A little belatedly, he realized he might've made a miscalculation. Though he had no clue why, the other man's gaze was full of sheer fury, and—like the revolver—it was all aimed toward Rush.

Move!

The internal scream spurred Rush to act. Cursing the fact that he couldn't fire his own weapon for fear of catching Alessandra in the cross fire, he opted for a more brutish attack. He pushed Alessandra aside more roughly than he would've liked, then dived for the gunman, who dropped his weapon but still managed to duck out of the way with a surprising amount of agility.

Rush stumbled forward. He cursed as he hit the railing hard enough to send his gut churning, and his own gun went flying over the side and tumbled to the ground below. Ignoring the frustration and pain, he quickly righted himself and turned back, expecting to find the other man going after Alessandra. Instead, their assailant's eyes were still on Rush, and he was fumbling to get his gun off the ground.

Growling, Rush sprang to action again. He slammed full force into the other man, knocking him to the ground. They wrestled, flinging back and forth for a few seconds before Rush used his superior strength to pin the man beneath him. For a moment, he was triumphant. He pulled back a fist, prepared to deliver the man a solid punch. Then the gunman unexpectedly regained the upper hand by pulling a wily maneuver that sent Rush down onto his back, and he was stunned enough that he couldn't come up with a quick solution. Thankfully, he didn't have to.

As his attacker pressed a knee to his chest and swung his weapon around, his face went abruptly blank. His eyes rolled back, and he toppled over. The man's fall gave Rush a view of Alessandra, who stood behind the gunman, her arms half-raised, a broken pole—a rake, maybe, or the handle of a shovel—in her hands. He'd never been so relieved to see a mess of sopping wet woman in his life.

"Red," he said, his voice thick.

"Rush," she said back in a relieved whisper.

He pushed himself up and folded her into his arms. "Pretty damned sure you just saved my life."

"Sorry it took so long," she replied. "I've never had to do that for anyone before."

He frowned. "Do what?"

"Save their life."

Rush couldn't help but laugh. He leaned back just enough that he could give her a tender kiss.

"Any time you want to save me…you take as long as you need."

Alessandra shook her head, and her gaze flicked from him to the prone man on the porch, and she swallowed. "What do we…um…"

"Do with him?" Rush filled in.

"Yes."

He kissed her again, then gave her a squeeze and pulled away. Even though he was sure the other man was out cold, he still approached cautiously. He'd already been surprised more than once. He had zero interest in letting it happen again. He gave the gunman a rough tap with his booted foot. Then a second one. Neither earned even a flinch. Satisfied, Rush crouched down beside him and retrieved the still-hot gun first.

He held it out to Alessandra. "You ever used one of these?"

She shook her head, but reached out and took it from him anyway. "No. Well. Once, when I was a kid. My dad let me shoot some beer cans on the beach, but my mom found out, and she made him swear he'd never do it again. I think I could do it again."

"Good enough," said Rush. "If he moves, shoot him in the knee."

He stepped back to the man on the ground and bent down a second time. First, his removed the rifle. Then he carefully pulled back the scarf to see if there was anything familiar about the guy's features. Unsurprisingly, there wasn't. His face was covered in a full, bushy beard. The skin that wasn't hidden by hair was thickly lined, and if Rush had to guess, he'd put the man's age at sixty-something. Rush stared for a moment longer, then moved on.

He dug into each pocket in search of some form of ID. His exploration was fruitless. The man had no wallet, no driver's license. Nothing that gave a hint as to who he might be.

"Is he with Garibaldi?" Alessandra asked softly.

Rush leaned away from the unconscious shooter and ran a frustrated hand over his soaked hair. "I don't know this guy personally, but unless you can think of another reason for a stranger to be firing at us, I think it's safe to assume that our mutual friend's decided I can't be trusted to do the job after all."

"Maybe I shouldn't have knocked him unconscious. We could've asked him some questions."

"It was the right thing to do, Red. Don't ever doubt that."

"So what now? Should we tie him up and wait?"

Rush thought about it for a second. Tying up the gunman had appeal, and not just because it would further incapacitate him, either. But a plan was forming in Rush's head, and leaving the other man completely overpowered wouldn't work well. He grimaced, then shook his head.

"Asking him questions will only give Garibaldi confirmation that his doubt was right." He pushed to his feet. "I think we're going to do something a little more creative. C'mon. I need to grab my phone."

Alessandra frowned, but she followed him without asking why, and it gave Rush a thrill of pleasure to have her absolute trust. He had to resist an insanely unreasonable urge to drag her to the tidily made bed, and instead settled for taking her hand after she'd grabbed her bags and he'd snagged his phone and his keys. He led Alessandra back out in the storm, cast a final irritated look toward the gunman, then headed down the stairs.

Now Alessandra did ask a question, sounding surprised. "We're leaving the cabin?"

"If I want Garibaldi to believe what I'm about to say, I need to put a reasonable distance between us and his hired guy. And I—" He cut himself off and stopped halfway down the steps as he caught sight of his vehicle. "Dammit."

Alessandra's eyes followed his gaze. "Does it looks like someone opened the hood?"

"Yes, it sure as hell does."

Rush let her go of her fingers and took the rest of the stairs at a run. The closer he got to the Lada, the worse the situation became. The hood was indeed open, and mechanical bits and pieces hung out everywhere. There was exactly zero possibility that the thing could be put back together without the help of a mechanic.

Reining in a need to kick a tire, he swung toward Alessandra, who'd reached the vehicle, too.

"Well," he said. "At least now we know why our friendly neighborhood sniper took so long to get up to the cabin."

Alessandra straightened her shoulders. "So then. We walk."

"We walk?" Rush echoed.

"You said we had to put some space between us and the cabin and that guy," she reminded him.

He narrowed his eyes and scratched at his beard, then cast a skeptical look at her sandal-clad feet. "You know that it's pouring rain and that walking is really hiking."

"It's windy, too," she said. "And don't look at my shoes like that. I've had these bad boys for four years, and they've hiked some pretty wet and treacherous bits of the coast."

"You hike the coast in—you know what? Never mind. I believe it. And that's all fine and good, but the nearest place to go is…" He trailed off, his mind churning.

"Is what?" Alessandra prodded.

"I've got another idea."

"Care to share?"

"How about I share while we move?" he said.

She shrugged and held out her hand, which he gladly took, and they made their way to the trees, where the overhead branches actually provided some cover from the rain and some protection from the wind. They were only a few steps in, though, when Rush's phone buzzed in his pocket. He dragged it out reluctantly, a hunch telling him who it would be. Sure enough, Garibaldi's name flashed across the screen. He signaled for Alessandra to be quiet, then slammed his finger to the answer key.

"Tell me why I should even be talking to you," he snarled into the phone.

"Atkinson?" Garibaldi sounded puzzled.

"Who the hell else would it be?" Rush retorted. "Expecting your sniper to answer, maybe?"

"What're you talking about?"

"Six feet tall, bushy gray beard, and oh…a long-range rifle. Sound familiar?"

There was a pause. "Back it up, Atkinson, and tell me exactly what you mean."

Garibaldi's voice was cool and demanding, but underneath that was a layer of genuine worry. Rush cast a glance toward Alessandra, wondering how much she could hear, and whether she was thinking the same thing he was—that maybe Garibaldi *hadn't* sent the armed man.

He infused a little more disbelief into his reply. "Do

you seriously expect me to believe that someone other than you has guys out here who have a specific interest in shooting at our favorite redhead?"

Another pause. "This guy shot Alessandra?"

Rush realized immediately that Garibaldi had misunderstood. It was the perfect opportunity. The perfect chance to bring his ruse to life.

"Damn right, he did," Rush said irritably. "Kind of rendered me prematurely useless."

"So Alessandra is…"

"No longer an issue."

He heard Alessandra's sharp inhale, and even in the rain, he could see her face pale a little. He shook his head in a silent apology.

"Where's this guy now?" Garibaldi asked.

"How should I know? I'm busy cleaning up his mess."

"Cleaning his—nah, never mind. I don't wanna know."

"He really wasn't your man?" Rush asked.

"If he was *my* man, he wouldn't have left you alive," Garibaldi replied evenly. "But I'd sure as hell like to know who he is."

"Then I guess that makes two of us."

"Put it on your list, Atkinson. Right after you clean up. And don't forget to check in."

"On it, boss."

He clicked the phone off, shoved it hard into his pocket, then dragged Alessandra in for a deep, rough kiss.

Chapter 13

By the time Rush let her go, Alessandra was breathless. Achy. Needy. The fact that Rush just left Jesse with the impression that he was off burying her body somewhere in the woods was irrelevant. The fact that they actually *were* in the woods, and that the rain was coming down harder, meant nothing. Less than nothing. The only important thing was how Rush was staring down at her, his eyes full of undisguised want.

Well, said a voice in her head. *That. And a few other things.*

Like the way his body molded to hers. Or how his lips came down to ghost over hers once more, gently this time. And how his hands squeezed her back, possessive and safe and strong. The rumble of his voice—a little raw and a lot sexy—mattered, too, even if his words didn't make much sense to her.

"I'm so sorry, Red," he said heavily.

Alessandra pulled back a little so she could think enough to form a coherent response. "You're sorry?"

"It made me feel sick to my stomach to say all of that to Garibaldi."

"You barely said anything."

"It was enough." He sighed and released her, a strangely pained look on his face. "I'm not a callous jerk, Red, but I can literally count on one hand the number of people who matter to me enough to make me think twice about something like this. Brayden, Harley and Anderson. And my mom, even though it's been years since we've been in contact. But somehow, in the last twenty-four hours, you've managed to get added to that list. So the thought of something like any of that happening to you..." He shrugged a little helplessly.

In spite of the cold, Alessandra was suddenly warm all over. She felt a ridiculous smile form on her face, and she wondered if the stress of it all was sending her into the deep end. She certainly felt more than a little crazy at the moment. But she didn't let it stop her from impulsively stepping forward to fling her arms over Rush's shoulders so she could initiate her own over-the-top kiss. And she made sure *he* was breathless this time, before pulling away.

"There," she said, satisfied.

"There what?" he replied with a half-amused, half-puzzled smile.

"Now you know I feel the same way." She paused. "Well. Not *quite* the same way. My list of people I care about is long. I'm even overly fond of the kid who bags my groceries, and I hand-make my neighbors' Christmas gifts every year."

Rush lifted an eyebrow. "So...you're adding me to an already-full list?"

A blush crept up her cheeks. "I'm putting you unreasonably near the top."

"Tell me something, then."

"What?"

"Who's above me? I need to know what the competition is like."

"Very funny."

"I'm serious."

"Shouldn't we start walking? Weren't you worried about the dark and stormy factor?"

"I think you're avoiding the question," he said, but he slid his hand to hers and started through the woods again anyway.

Alessandra expected him to push the topic a little more, but he was quiet as they moved through the trees. And she was thankful. She needed a few minutes to collect her thoughts. And to address the staccato beat of her heart every time she replayed Rush-related events of the last day. But trying to reason through it did no good. No matter how she came at it, she kept coming back to the same conclusion. The more moments she spent with Rush, the more she liked him. The more she thought he might be—*should* be—a longer-term part of her life. And weirdly, the rapid conclusion didn't scare her. Maybe because there was so much other, truly frightening stuff happening. Things that put her feelings in perspective. Life was short. Precarious, even. Particularly right then.

She stole a look at Rush from the corner of her eye. Even the sneaked glance made her pulse thrum and her chest compress pleasantly. What was it about the man that stole her breath so thoroughly? The intense physical attraction was a given. Every time he touched her, she lit up. His tattoos, his beard and his compactly muscular body made her mouth dry. And that wasn't even factoring in how it felt to have him in bed with her. But even when things were short-term, as they tended to be for Alessandra, she typically chose men who played it safe. And Rush had said himself that wasn't what defined him. Normally, it was the kind of thing that made her worry. Or at least take a step back. But right then, all she wanted was to dive in. She liked Rush's touch of gruffness. She like his dogged determination to pursue his father's killer, and she liked the passion he exuded in everything he did. In fact, so far, she'd liked everything about him. And that wasn't even factoring in the strange spark of rightness she felt when she thought about him.

As her mind turned it all over in her head, a sudden memory—one she hadn't recalled in a good decade or more—sprang to the forefront of her thoughts. She'd been about six, and playing with the Barbies her mom had always grumbled about. "Unrealistic expectations of the female form" was one of the favored descriptions. But she'd let have Alessandra have them anyway. And a Ken doll, too. Which inevitably meant a romance would come to life. On this particular day, Alessandra had created a destination wedding. Oceanside in the form of a bathtub. She'd been a little lost in play when a sudden thought occurred to her.

"Mommy, how did Barbie know?" she asked.

"How did she know what, Love-bug?" her mom replied.

"That she wanted to marry Ken?"

"Oh. I imagine it was the perfect plastic hair that cinched the deal."

The facetious statement went over Alessandra's head,

and she was already moving on anyway. "Is it the same way you knew with Daddy?"

Her mom had laughed. "Minus the plastic hair...yes. I knew the second I laid eyes on your dad that I was going to marry him. Took him about a month to catch up, though."

Alessandra had looked up from the dolls and the bath time suds, another question on her lips. But when she saw her mom's face she'd closed her mouth instead, and the chatting moved on.

She's seen something in her mom's expression all those years ago—something happy and dreamy—that she'd sensed was grown-up and private. Much later, she'd figured out that it was love that inspired the look. And not just any kind of love. The head-over-heels, meant-to-be-together, once-in-a-lifetime kind.

Alessandra herself had never felt that pull. She'd liked a few men. A couple of them she'd even say she'd liked a lot. But never enough to call it love. Never enough to think it might *become* love.

And thinking about it now is just plain crazy, she told herself in a stern voice.

But once again, reason didn't seem to matter. And right then, that look on her mom's face hovered there, so close that Alessandra wished she had a mirror so she could check her own face. She was almost certain of what she'd find. And maybe being so sure should've made some nervousness creep in. Maybe it *would* have, if she hadn't abruptly noticed that both the terrain and the weather had changed. And so had their trajectory. The trees had grown thinner, the ground was more even, and the rain had tapered off to nothing. But most importantly, they seemed to be *descending* instead of *ascending* now.

"Are we moving *down* the mountain?" Alessandra asked in surprise.

Rush nodded. "This is an ATV trail. They're all over the mountainside."

"And I take it you know where this one leads?"

"I've spent some time out here. I can only stand Garibaldi's company for so long before I need to escape." He turned her way and smiled.

She narrowed her eyes. "Now who's avoiding a question?"

"All right. I admit it. But it's only because I don't think you're going to be too crazy about where we're headed."

"You might as well just tell me."

"Garibaldi has these cabins," he said. "They're old. Original to the town. Used to be lodging for the temporary, seasonal logging staff. At the moment, they're empty."

"Okay," Alessandra replied. "Why are you worried I won't like the idea? Are they haunted? Overrun by rats? Full of holes and mold and lions and tigers and bears, oh my?"

He laughed. "No. They're nicely done up. Rustic, but clean. Especially the main cabin. Bigger and with more amenities than the one we just left."

"So…"

"Didn't you hear me say who owns them?"

"Yes." She paused in her walking, and when Rush swung to face her, she took a hold of both his wrists and lifted her gaze to meet his eyes. "I heard you say that they belong to Garibaldi. But would you take me somewhere unsafe?"

"No," he replied, "I sure as hell wouldn't."

"I trust you. If you think being under Jesse's nose is the right place to be, then it's the right place to be."

A smile tipped up one corner of his mouth. "Under his nose. That's funny. Those are the exact words my partners used."

"Oh, so this isn't *your* genius idea?" she teased as they resumed their walk.

"Might've stolen a play out of the other guys' books."

Alessandra wondered if Rush knew how he softened when he talked about his friends. If he was aware of how his eyes crinkled in the corners, or how his mouth stayed in a slight curve.

Add that to the list of things I like about him, she thought, while aloud she said, "Tell me more about them."

"You want to hear about my friends?"

"Yes."

"Okay, then. But be warned. They're a bunch of goody-goodies."

"I'm prepared."

Rush grinned, then launched into a description of each of the other men.

Brayden was, as he'd said previously, their fearless leader. A take-charge, do-it-right kinda guy. He'd kept them on track over the years, pursuing Jesse unwaveringly. He'd led the way into Whispering Woods, too, uncovering the first clues as to what the man who killed their fathers was up to.

He called Anderson "Mr. Nice Guy," and said that his friend was almost too patient and kind. He laughingly explained how he'd always believed that in another life, Anderson would've become a school counselor. He wondered aloud if the other man would stay with the police force when the case wrapped up.

Harley, he told her, was the baby. Who, in spite of his burly appearance, had a sensitive side, which he put to good use in his sculpting and painting. He was also talented in the tech department, and his skills had proved invaluable over the course of their investigation.

"So what about you, then?" Alessandra asked when he was done talking.

"Me?"

"Brayden is in charge, Anderson is there to placate the masses, and Harley fixes things from behind the screen. What's your hidden talent?"

"Don't know about a hidden talent, per se, but I think—and don't laugh—I'm the street cred. Going undercover was my idea. Infiltrating Garibaldi's merry band of thugs was all me. Hell. I didn't even *tell* the other guys that I was doing it. They caught me in the act." He chuckled. "Poor Harley. Probably scared the crap out of him when I showed up."

Alessandra hesitated. "Can you tell me about the case?"

She expected him to immediately say no, but after a second, he nodded instead. "Those foolish friends of mine told their girlfriends, so I don't see why the hell not."

Alessandra's heart skipped a beat. Had he heard himself use the word *girlfriend*? Was it a significant slip? She wanted it to be. But if Rush had noticed, he didn't comment. He just went on, telling her a little more about what they'd accomplished so far.

Brayden had come into town first, figuring out pretty quickly that Jesse's business was a front for something else. With the help of Reggie Frost, a local woman whose family owned The Frost Family Diner, he'd uncovered a secret basement under the businesses on Main Street. When Brayden and Reggie couldn't do any more without being caught, Anderson stepped in. Under the guise of protecting Whispering Woods' third-grade teacher, Nadine Stuart, he discovered that the secret room was used in some kind of art scam. Which, of course, brought their very own art expert—Harley—to town. The art scam was tied to a shop owner named Liz, who turned out to know nothing about what was happening in her store.

"What *was* happening?" Alessandra asked.

"Opiates." Rush's voice was grim. "Hidden in the paint of some pieces Garibaldi had in Liz's Lovely Things."

"And you couldn't bust him for any of that?"

"You mean murder, mayhem, arson and a dozen other misdemeanors and or felonies? Nope. Not the way we need to. The man's a genius at passing the buck, and we need to make a hundred percent sure that *he's* going to be the one put behind bars. And at the moment, every guy working under him is sharing rumors about a big buy of some kind. My personal opinion is that it's a liquidation. Cutting out of Whispering Woods and going underground. Which is why I need to catch him. Redhanded, as they say."

Abruptly, Rush stopped talking, and his arm came out to stop Alessandra from moving forward any farther, and his voice dropped lower. "Look through the trees up there on the left."

Alessandra squinted. She could just see the outline of a building of some kind.

"That's a storage shed," he told her. "What I want to do is take you up behind it and have you wait there while I make sure Garibaldi hasn't decided to start using this place. Have you still got that revolver?"

She lifted her purse. "In here."

"Okay. Let's make a trade. My gun's a little easier to fire."

Worry rushed in as he slid open his coat, reached for his weapon, then held it out to her.

"Do you think I'm going to need it?" Alessandra asked as her fingers closed on the warm metal.

"I hope to God not," he replied as he put out his hand expectantly. "But I'll feel better if I know you've got the means to protect yourself."

She shoved the old gun into his palm. "If the stupid revolver jams and you die as a result, I'll be *really* mad."

Her attempt at bravery-inducing humor only lasted as long as it took Rush to tuck the weapon awkwardly into the wrongly sized holster. Because Alessandra realized something. If something happened to the man beside her, she wouldn't be mad. She'd be devastated.

As soon as they reached the shed, Rush gave Alessandra a quick kiss, then took off. Leaving her made him grit his teeth, but he knew if he lingered, it'd be even harder for him to do what needed to be done. He had to trust that she'd be safe, and also to trust that if something *did* go wrong on her side, she'd be able to protect herself. Or if something went wrong on Rush's side, she'd make the right decision and stay away. Run like hell, maybe.

Would you, if the roles were reversed? asked his conscience.

He silently growled back at it as he skulked along the perimeter of the cabin site. Not a denial, because he didn't want to lie to himself. Just a general snarl. Truthfully, he knew there was no way he'd simply walk away from Alessandra. He'd fight for her. To the death, he was pretty sure. In fact, just the *thought* of the possibility of an unexpected attack made him want to hurry back to her side. He had to force his feet to move slowly.

No need to get sloppy.

He'd be no good to her—or anyone—if he missed some key detail. So far, though, the site looked clear. There was no sign of recent visitation. No tire tracks in the mud, no open doors flapping. And since Rush himself was the last one to shut the place up, he knew what to look for. It was as clean and undisturbed as when he'd left it. Even the broken branch he'd noticed lying in the middle of the dirt driveway as he'd left was still there.

"You can never be too careful, though," he murmured to himself as he moved from the perimeter of the whole site to the perimeter of the first cabin.

He checked the windows and the doors of each space. He checked the porches and the stacks of firewood. When he was done with the exteriors, he oh-so-cautiously inspected the interiors. Closets. Beds. Cupboards. His final inspection was of the big cabin, and there he lingered for a moment. Not because it had two hundred extra square feet or because there were more places to hide, but because it was where he was bringing Alessandra. And as much as he hoped her stay would be short, he wanted her to be comfortable. So even though it kept him away from her for another few minutes, he took the time to ensure things were up to par.

He made sure the linen on the bed was fresh, and he checked to see if there was tea and coffee. He stacked some wood into the fireplace, then turned to go. At the last minute, though, a crazy idea occurred to him, and he had to run with it. He hurried around the cabin, arranging things perfectly, then slipped back out and headed eagerly toward the spot where he'd left Alessandra.

By the time he reached her, her teeth were chattering.

"Wh-wh-what t-t-took you s-so long?" she asked. "And wh-why d-d-do you look like th-th-the Cheshire c-cat?"

"I'm sorry," he said, meaning it, but still grinning. "But I'll make it up to you."

"Oh, r-r-really?"

"Yep."

Feeling extra spontaneous, he reached down and scooped her from the ground. She squealed a girlish protest and almost dropped his gun, but Rush was determined. If he had to meet an incredible woman under the worst circumstances, then he was going to make the best of it. Gripping her tightly against his chest, he carried her past the woodshed and smaller cabins. He lifted her up the steps, across the deck, then pushed open the door with his hip and brought her over the threshold. Inside, he kicked off his boots, brought his foot up to the stool near the front door, and yanked off Alessandra's very muddy sandals. Then he spun in a circle so she could get the full effect of his efforts.

"Are those *emergency* candles?" she asked.

"A man's gotta work with what's available," he said.

"I hope we don't have a *real* emergency then."

"Hey. The romance doesn't make itself."

"Doesn't it?" she replied, her voice breathy enough that Rush almost forgot he had a plan.

Perfectly good couch over there, his libido pointed out.

He ignored it—barely—and instead carried Alessandra past the living room and to the bathroom. He shouldered through and at last set her down.

"Ta-da!" he said with a flourish toward the still-filling copper tub.

Alessandra's baby blues widened. "Is that a bath?"

"Damn right."

"With bubbles?"

"Interested?"

"God, yes. Thank you, Rush. It's amazing, and I—" She cut herself off, a fierce shade of crimson slamming across her face at an incredible speed, and she cleared her throat. "Really. Thank you. I'm kind of hurting head to toe, and a bath will be fantastic."

He tipped her chin up and pressed his lips to hers. "Good. I'll get you a towel."

He slipped out of the bathroom and decided to use the moment alone to place another call to Garibaldi, too. The last thing he needed was for the other man to get antsy about where he was and what he was doing.

His boss picked up on the first ring. "Atkinson. Made it out alive, I see."

"Disappointed?" Rush said.

"Not in the slightest. You're still useful to me."

"Should I thank you for that comment?"

"You can show me your gratitude by telling me you figured out who the hell shot Alessandra."

Rush's gut roiled, but he made himself answer evenly. "When would I have had time to do that, boss? Before or after I dug a six-by-three hole in the clay?"

Garibaldi let out a dark chuckle that made Rush feel even sicker. He *had* to be riding a sociopathic line of some sort.

"All right," the other man said. "I want you to drive back into town. Meet up with—"

Rush didn't let him finish. "No can do, boss. Our trigger-happy friend tore apart the Lada's engine."

Garibaldi dropped a curse, then said, "Who the hell *is* this guy? I want to know. Like, yesterday."

"Me, too," Rush replied vehemently.

The gunman was still loose. God knew where he was or what he was planning.

"I'll send someone to get you," Garibaldi said. "Tell me where you are."

Rush closed his eyes. He wished he could argue, but he knew he couldn't. It would only arouse Garibaldi's suspicions.

"Right this second, I'm in the middle of nowhere," he said instead. "Give me two hours or so to get somewhere reasonably easy to access by car."

"You need two hours?"

"Sorry. Did you think I was going to dump the redhead a few yards off the road?"

The pause in the other end was almost too long, and Rush half expected his boss to call him out for the continuing deception. But after a moment, a sigh carried through the line.

"All right. Two hours, Atkinson. Then you're on this until it's figured out. I've got a major deal coming through, and the last thing I need is a complication."

Rush hung up and moved to grab a towel from the cupboard. He paused, though, with his hand on the off-white plush, then turned for the door instead. He locked it—dead bolt and slide lock both—and took a quick look to make sure all the windows were secure and the curtains drawn. He didn't really believe the gunman would be able to track them, but his conversation with Garibaldi had reminded him that he hadn't put as much thought into identifying their attacker as he should've.

Who was he? Was he there because of Alessandra, or was it Garibaldi? The latter seemed more likely, but for some reason, the former stuck in his mind. He just wasn't sure why. The thing that nagged at him most was the way the gunman had stared at him. Why would a man he'd never met give him that kind of death glare? His eyes drifted to the slightly ajar bathroom door, considering it.

Then—like she could sense his invisible scrutiny—Alessandra's voice cut through his thoughts. "Rush? Are you still out there?"

"Coming," he called, stepping toward the bathroom. "Hey, can I…"

His question trailed into oblivion as he caught sight of her. Long, honey-kissed legs bent up out of the tub. One hand resting on the edge of the tub and the other swirling on the surface of the water. Perfect, full breasts just barely covered by a sea of bubbles. Her blue eyes glittered, catching him and holding him.

"You know it's kind of weird to stand there and stare, right?" she said softly.

He swallowed. "Is it?"

"Yes."

She sounded so serious that he shifted from one foot to the other. "Sorry. I'll wait out in the living room."

"No," she replied quickly.

"No?"

"I don't want you to leave. I want you to get *in.*"

And Rush couldn't say no to that.

Chapter 14

Rush watched lazily as Alessandra fastened the second-from-the-top button on the shirt she'd borrowed from inside one of the drawers in the bedroom. It was a men's shirt, which might've made Rush a bit jealous if not for two things. One, he knew it was from the pile of stuff left behind by Brayden. And two, it was brand-new with the tags still attached.

And don't forget three, added a voice in his head. *She looks damned good in it.*

It was true. Even though she was decently covered, there was something undeniably sexy about the way the too-big shirt hung off her body. It made him want to drag her back into the bed all over again. Hell. He might've even done it if she hadn't turned a skeptical eye his way.

"Are you going to get dressed, too?" she asked. "Or just sit around in your underwear until your chauffeur arrives?"

He cast her a lascivious smile. "What makes you think I'm wearing anything under this sheet?"

In spite of the fact that they'd spent the last hour together naked, she blushed, and her gaze skidded over the sheet. "I guess if you want to greet your driver that way, it's up to you."

He winked, tossed back the sheet—which revealed his perfectly respectable pair of boxers—and swung his legs over the side of the bed. "Satisfied?"

"He could be early, you know."

"Lackeys tend to run late. I should know—I *am* one."

She rolled her eyes and pulled her brush through her cascade of red hair. Rush watched that, too. He wanted to enjoy the last few minutes he had with her. He was loath to leave her at all. In fact, they'd argued about it, and he'd tossed out a few ways to make sure he could stay. Not the least of which was taking whoever turned up, tying them to a chair and leaving them there until Rush found a way to solve every bit of his case while also protecting Alessandra. It was she who insisted he go. She used logic and reason. Then the threat of walking away from Whispering Woods and him forever. And even though he didn't think the threat was credible, the thought of it was enough for him to relent and come up with a more practical plan.

Rush would leave, as planned. He'd do his bit to help Garibaldi search out the identity of the man who'd attacked them. He'd even put some solid effort into it, since he genuinely wanted to know who the guy was, and his motivation, too. Regardless as to the outcome, though, he'd get a hold of a vehicle and find a way back to the cabin in two hours. He was leaving behind his phone— the perfect excuse to return if nothing else came up first.

For Alessandra's part, she was going to hide in the closet the moment they heard the tires on the gravel. She'd promised to stay in the bedroom once Rush was long gone. The room would be locked from the inside, and she'd have Rush's gun within reach, and a book in her lap to keep her mind occupied. She'd sworn she'd only leave to use the bathroom. They were going to pull in the armchair from the living room and position it in the corner so she'd be out of sight. It wasn't a perfect plan, but it was something. Or it had *seemed* like a plan, when he was tangled in her arms and legs. Now he was doubting it again.

"We can just leave," he said abruptly. "Run away."

She'd finished brushing and was now twisting her hair up into a bun. "Very funny."

He sat up a little straighter. He *had* been half kidding. But it suddenly seemed like an almost plausible idea.

"Do you like margaritas?" he asked.

She stopped mid-twist and turned to face him, answering slowly. "I'm more of a piña colada girl. Why?"

"What if I said we could go right now?"

"Go where?"

"Somewhere hot. Tropical, even. Nice pool. Or the ocean. I know you like the ocean."

"Right. And you'll just leave your job and your friends and the case you've been chasing for the last fifteen years. All to run away with a woman you met yesterday. Sounds like a legitimately reasonable idea."

Rush pushed to his feet and strode over to Alessandra. Her hands fell away from the work they were doing on her head, and her hair sprang free. Rush reached out and ran his fingers through the loose tresses, then slid both of his hands to her hips and met her eyes.

"You're telling me you can't feel whatever this is growing between us," he said, the intensity in his tone obvious even to his own ears.

Her response was equally intense, but her voice was far softer. "Of course I do. And I like it. I like *you,* Rush. More than I should, considering how little time we've known each other. But that's the whole reason you need to finish with this case. I don't want to start off a relationship by hiding."

He brushed away a strand of hair. "You're already hiding."

She made a face. "By hiding *permanently.* And I don't want to be the person who stopped you from getting justice for your father."

"Red…"

"No. Don't say it."

"What?"

"That you don't care. Or that I'm more important."

"Red," he said again, more firmly because it was pretty damned close to what he'd been about to tell her.

She vehemently shook her head. "Seriously, Rush. Imagine introducing me to your partners. 'Hey guys… this is Alessandra Rivers. She seduced me, then stole me away from the case. Sorry we'll never get the closure we were always hoping for.' How would that go over?"

He couldn't help but chuckle. "Hard to say. The guys are kinda soft."

She started to say something else, but the low rumble of a vehicle's engine stopped her before she got started.

"Dammit," Rush swore. "They're early. Time for you to hide. I'll get dressed."

"I hate to say I told you so," Alessandra said, and

grabbed her bag from the floor and hurried toward the near-empty closet. "But I did tell you so."

Rush slipped into his jeans and T-shirt, then stepped over to grasp the bifold door from the outside. "You're going to be smug? Now?"

"When I'm right, I'm right." She kissed him quickly before pulling away to send a serious look his way. "Promise me you'll be safe."

"I will," he said.

"Two hours or less."

"See you then, Red."

He kissed her again, then closed the closet and made his way out of the bedroom. When he opened the front door, though, he was greeted by an unpleasant surprise. Garibaldi hadn't sent someone. He'd come himself.

Ignoring an urge to slam the door, Rush crossed his arms, channeled his inner thug, and issued a displeased greeting instead. "Checking up on me, boss?"

Garibaldi replied with a smile that didn't reach his eyes. "Thought I'd make sure you were all right and offer you the grace of my company and benefit of my years behind the wheel."

"I didn't even know you *could* drive."

"Funny as always, Atkinson."

Rush offered the other man a shrug. "You wanna come in while I grab my coat and boots?"

He hoped the offer would be declined—enough of a show of good faith on its own—but Garibaldi's eyes lifted over Rush's shoulder to the interior of the cabin, and he shrugged back. "Sure. Why not?"

Rush stepped aside to let his boss enter first, then followed him in, careful not to let his eyes stray to the open bedroom door.

"Smells like soap in here," Garibaldi stated.

It wasn't what he was expecting to hear, but Rush didn't let himself be caught off guard. "Had about six layers of dirt and blood to wash off. Helped myself to a soak."

The other man's eyes flicked around curiously. Rush ignored it in favor of getting himself ready to go.

"So where's your sidekick, anyway, boss?" he asked as he pulled his coat from the hook.

"Ernest is running some errands," Garibaldi replied. "He already went by the other cabin and made sure it was secure. You guys did a hell of a number on the inside, by the way."

Rush made sure his own response was dismissive as he bent to force his feet into his boots. "Yeah. Well. I was a tad more concerned about saving my own hide than I was about keeping things tidy. Ernest find out anything useful?"

"Not a thing."

"So still no clue what this guy wanted?"

"Not yet," Garibaldi said. "That's another reason I came for you myself, though."

Rush frowned. "What is?"

"Wanted to get a better feel for who the guy was."

"There's not a lot to tell. Bushy beard, like I said. Older and rough-looking. Wouldn't have looked out of place begging for change. Does that mean anything to you?" He stood up and found Garibaldi studying him intently.

"Can I ask you something, Atkinson?" the other man said.

"You're the boss."

"Did the guy seem more interested in you, or in Al?"

Rush made sure not let on that he'd had the same question. "Dunno. There were too many flying bullets and fists for me to really pay attention. Why? You got an idea? You're thinking someone was specifically targeting the redhead?"

Garibaldi sighed. "Something's not sitting right."

Rush hesitated, his mind on whether or not Alessandra could hear them. After a moment, he decided to plunge in anyway.

"Can *I* ask *you* something, boss?"

"Go ahead."

"Why couldn't we just let the girl go?"

"Buyer's remorse, Atkinson?"

Rush shook his head. "Just a waste of a pretty face."

"True," the other man agreed. "But she couldn't be trusted. You wanna hear a little story?"

"Sure."

"The reason Alessandra and I go—*went*—way back is that our fathers used to do some small-time jobs together. Her dad, Randall, was a backstabber who repeatedly chose his family over the obligation he had to *my* dad and the crew. He kept leaving, then complaining about being coerced to come back in. Don't know why it was such an issue."

For once, Rush couldn't contain his reaction. "You think staying in the game should've won out over his kid?"

Garibaldi didn't even blink. "It's fine to have a family. But you don't make a commitment, then screw over the people whose backs you're supposed to protect. When you're in, you're in. Or else men wind up dead. And someone has to pay for that."

Rush stared at his boss, realizing the situation was

personal for the other man. "You hold him responsible for your father's death."

"Over the years, I've discovered the old apple-not-falling-from-the-tree thing is very, very true. End of story. Let's go."

And as his boss smiled a dark smile and clapped a hand onto his back, Rush was filled with a dangerous wave of foreboding.

For a good five minutes after Alessandra was sure Rush and Jesse were gone, she continued to sit in the closet with her back pressed to the wall and her eyes closed. Though the conversation between the two men had been reasonably brief, it had thrown her.

She'd known about her father's questionable past. She'd known about his friendship with Jesse's dad, too. But she hadn't been aware that he'd tried to get out of the life and been sucked back in. And Jesse had never, ever indicated that he thought her father had somehow gotten his own dad killed.

Alessandra inhaled and tried to tell herself that Randall Rivers was still the same good man he'd always been to her. The one who'd disclosed his past discretions and told her that she and her mother were the reason he'd finally seen the light. The man who'd read her stories at bedtime and taken her to get her ears pierced when she was twelve. Who'd worked long hours on construction sites to save for her college degree, and who'd told her she could only get ahead if she got herself educated. The man she'd loved and respected, and who created that dreamy sparkle for her mother.

But was he really that man at all?

She breathed out. It was almost impossible to shove

off the question. And it brought more with it. Had her father, the criminal, ruined lives? Taken them? Was he like Jesse, perfecting the wolf in sheep's clothing? She didn't have any answers. She wouldn't *get* any answers. The only one who knew for sure was her father, and he'd been dead for a decade and a half. And even if Alessandra *had* been able to ask him, would she have been able to trust that whatever he told her was true?

She swallowed. It was awful, to have so much doubt cast upon the things she'd always believed to be fact. And worse to be forced to question her dad's character. She felt like her entire childhood had been turned on its head, and she couldn't shake it.

What I need is something to distract me, she thought.

Her mind went to the book Rush had pulled off the shelf for her. A romance. He'd winked and told her to think of it as a how-to book. She'd laughed and blushed and cringed a little at the cheesy joke. But now, she thought it might be the perfect escape.

She stood up, pushed open the closet door and stepped out into the bedroom. She moved toward the nightstand, where Rush had left both the book and the gun, but she paused when she realized that the door still hung ajar. Remembering her promise to lock it from the inside, Alessandra started to walk toward it. Then she froze as a noise carried to her ears. She could swear it was the sound of feet, hitting wood.

Holding her breath and afraid to move, she strained to hear it again. She didn't. But what she did hear was even worse. It was the rattle of the front door handle. And worse again. The sound of something heavy smacking against the door.

No!

The silent protest was accompanied by immediate action. Alessandra sprang forward. She closed the door—not a slam because she didn't want to give herself away—and locked it. Then she turned and sprinted for the weapon. Before she even reached it, the bang outside came a second time. It sounded a third time as she lifted the gun, then a fourth as she turned back toward the door. She willed her hands to stay steady. But when the crack of splintering wood followed the fifth boom, her whole body shook.

The intruder was inside. All that was between them was the locked door and a gun she was probably incapable of using effectively. A whimper escaped from her lips before she could stop it.

Why did I tell Rush to go?

She wanted to tell the self-directed question to go stuff itself. To insist that she was perfectly capable of protecting herself. She was strong, independent and resourceful. But each new sound carrying through made her doubt the claim. Whoever was on the other side of the door wasn't trying to disguise his presence. He was tossing through things, clearly searching for something. Or for *someone.* For her, in all probability. And for all Alessandra's capabilities, none seemed like the right ones for this scenario. What she needed was the know-how. The experience. The training. Or someone by her side who had those things. Like Rush. Whom she'd sent away.

Oh God.

Any second, the man out in the main part of the cabin was going to try the bedroom door. She was going to be forced into a confrontation. Forced to battle for her life, and possibly—*likely*—have to use the gun. And inconveniently, the "fight" half of her fight-or-flight system seemed to be missing completely. Unlike the need to run, which was tidal-wave strong.

Maybe I can do it, she thought with a glance toward the window. *Maybe I can get out and get away.*

But even though the curtain blocked out the view, Alessandra knew what loomed on the other side of the glass. An endless mountain of forest. She *might* be able to get through the window undetected. She might even make it as far as the woods without being seen. But once there, what would she do? Hide, and hope for the best? Try to make her way into town, and pray that she could get in contact with Rush? Would she even make it that far successfully?

But then the decision was taken away from her anyway. The bedroom doorknob rattled. Hard. And as much as she tried to brace herself for the forced entry, the sudden, violent shudder of the wood as someone slammed a foot into it still caught her off guard. Startled, she jumped back. And it was a good thing, too. Because the bedroom door was nowhere near as strong as it should be. Or rather, its hinges weren't. The solitary blow sent them flying off, and the wood fell inward. And with it came the man behind the kick, a stream of swear words accompanying his fall.

For a second, Alessandra just stared down at him, too startled to do much of anything.

He was stuck in an awkward position. Almost the splits. One foot forward and the other behind him. The front knee bent at a cringeworthy angle, and the rear wasn't much better. Based on the amount of noise he'd made, Alessandra had been picturing a big man. But he was small. No more than five and a half feet tall, and definitely not topping a hundred and fifty pounds. When he lifted his near-black eyes to her face, though, she could tell that his size didn't make him any less dangerous. His gaze was cold, and it glittered unpleasantly. For the first time in her life, Alessandra truly understood what people meant when they said they wouldn't want to meet someone in a dark alley.

So why are you just standing around? screamed a voice in her head. *Do something!*

He clearly had the same thought at the same moment. As Alessandra raised her gun, he dropped a hand to his waistband in search of his own weapon. Alessandra's eyes followed the motion, and she realized more quickly than he did that the gun was missing from its holster, which had managed to snap open in the wild fall. A quick flick of her gaze told her that the gun was on the ground a few feet away. Out of reach.

Alessandra sent up a silent prayer of thanks, then said, "Don't move," and she was pleased that her voice sounded surer than she felt.

"You won't shoot," the man snarled back at her.

She shook her head and countered, "No. I don't *want* to shoot. But that doesn't mean I won't. I'm pretty attached to my own life, so if it's a choice between me and you…" She shrugged with as much casualness as she could muster. "Who are you?"

"Do you seriously think it's—" He cut himself off as she lifted the gun from his chest to his head. "I'm Val."

"I don't mean your *name*," Alessandra replied impatiently.

"If you aren't smart enough to figure out why I'm here, I don't know why my boss would waste the resources on you in the first place." His dismissive tone made her stomach drop.

She made herself shove aside the sick, nervous feeling, and she tried to scoff. "So you think of yourself as what? A glorified executioner? Did you really think I'd be that easy to kill?"

"I hoped." He eyed the gun. "Told you that you wouldn't shoot."

"And I told you that I didn't *want* to. Just explain to me in detail why you're here, and—"

"What? You'll let me go?"

Alessandra resisted an urge to bite her lip in a show of further indecision. Obviously, she couldn't just let him walk away. He'd turn around and tell Jesse that she was alive. And that Rush had lied about her death.

But he probably already knows all that, doesn't he? she reasoned. *Which is also probably why he sent this guy, Val, in the first place.*

Where did that leave her, though? She couldn't shoot him in cold blood. She still wasn't convinced she could shoot him in *hot* blood.

"You won't shoot me," he repeated yet again, his voice low, but with an edge.

"I already told you, I—"

He lunged forward, cutting her off. And belatedly, Alessandra realized everything he'd said was a ruse. An attempt to distract her from the fact that he'd been plotting an attack.

Chapter 15

Alessandra jumped back as Val's hands came for her ankles. The move pushed her off-balance, and as she tried to stay on her feet, she could barely hang on to the gun in her hands.

The gun. His gun. Crap.

He was already going for it. And she clued in that his dive toward her had been a distraction, too.

Furious at herself for not catching on, Alessandra fought to regain control of the situation. She had the advantage of being on her feet while Val was still on the floor. So she used it. She slid past her attacker, one foot extended. Her toes hit the weapon, and the gun slid over the hardwood and disappeared under the bed. A space far too narrow for even the small man in front of her to squeeze into. She almost wanted to cry with relief. But she didn't have time. The fight wasn't over. And now Val was even more furious than he'd been before.

He snarled and turned his attention back to Alessandra. He'd made his way to his knees, but was clearly impatient to get to her, because instead of coming to his feet, he simply lunged again. Alessandra leaped back out reach. She tried to train the gun on him, but her lack of experience wielding a weapon made it hard for her to move and aim at the same time.

Just squeeze the trigger!

She tried to obey the silent, self-directed command. But her finger slipped, the gun wobbled, and she had a sudden feeling that if she continued to try to use it, especially in such small quarters, things weren't going to go in her favor. What she had to do was escape. Or at the very least, get some space. And for that, she had the right tools. Speed, agility and wits. All she needed was a clear path to the door.

With renewed determination, Alessandra feinted left, then dodged right. Val followed. She danced backward, and Val growled and tried to stand.

Don't want that, she thought.

She pretended that she was going to try to jump past him, hoping it would deter him from wasting time trying to right himself. It worked. The snarly man gave up his effort to stand and dived sideways instead. Alessandra stepped easily out of reach. The dodge made her assailant stumble, and it gave her just the break she needed. But she didn't take the time to be grateful, or to turn around and check on Val's recovery. She just bolted out the bedroom door. Then she flew through the living room, knocking over an rustic-looking antique barstool in the process. She ignored the clatter and moved on, so close to freedom that she could already taste the rain-heavy air outside. But the second before her fingers landed on the knob, a *bang* and *crash* from behind told her she was going to have to fend Val off again.

She spun, her hands coming up, ready to shove away her attacker. But her adrenaline-fueled defense was unnecessary. Val was on the floor, tripped up by the same barstool that had impeded her progress. He'd knocked over a wall-mounted shelf, too—probably in an attempt to stop himself from falling over completely—and he was flat on his stomach, blood pouring from an ugly open gash on the side of his head.

What in God's name...

Alessandra's gaze found the cause a heartbeat later. It was a stone knickknack, carved into the shape of a mountain, and its already-jagged edge was split and covered in crimson.

"Val?" She said his name, took a step forward, then immediately, "Oh God."

Her attacker's eyes were already wide and unseeing. There was no doubt that he was dead. And in spite of the fact that he'd been sent there for the sole purpose of killing her, Alessandra couldn't stop herself from doubling over and dry heaving. Even when she was done, and her stomach was aching from the pain of it, she couldn't quite bring herself to be thankful he was dead. She just felt sad and defeated and scared.

But you still need to keep going.

"But where to?" she whispered aloud.

She eyed the door. Obviously, escape wasn't an issue now. She flicked a glance toward Val's body. But staying in the cabin didn't exactly have appeal. She turned back to the door. Anything had to be better than sitting inside with a body. Even waiting in the storage shed outside sounded good in comparison. But she no sooner made the decision and took a step toward the door than the musical tone of a ringing phone—not hers and not Rush's, which were both in the bedroom—came to life.

She swallowed nervously and eyed Val. It had to be his. And Alessandra had a feeling she should at least see who it was. She sucked in and held a breath, then moved closer. Tears threatened. But she pushed through them and bent down.

"Oh, thank God," she murmured when she saw that the phone was sticking out from the dead man's jeans pocket.

She yanked it free and glanced down. As impossible as she would've said it would be, her stomach twisted even more. Jesse's name was scrolling across the screen. She stared at it, wondering what would happen when Val didn't answer.

Nothing good.

Alessandra stared for a second longer, a simple plan— maybe a stupid one, too, she wasn't sure—forming in her head. She would answer. Say nothing. And hope Jesse assumed it was bad cell phone service. Telling herself it would work, she tapped the screen, then lifted the device to her ear. But instead of Jesse's angry voice coming on the line, it was Rush's rough and angry tone.

"Val," he snapped. "Where the hell are you? Boss says you were supposed to be done with a job fifteen minutes ago."

Alessandra exhaled, her voice wobbling. "He failed."

There was the briefest, heaviest pause on the other end. Then Rush spoke again, his words no softer and no less tinged with anger.

"Good news," he said. "Boss'll be happy to hear it. And speaking of the boss…he wants me to pass along the message that we're already on our way to the warehouse. But don't worry. I'm sure I can take care of the second job on your behalf."

Then there was a *click*, and Alessandra was left staring down at the phone. It was obvious that Rush's reaction—or lack of reaction, really—to her answering the phone was a result of him not being alone. But his words...she was sure they were meant to convey a message.

She was the job. Or rather, her *murder* was the job. Which meant that the dead man wasn't just a glorified errand boy. He was a working class assassin. She shivered at the thought, and forced herself not to dwell on that fact. She needed to figure out what it was Rush wanted to communicate to her.

What else did he say? That they were on their way to the warehouse?

Alessandra thought about that for a second. On account of his audience, Rush had to have meant it literally. So maybe he was just disclosing his location. And if that were true, then it'd worked. She knew there was only one area in Whispering Woods that even *had* warehouses. It was a small industrial complex that she'd read about online when briefly researching the town.

A tiny lick of relief at knowing where Rush was filled her. But as quick as it came, it was gone. Because she recalled the next part of what Rush had said.

Taking care of a second job.

She knew what that meant, too. At least as far as Val was concerned.

But Rush wasn't a murderer. Even undercover, he wasn't going to kill someone. Not for Jesse. Not for anyone. So...what?

Then it hit her.

Val was supposed to *do* the job. The only reason Rush would've mentioned it all was if it was important to Alessandra in some way. And there only one person in all of Whispering Woods who mattered to her.

Rush.

Rush was his next target.

Alessandra sucked in a breath that burned through her lungs.

She needed to get to him. Now.

No.

Before now.

Urgency overtook horror and disgust, and she bent down to Val's body. She stuck a hand in one coat pocket and came up empty, but a reach into the second pocket yielded triumph in the form of keys. Squeezing them tightly in her palm, she moved quickly through the cabin. She grabbed her bag, Rush's gun and phone, then slid into her shoes and ran straight out the door.

Rush glanced over at Garibaldi's too-relaxed hands on the steering wheel, his mind slipping repeatedly to Alessandra and to the phone call.

Stop obsessing over it, he ordered silently. *If she wasn't fine, she would've found a way to tell you, even with the twenty-second length of the call. And if you don't stop, Garibaldi's going to notice. If he hasn't already.*

But it was exceedingly hard to distract himself when he was sure they were headed toward his own execution.

Before the call—*God, how he hoped Alessandra had picked up on the fact that he didn't want her to follow them*—he hadn't been able to figure out what the purpose of their trip was. They'd completed one mundane task after the other. Time wasters, every one of them. First they'd grabbed a to-go coffee from the gas station in town. Then they'd snagged a piece of certified mail from the post office and dropped it off with another of Garibaldi's lackeys. Finally, they'd checked in on one of the souvenir shops Garibaldi owned, and made small talk with the owner. And even though he'd chatted the entire time, Garibaldi didn't once bring up their current situation. He didn't mention the shooter at the cabin, or Alessandra, or where they were ultimately going. Instead, he'd talked about a movie he'd seen recently. About sports. About a job he'd pulled off in his twenties. Hell. He'd even repeated a series of terrible jokes he'd recently read online.

Rush had grumbled about it all, as would be expected. That, at least, there'd been some truth to. Everything else about their meaningless tasks reeked of falsehood. With each passing minute, the deep sense of wrongness in Rush's gut had grown. It *still* grew, even though he now knew that the little stops and overzealous chattiness were a deliberate distraction. Not so much a time *waster* as a time *buyer*. To give Val a window to accomplish whatever terrible task he'd been assigned. Which was a whole other freshly opened can of concern. The man set Rush's teeth on edge at the best of times. He was a sadist. A criminal who committed crimes for the sheer pleasure of it. Rush had once seen him *grin* as he blew through a crosswalk, narrowly missing the three kids using it at that moment. Garibaldi saved Val for the jobs no one else would do. So the thought of him anywhere near Alessandra…

But he failed. Alessandra said so.

Rush was relieved that she was okay. He wished like

hell he'd been able to say more to her. Or *anything* to her, really. But all he'd been able to do was to deliver his pseudo-boss's cryptic message—which had been abrupt and accompanied by zero explanation—to Val. At least the part about heading for the warehouse appeared to be true. Garibaldi was turning into the industrial complex now, and Rush itched to ask questions.

The other man spoke first. "Recognize this place, Atkinson?"

"Yeah, boss. Why wouldn't I?" Rush replied.

Garibaldi shrugged. "Thought it might mean something to you. My guys and I have been running merchandise through a unit here for the last few months. Thought you might've noticed."

There was an edge to the comments, and Rush had a sudden urge to grab Garibaldi by the collar and demand that he just say what he meant. Instead, he just grunted.

"Try to mind my own business, boss," he said.

"Do you now? I've been getting the feeling you've been champing at the bit to know exactly what this little project is all about." The edge was still there—a threat under a casual observation.

Rush responded with an equally offhanded tone. "Always trying to go after whatever's bigger and better."

Garibaldi said nothing as he slowed the car and pulled up to the only privately gated warehouse in the bunch. He rolled down his window, punched in a code and guided the vehicle through the gate as it slid open. He stayed silent as they rolled over the concrete, and that was just fine with Rush. It gave him a moment to assess his surroundings.

One way in and out. Two armed thugs at the door. No signs. Nothing good about any of this.

"What the hell is this, boss?" he asked, his voice infused with all the curiosity and none of the concern he felt.

Garibaldi brought the car to a halt in a stall directly in front of the warehouse and cut the engine.

"You'll see," said the other man, swinging open his door. "Come on."

Rush rolled his shoulders in a useless attempt to ease some of the tension stiffening them, then climbed out of the car and stared up at the nondescript building. He pretended not to feel the guards' eyes on him as they stepped up to the door. He couldn't keep ignoring them, though, when one shot out a hand and grabbed his elbow. The grip was like being squeezed by a slab of meat, and Rush's immediate inclination—that he just barely managed to rein in—was to deliver a perfectly placed punch to the man's solar plexus. He settled for a glare.

"What the hell, man?" he said, flickering a narrow-eyed glare toward Garibaldi.

His boss shrugged. "Sorry, Atkinson. Rules are, you've gotta turn over your weapon."

Dread hit him in the gut. "You can't be serious."

"Deadly. Unless there's some reason you think you *need* your gun when you're with me." Garibaldi smiled darkly.

Rush rolled his eyes—deliberately dismissive—and yanked open his coat to reveal the antique revolver. "Should I hand it over myself, or initiate a wrestling match so the Testosterone Twins feel validated?"

The other man's gaze rested on the weapon. "Interesting choice. New to you?"

"A souvenir," Rush said. "Belonged to our gray-haired friend at the cabin."

Garibaldi's face tipped again up, any disbelief hidden behind a blank stare. "Go ahead and hand it over."

Rush grunted and dragged the weapon free. For the briefest second, he considered whether or not he might be able to shoot all three men in rapid succession and still come out alive. He shoved off the idea almost as soon as it came, though. The revolver wouldn't fire rapidly enough, and there was a damned likely chance there were other thugs lurking in unseen places, prepared to act under the slightest provocation. So he simply held out the gun, butt end first, and let the other guard—the one not trying to crush his shoulder—take it without protest.

"Good," said Garibaldi. "Let me show what I've been working on."

Rush nodded wordlessly. The thick concern was still rolling over him like a fog, and it didn't lessen any as he followed his boss into the building. The interior was dark, the air so dry that Rush had to let out a little cough. But the cough died abruptly when Garibaldi flicked on the lights and the space became illuminated in a yellow glow that revealed the contents of the warehouse. Paintings. Dozens and dozens of them. And Rush recognized them for what they really were—a cleverly disguised means of transporting and distributing an opiate. His partner Harley had been the one to figure it out.

The method was ingenious, really. A specialized paint was mixed with the drug in question. A local "artist" was hired to create the landscapes, and an unknowing art dealer sold them to predetermined buyers. The people who knew what was up were limited. There was Garibaldi himself and the men who created the paint. There were the guys who received the painting and extracted the drugs, and a few select men inside the crew.

And you aren't supposed to be one of them, Rush reminded himself.

He started to turn and face his boss, feigned ignorance on his lips. He only made it a half a spin before he realized there was no need to pretend. Three men stood around him in a triangle, each with a weapon trained at his head.

Garibaldi nodded. "There's a chair right there, Atkinson. Why don't you have a seat? We can have a little chat about how I feel about betrayal."

And Rush had no choice but to obey.

Chapter 16

Alessandra had stopped the little hatchback in the middle of the road, and now she sat there, tapping her fingers restlessly on the steering wheel. She sucked in her bottom lip. Up ahead, she could see the industrial complex. It wasn't huge, even if the buildings were some of the biggest in town. She'd learned from a sign just a few miles back that among other things, there was a self-storage space and a furniture wholesaler and an ATV rental place. Jesse's company logo sat on the very top of the sign, and Alessandra was sure that was because he probably owned the whole thing. But there was no clue as to which area he was in now. Or if he was there at all.

He has to be, she assured herself. *Rush wouldn't steer me wrong.*

She squinted at the buildings again, searching for a hint. And then she got one. Or she thought she did, anyway. On the back edge of the property was a building that stood out. Sort of. It was the same grayish color as the rest of them, but it had one feature the other didn't—its own fence. It seemed like the kind of thing Jesse would need. An extra layer of protection for whatever illegal activities he currently had underway.

"Or…" she murmured to herself. "It might not mean anything."

But as she continued to stare at it for a few more moments, a flash of movement caught her eye. And with no other leads, that was enough to convince her that it was at least a place worth starting. She started to shift her foot from the brake to the gas, then stopped. She couldn't very well just drive up and park. Someone would undoubtedly recognize the vehicle. It was Val's, after all. In fact, she was probably lucky that she hadn't been spotted already.

What I need to do is go in on foot, she thought. *In stealth mode.*

She glanced from side to side in search of a place to stash the car. The street was more or less empty, so after the briefest look around, she decided simply to pull over and park beside a largish bush at the end of the road. It gave the vehicle enough cover that unless someone was looking for it, they wouldn't find it. She pulled into the spot, checked to see if anyone was in sight, and when she was sure she was alone, she climbed out and started the trek toward the warehouses.

In spite of the way she worked to stay out of sight, the walk was still almost too quick. In minutes, Alessandra was standing at the nearest warehouse in the industrial complex, her back pressed to the side of the building. Given that it was the middle of the day and the middle of the week, the air was surprisingly quiet.

The only thing she could hear as she skulked along was the sound of her own thumping heart, and the feel of its ever-increasing thud did nothing to calm her down. By the time she reached the gap between the first and second buildings, her hands—which clutched the bag that held Rush's gun—were already sweaty. They ached, too, from her tight grip. But even when she made an effort to loosen them, she couldn't quite do it. Her feet were heavy, and her mind argued that taking another step would expose her.

Just breathe, she told herself firmly. *Rush needs you.*

The reminder was enough. She counted off ten inhales and ten exhales, then darted to the next warehouse. This time, she pushed along more quickly, and five breaths sufficed between the second building and the third. Her steps were still cautious, but they were surer, too.

You can do this, she said to herself every few steps.

And when she reached the final warehouse before the singularly fenced one, she actually believed it. Even when she leaned out and spotted the two burly men standing outside the main door, she wasn't deterred. She just jerked back and flattened herself to the exterior wall, satisfied that their presence affirmed her suspicions. She was in the right spot. All she needed to do was make sure that Rush was inside.

She eased forward the tiniest bit and searched for a good place to get a look inside. The fence was just a regular chain-link one. Six feet high, with no barbs or spikes or electrical wires at the top. But Alessandra could see that it wasn't completely devoid of reinforcements. There were a least two cameras attached to the posts, and maybe more that weren't within her vision. It didn't take a security genius to figure out that the electronic surveillance was meant to pick up where the human surveillance fell off, and vice versa.

Which isn't good for me.

She nervously tapped her thigh and scanned the area for an alternative.

There wasn't much to find. Aside from the other buildings and a couple of vehicles, there was nothing nearby. She paused, her mind working at a crazy idea. If she could get *inside* the warehouse she was standing *outside* at that moment, then somehow make her way up onto the roof…

She looked up toward the flat bit sticking out. "That's a truly insane plan, Alessandra."

Except she was already mentally mapping it out.

The main door was too risky. But there was a metal door on the side where she stood, and it had zero exposure to Jesse's building. She knew it was probably locked—the warehouse was too silent and too dark to be occupied—but she was pretty sure she could probably pick it anyway. It was a skill her father had taught her, joking that she never knew when she might need it. She wondered for a second what he would've thought about being right, then shook off the sad turn of her mind and moved on to what the next step would be.

Assuming no one was inside, she'd simply have to find a way up. From there, she just needed something she could use as a makeshift bridge. And not even a long one, because by Alessandra's estimate, there was only about four feet between the two buildings.

Great, she thought. *From there, I just have to get down, find a way to look inside, make sure Rush is there, then break in and save him. And not get caught at any point.*

"Piece of cake," she muttered sarcastically.

But that didn't stop her from moving anyway. She stepped to the side door and put her hand on the knob. A quick twist confirmed that it was locked, so she dropped to a crouch to examine the keyhole. Thankfully, it looked uncomplicated. Just a standard slot.

Alessandra opened her purse wide and dug through until she found two loose bobby pins. She gave them a skeptical look, then closed her eyes and pictured her dad's slightly devilish face as he explained the steps. It was easy to hear his voice in her head, too—both patient and authoritative as he laid out each bit of what had to be done.

First, you need to bend one of the bobby pins at a ninety-degree angle. You can use your teeth. I promise not to tell the dentist. Or your mom.

Smiling—and with her eyes still shut—Alessandra followed the remembered instruction.

Good work. Now take the second one and flatten it out. It should be as straight as you can make it. Like a ruler.

She did that, too, pleased that it seemed to come easily.

Great. Okay. Keep holding that second one. You need to bend the tip a bit. What you're trying to do is create a pick.

Alessandra worked to make it happen, then opened her eyes and dropped her gaze to the tools. They looked right. And her dad's voice in her head prompted her again.

You're doing awesome, Munchkin. Now what I want you to do is to take that first bobby pin and stick it into

*the bottom half of the lock. Not so hard that you bend it,
but make sure you put it in as far as it'll go.*

With her tongue between her teeth, she inserted the
pin until she couldn't force it any farther.

*Fantastic. Now take the other bobby pin and stick the
bent bit in just above the first one. And here comes the
tough part. You're using that bent bit to search for some
little bits that move up and down.*

Alessandra found the first one with relative ease.

*Good. Push it up until it clicks. Excellent job, Lessie!
You're a natural, just like your old man. Now you need
to do the next four, and you'll be a real pro.*

She worked slowly, sweat forming on her brow as
she carefully forced each locking pin into place. It was
painstaking. But worth it when she heard the final *click*,
and not one of the pins had dropped back down. As she
exhaled and let a small, triumphant smile lift her lips,
she could see her father's responding grin.

*You're amazing. One step left. Turn the lever in the
same direction as the key would go, and the door will
unlock.*

She inhaled again, holding her breath as she carefully
twisted to right. When she heard the release, she started
to breathe out. Then stopped.

What if it's alarmed?

Her eyes widened at the thought, and she wondered
why it hadn't occurred to her before. Of *course* it might
be alarmed. Maybe not even with the loud, blaring type.
Maybe with the silent, trigger-a-call-to-the-cops kind.
What would happen if the local police suddenly came
tearing in, lights flashing? How would it affect Rush's
safety? Or her own, for that matter? Should she even

open it, or should she seek out another way to get a look into Jesse's warehouse?

But as it turned out, she didn't get a chance to make the decision. A dark, dangerous voice made it for her.

"Go ahead, sweetheart," it said. "Let yourself in. You won't get caught."

Alessandra let out a startled yelp, and at the same time, she reflexively released the doorknob, which sent the door flying open inward. She tumbled blindly forward into the pitch-black. She started to run, and for a moment she thought she was free. Then a thick hand closed on her shoulder, and when she tried to scream, a second palm sprang to action, cutting off both the noise and her oxygen.

Rush's head was spinning. Aching from the last blow delivered by the thug he'd dubbed Meat-Fist. But just a heartbeat earlier, something had cut through the throb. He could swear it was the sound of a half-formed scream. And under the haze of pain that hung over him, he half thought it sounded familiar.

Alessandra.

His head jerked up as her name popped into his mind. He swung his bleary gaze around, afraid of what he might find.

If she gets hurt because of me...

He blinked. His position hadn't changed. He was still tied to the wooden chair. Still stuck in the middle of the painting-filled warehouse. There was no Alessandra, thank God. Just Garibaldi and the three gun-wielding men. Though to be more accurate, it had rapidly become *two* gun wielders and one *fist* wielder. A man who punctuated Garibaldi's questions with a jab here and a jab there. Rush's ribs and face were the bruised evidence. But none of it had induced the explanation his so-called boss wanted.

Ask whatever you like, I'm not telling you a damned thing.

The thought was infused with more bravado than he truly felt, and Rush knew it. He sagged back down, his chin hitting his chest. He wasn't a weak man. If he had been, he wouldn't have lasted as long as he had so deep in the undercover world. But this was the first time he'd been caught, and it was a true test of his stamina. There was a hell of a difference between engaging in a fight and taking a concentrated beating while rendered immobile. He didn't like it one bit.

He was glad, at least, that Garibaldi hadn't figured out his real association. The other man only knew that Rush was playing two sides of *some* kind. Not that he was a cop, or that he was with the Freemont PD. Which meant that his partners were safe. That no matter what happened to him, they'd be able to carry on and find some other way to put the man who'd killed their fathers behind bars.

And even more importantly...he believes Alessandra is dead.

Thinking about her again made his heart ache as hard as his body. He was sad and angry at the same time. If—when—Garibaldi grew tired of getting nowhere with his questions, he wouldn't leave Rush alive. The future Rush had just barely glimpsed would be ripped away. Worse than that, he'd never get the chance to tell Alessandra that he *wanted* that future. He couldn't explain that for the first time in memory, he cared about something more than he cared about meting out justice. He could almost hear her voice, crying softly somewhere in the back of his mind.

His chin sank even lower. Garibaldi be damned. He'd trade the man's fate in for five minutes with Alessandra. The woman he'd barely gotten a chance to know, but who he was already certain was the piece he'd been missing his whole life. Something he felt she deserved to know.

Gives you a damned good reason to get out of this situation, doesn't it?

He breathed out and forced his thoughts back to finding a solution. Until the last couple of minutes, he hadn't actually been given enough time to be thinking about a way out. He'd been questioned. Punched. Kicked. Questioned again. Then punched and kicked and questioned some more. Almost without any reprieve, and with increasing frequency.

So maybe you should be wondering why you're being allowed to breathe now.

He dragged his head up again, and was surprised to find that the scenery had changed. Only the two gunmen were present now, and they both had their weapons trained straight on Rush, their matching indifferent gazes unwavering.

What had happened to the others?

Rush swung his head to the side, searching.

Aha. There they are. His forehead bunched into a painful frown. *But who's the bonus guy, and why is he standing so awkwardly?* He stared for another second before placing the somewhat familiar figure. *Oh. Right. The guard from outside. The one with the grabby hands.*

Then Rush's blurred vision abruptly cleared. Because Grabby Hands stepped just a little to the right, giving a better view. And that view was of Alessandra, being handed over to Meat-Fist like a piece of property. Her tall, slim body was hunched over. Her crown of red hair was a disaster. But she was still the most beautiful damned thing he'd ever seen, and he hated the way she sagged in defeat.

Hell.

Rush wanted to call out to her in the worst way, but he didn't dare draw attention to himself. The last thing he needed was for Garibaldi to pick up on his feelings. The other man didn't need to know that witnessing Alessandra be manhandled like that filled Rush with fury, or to figure out that the woman meant far more to him than she ought to. So he settled for staring. Watching. Waiting for her to see him, and to hopefully find a way to believe that he'd get them out of the current situation.

She tipped up her face, and Rush tensed as he prepared to be spotted. She didn't look his way, though. Not yet. Instead, she turned a defiant glare toward Garibaldi.

"How could you, you son of a—"

Garibaldi cut off her furious question with a swift rap of his knuckles to her jaw. The blow made Rush jerk angrily in his chair, and all eyes turned in his direction. Meat-Fist remained indifferent. Alessandra's pain-laced expression morphed into mix of concern and relief. Garibaldi, though...he looked *pleased.*

A string of self-directed curses rolled through Rush's head. They'd given themselves away. *He'd* given them away with his instinctual need to protect her. Whatever it was the murderous crook wanted to know, he would find out. All he had to do was to threaten Alessandra, and Rush would tell him.

Smiling knowingly, the other man grabbed Alessandra by the arm and propelled her toward Rush.

"Well, Atkinson," he said. "I'm guessing that vow of silence you seem to have taken is about to end."

Rush focused on Alessandra. Swiftly, he drank in her blue eyes and honeyed skin. He stole a look at her lips and committed to memory the feel of them.

Then he turned to Garibaldi and said, "Leave her alone and I'll explain it all."

The other man's smile widened. "You have to know I'm not going to let her go, no matter what it is you tell me."

Rush struggled uselessly against his bonds. "If you hurt her…"

"What?" Garibaldi countered. "You'll yell at me from there? Relax, Atkinson. I don't want to drag this out. And I'll make it quick, so long as you speak up now. Who do you work for?"

Rush started to answer, a lie on his lips, but Alessandra beat him to it.

"Me," she said, her voice a barely-audible whisper.

He tried to protest. "You don't need to get involved in this, Red."

She shook her head and looked him in the eye. "I can't let him hurt you because of me," she said, then drew in a breath and switched her attention to Garibaldi, her voice a little stronger, but full of defeat. "I hired him."

The statement surprised Rush, but it seemed to intrigue Garibaldi.

"*You* hired him?" the other man replied. "When? For what?"

"A few months ago to do some private investigative work," Alessandra said, the words flowing smoothly from her mouth now. "I've got the receipts somewhere.

Or you can look at my online statements. I think they come up labeled as the Atkinson Agency."

Garibaldi's gaze flicked between them for a second, and then he nodded. "You were looking into your father's death."

Alessandra didn't miss a beat. "I found a box of stuff. I wanted to know more, and I didn't know where to start. So I sought some outside help. Then I lost contact with him, and I started to worry, so I went to the police. And I think you know the rest."

"I think I do," Garibaldi murmured. "And since you've made this much effort, I'm going to do you a solid and let you in on a secret. You want to know why your father died?"

"There's no reason for you to listen to this," Rush interjected.

Alessandra shook her head. "I'm sorry. I *want* to know, Rush. And I think Jesse's the only one who can tell me."

Garibaldi's eyes glittered. "I don't think you'll be disappointed in him, Al. In fact, you'll probably be pleased."

"Just spit it out," Rush snarled.

The other man lifted his hands in a gesture that managed to be surrendering and mocking at the same time. "It's all about loyalty in this business. And Randall had none to his crew. He chose to work with someone else instead. Feel like making a guess about who?" He paused expectantly. "No? Okay. I'll straight up tell you. He aligned himself with the friendly neighborhood police. Freemont PD to be exact. Your dad set up *my* dad, Al."

He paused again, as if to either let it sink in, or let them question the validity of the claim.

But when Rush met Alessandra's eyes, he knew she

was thinking the same thing as him. There was no need to question anything.

The Freemont PD.

It made sense of the envelopes Randall had used for his notes. It explained why his loyalties seemed divided, and how he kept getting pulled back in.

Alessandra issued a short nod, then breathed in and asked, "Set him up how?"

"Easy peasy," Garibaldi replied. "Gave the cops intel on a drug deal that could've *made* them. I figured it out, actually. My dad, though…he didn't want to believe it. Kept on *not* believing it, right until those three cops came at him."

"Did you kill him?"

"Your dad? No. The car crash was real, as far as I know. But the damage was already done. The setup was in play. And it might've been successful if it weren't for me letting the metaphorical cat out of the bag. But I did. And I earned the privilege of watching the whole thing happen from right beside the dealer your dad had betrayed. He shot my dad first, for being a fool, which is why the cops got away. But no one's perfect, right?"

"But Jesse. You could've stopped him from killing them. You could've saved your father's life." Alessandra's voice quavered as she said it.

"I could've," Garibaldi agreed, apparently unaffected by the obvious emotion. "But why would I? That drug dealer who shot my dad made me an offer. If I could take out those cops—and the evidence they had against my new friend—he'd give me a job."

Rush knew what was coming next, and he closed his eyes to brace himself. It still didn't provide enough of a buffer. Garibaldi's voice penetrated the air in a most unpleasant way.

"So I did it," he stated, his tone self-satisfied. "I walked into that police station, I laid a bomb, and I timed it to go off. Lit the place up like a firecracker. Three dead cops, no more evidence and a brand-new career for me."

The confession kicked Rush in the gut. But unexpectedly, he found no relief in hearing it out loud. Fifteen years, he'd been waiting to have the truth set free. Yet there it was, and all Rush felt was the same frustration. He needed to *do* something. To act. But his hands were literally tied.

Rush was so caught up in the futility that he nearly missed the fact that Alessandra was speaking again.

"You're sick," she said. "Those were *people,* Jesse. With lives and families, and…what is *wrong* with you?"

"I look after my own interests, Al. Who else would've done it for me all these years? Mom decided to die when I was born, and Dad was too stupid to do the job."

There was a shuffle then, and when Rush opened his eyes, he saw that one of the thugs was moving toward them, a chair in his hands. The big man positioned it against the one where Rush already was, and Garibaldi gestured toward it.

"Have a seat, Al," he said.

When she didn't immediately move, Meat-Fist grabbed her and shoved her down, then started winding a piece of cord around her torso. The rough treatment brought Rush back to life.

"What the hell are you doing, Garibaldi?" he growled.

"Me?" the other man replied with far too much lightness. "I'm completing my last transaction here in Whispering Woods. And I'm letting you two take the fall." He nodded toward his lackeys. "Go ahead, boys."

Grabby Hands reached obediently into his coat pocket and dragged out a small tube. He popped the top, turned toward the nearest paintings, and squeezed. It only took a moment—and a single inhale—for Rush to figure out the end game. They were going to light the place up.

Chapter 17

From behind him, Alessandra's inhale was sharp enough to rock their back-to-back chairs, and Rush knew she'd also figured out Garibaldi's plan.

He wanted to murmur a reassurance. To tell her to bide her time and not react. They'd stand a far better chance of getting out alive if they made their move once Garibaldi and his crew were gone. But his concern that she might lose it was unfounded. After the initial breath, all she did was say his name in a soft, worried voice.

"Rush."

"It's all right, Red," he murmured back.

"I'm scared."

"I'm right here."

"You're hurt."

"I've seen worse."

Then Garibaldi cut in, his voice an unwelcome in--

trusion on the moment. "This is all so sweet that I almost feel bad."

"So let us go," Rush snapped. "Or at least let Alessandra go."

"Not a chance in hell," said the other man. "But at least you'll die together. Very Shakespearean, I think. Romantic and tragic."

Then he imperiously snapped his fingers. A heartbeat later, the smell of sulfur whipped through the air, and the crooks were on the move. At the door, though, Garibaldi paused.

He sent a final smile their way. "Don't worry about the competency of the police, kids. I'm as good at manufacturing evidence as I am at destroying it."

Then he was gone.

For a full thirty seconds neither Alessandra nor Rush said a word. The hum of an engine and the sound of rolling tires carried in, then silence reigned again for a few moments before a new noise took over. The crackle of flames.

Rush jerked to action, sliding as far forward as he could, then grasping for Alessandra's bonds.

"What are you doing?" she asked.

"My best to get you free," he replied. "Fire moves more quickly than you can imagine."

As if to emphasize his statement, something in the room snapped, and acrid smoke billowed out.

"Fire took my entire livelihood in under ten minutes," Alessandra reminded him. "I'm aware of its power. I just think it makes more sense to free yourself first."

Rush didn't halt his efforts. "I promise I'll let you untie me as soon as I've got you free."

"Right. And if you think that I don't have enough *time* to untie you, then what?"

"Then you run. Without me."

"I didn't sneak in here just to let you die!" she exclaimed.

Rush's fingers finally found purchase in something that felt like a knot. "You *didn't* sneak in here. Grabby Hands dragged you in."

"Grabby—what?"

"Lean back a little."

She obliged, and Rush performed a mental fist pump as his thumb made its way through a loop. He didn't have time to celebrate. The smoke was growing steadily thicker, and the smell was worse. Rush couldn't help but wonder how much of the opiate was mixed in with the burning paintings.

"I did try to warn you not to come," he said as he worked the cord marginally looser.

"You told me where you were. And that you were a target."

"I also said I would take care of the job."

"Is that what you were doing when I got here? Because it looked like—" Her words cut off in a racking cough.

Rush looked up. The air above face level was so clouded that it looked like night, and the smoke was still building.

Move faster, urged a voice in his head.

But his fingers were burning, and his mind felt a little sluggish. Another breath in, and he was choking, too. If it weren't for the bonds holding him up, he would've doubled over.

"Dammit," he muttered between coughs.

When they subsided, it took a moment to regain his

grip on the knot, and a moment more to find the loosened bit.

"Rush?" Alessandra's voice was a little weak.

"I've got you, Red," he said.

"I don't feel all that well."

"Just a second longer."

The tie resisted for another moment, but he gave a hard yank, and it finally came free. He felt Alessandra sag forward, and worry thrummed through him.

"I need you to stay with me, sweetheart," he told her.

She coughed again, then croaked, "I'm coming."

Rush heard her hit the floor, and the sound was followed by a tug at his own bonds. Though her efforts were punctuated by wheezy breaths and hacks, she still managed to free him more quickly than he had done for her. The ropes dropped off and Rush pushed to his feet, immediately spinning with the intention of pulling Alessandra into his arms. When he turned, though, his heart dipped down to his knees. She was on the floor, her hair a pool around her head, her chest rising and falling far more quickly than was normal.

"Red," he said, dropping down to place a hand on her face. "Come on, love."

He got no response.

Damn, damn, damn.

With his own lungs protesting against the blackened air, Rush slid his hands under Alessandra's body, then heaved to his feet. Dizziness hit him hard, but he pushed through it. He had no choice.

Rush squinted. The warehouse was not only engulfed in smoke, but was also hot enough that he was sweating. Grimy, salty drips were making their way down his forehead, over his brows, and into his eyes. The only reason he could tell at all which way to move was because the smoke was traveling, and he knew it had to be toward an opening.

Tucking Alessandra closer, he took one wobbly step forward. Then another. He was more than light-headed now; he was downright spinning. He hurt everywhere from the inside out. His lungs and rib cage. His arms and legs. He wanted to collapse.

Just one step more, he said with each move. *And one more.*

At last—when he didn't think he could go another foot—he smacked into something solid. A little shove, and it moved.

The door. Thank God.

"Hang on, Red," he whispered roughly.

He pushed harder and was rewarded with a burst of light and a lungful of air. But it wasn't quite soon enough. As he bent to put Alessandra on the ground, the world swayed all around him. He sank to the ground and fought to hold on. It was a losing battle, though, and Rush knew it. He rolled to his side, noting that—oddly—as the world slipped away, a very real-seeming voice filled his ear, and an even realer pair of hands seemed to be grabbing his shoulders. But then that faded away, too, and nothingness took over.

Consciousness came to Alessandra in steps.

First came the pain. Rawness in her throat. A pounding in her head.

Second came awareness. The movement of a vehicle underneath, the fresh air streaming around her and the stiffness of an awkward sleep.

Finally came the panic. *Rush. The fire. Jesse.*

She tried to focus, but her head was swimming with fear and confusion. And when her eyes flew open, and her surroundings assaulted her, the fear only grew. It was light out. Her face was pressed against a cool glass window, and she could see foliage whipping by, and for a second it confused her. Her mind was too hazy to make sense of it, and her heart thundered so hard it hurt. Then she clued in. The vehicle she was in was rolling unevenly through the woods. And not on any kind of road, either.

Why?

She started to ask the question aloud, then thought better of it. Instead, she closed her eyes again and let her head flop down just a little. Then she cracked her lids and sneaked a look through her lashes. And what she saw made renewed fear bowl through her. She was in the passenger seat, and the man driving the car was the same one who'd attacked her and Rush at the secluded cabin. There was no mistaking the bushy beard sticking out from under his scarf. Alessandra squeezed her eyes shut and bit her lip to keep from making a sound.

Where was Rush? Where was *she*? How had she gotten into the car, and why was the gunman driving her into the woods?

She tried to make herself sort through what she remembered last. It was nothing but smoke and desperation and the surety that she wasn't going to make it out alive. And of those three things, the surety was the only thing that remained.

I need a way out.

But she wasn't certain what that would entail. She had no idea where they were or where they were headed. The man driving the car could simply be looking for a place to he could kill two birds with one stone—a spot where he could shoot her and dispose of her body at the same time. And even if she managed to avoid that particular fate, what was she going to do after? Run into the woods? God knew what kind of shape she was in. Her head felt like it was stuffed with fluff. The adrenaline that had helped her do what needed to be done in the warehouse...that was all gone. Maybe she wouldn't even be able to put one foot in front of the other.

But you have to try, urged a voice in her head. *If not for your sake, then for Rush's.*

Thinking his name again made her heart lurch. For all she knew, he was dead.

Oh God.

The despondent idea hit her like a blow. From behind her closed lids, she could see his face the way it'd been in the last moments. One eye bruised and puffed up. A lip so swollen that she wanted to kiss it better but would've been afraid to actually do it for fear of hurting him.

The ache in Alessandra's chest changed from physical to emotional. Life wasn't fair. Her mother had always said so. But this was the worst of the worst. A glimpse of something greater, ripped away before she could even acknowledge what it might truly become. The chance to love someone. Gone.

Tears slid out from under her eyelids, thick and hot. She could feel them sliding down her cheeks, and she knew that if the gunman turned her way, he'd see them and she'd give herself away. But she couldn't stop them. The pain of loss was too acute. Far greater than the need for self-preservation.

"He's still alive, if that's what you're worried about."

The gruff statement made Alessandra jerk involuntarily toward its speaker. Strangely, it wasn't the words or the acknowledgment of her silent concerns that gave her true pause. It was the fact that there was something vaguely familiar about his voice.

Because you heard him talking back at the cabin.

But that wasn't it. Yes, he'd said a few things. But she couldn't remember what they'd been or what he'd sounded like. She'd been too scared to notice. Now, in the small space, this feeling of familiarity was distinct.

Alessandra studied him for another moment, trying to place the odd sensation. The man's attention was fixed straight ahead, his hands tight on the wheel. And there wasn't anything about him that she could say she recognized—not on a deeper level. He was dressed the same as he had been when he'd confronted them at the cabin, and he was definitely the same man. But aside from that, he was a stranger.

When he spoke again, though, the same jolt of remembrance hit her.

"You can go ahead and look, if you don't believe me," he said without moving his gaze from the windshield. "Your guy's in the back seat."

As much as Alessandra wished she could've stopped herself—it left her feeling too vulnerable—she couldn't help but turn to check. And she couldn't stop the exhale of relief, either. Rush was lying straight across the back. Battered and bruised. Covered in soot. But his chest rose and fell evenly.

Thank God.

Alessandra stared for another few seconds, counting off ten perfectly healthy breaths before she faced the driver again. She couldn't think of the right question to ask. "What do you want?" seemed too vague. "Are you going to kill us?" seemed like too much of a lead-in. But he beat her to it anyway.

"I thought he was trying to hurt you," the man stated, and his voice held a surprising amount of emotion.

Alessandra blinked. "What?"

"At the cabin," he elaborated. "I assumed that because he was working for Jesse Garibaldi, he couldn't possibly have your best interests at heart."

"I…" She trailed off. *Why does he even care?*

"I'm sorry, Lessie. If I knew he was helping you, I would've approached it all differently."

He said something else. Possibly a *few* things. But all of it was lost. Because the jumbo jet of realizations had just crashed straight into Alessandra's brain.

There was only one person who'd ever called that nickname. One person she'd let get away with it. But it was impossible that this was the same man.

Because he's dead.

She didn't realize she'd said it aloud until the man stopped talking and turned his head. Then she saw his eyes, and she *knew*. It was him.

If Alessandra had though the world was swimming before, it had nothing on that moment. She met that blue stare—one she knew as well as she knew her own—and then the world winked out, this time in a faint.

It was the silence that woke Rush. Or maybe it was just that the noise—an indefinable hum and the comforting whistle of the wind—had kept him under. It was hard to say which. Either way, both sounds were gone, and it was far too quiet. And he was cold, when he could swear just moments earlier, he'd been surrounded by blistering heat.

Trying to stave off the chill and sink back into oblivion, he reached for the warm body he knew should be beside him. He tensed pleasantly in anticipation of her soft breath and the smell of her hair.

Maybe sleep *isn't what I'm after at all.*

The thought was tinged with drowsy desire, and when his fingers whacked into something cold and unyielding instead of warm flesh, it had the same effect as an icy bucket of water. He jerked up. Or tried to. His chest met with resistance, and his body slammed down again so hard that his eyes watered. He was left staring straight up at a strangely textured roof and wondering what the hell was going on.

Then he remembered it all, and for a few seconds, he assumed he'd been captured and tied up again. His mind immediately went to Alessandra. If he was tied up, where was she? Fearing the worst, he brought his hands up to feel his bonds and to seek a way out. What his grabbed at instead of rope was a familiar-feeling piece of nylon. It only took a moment to place it.

A seat belt.

The realization made Rush pause to quickly reexamine his current situation. His flicked his gaze back and forth. Yes, he was definitely in a car. The back seat, to be exact. Someone had taken the time to strap him in, albeit awkwardly. So he didn't think he was truly being held against his will. Which was good.

Still...

The whole thing was as puzzling as it was encouraging, and he didn't think he should just jump straight up.

Moving cautiously, he brought his hands back to the seat belt. He searched for the latch, found it, then depressed the latch. An audible *click* made him wince, but there was no reaction from anywhere else in the car, so he slowly sat up. His body hurt more than it ever had in his life, but it seemed insignificant at the moment. And another glance around only added to the strangeness. The car where he sat appeared to be in the middle of the forest. Tall trees were visible on either side of the vehicle. The windows were open, letting in a light breeze that brought with it a woodsy scent.

What the hell...

Rush sat up a little straighter. His new position confirmed it; he was definitely in a car in the forest. The fresh line of vision made more sense of it, too. It looked like whoever had driven the vehicle to its current spot had used one of the ATV trails. The why was still a mystery.

Rush started to move again, this time to reach for the door handle. He froze, though, when the wind whipped in, and a masculine voice carried with it into the car.

"Come on, Munchkin," said the unseen man. "Open your eyes for me."

Munchkin?

Even more confused and more cautious than before, Rush adjusted again, his gaze scanning the area for the source of the strange comment. Then he spotted it. A shadow-shrouded figure, crouched down and slightly hidden behind an enormous fallen log. The figure shifted, extending an arm downward. Rush followed the motion with his eyes, and as he caught a glimpse of what was on the ground below the man, every protective urge he had roared into high gear. Because what he saw was the undeniable glint of red hair, catching the minuscule amount of sunlight that pushed through the thick foliage overhead.

Alessandra.

Then things got worse. The shadowy figure lifted its head—*his* head—and looked straight at Rush. Recognition flooded in. The figure was no stranger. It was the man who'd tried to kill them at the cabin.

Instinct took over.

Rush grabbed the door handle and pushed out. He obviously couldn't catch the gunman by surprise, but he was also sure that waiting wouldn't do any good, either. So he leaped from the car. Ignoring the everywhere-pain, he charged forward with the intention of doing nothing more than knocking the other man straight to the ground. He held on to the hope that the outright attack would be unexpected. The hope grew as he got nearer because the man made no move to get out of the way. When the guy lifted his hands and put them on his head, though, Rush faltered.

The slight hesitation gave him a moment to take in a few more details. Like the fact that Alessandra's head was propped up on a folded coat, while her body was tucked under a blanket.

Rush stumbled to a stop, and he snapped a glare back to the gunman.

"I need you to tell me what the *hell* is going on." His voice was harsh with the residual effects of the smoke from the warehouse.

The man's hands didn't move from their secure spot, and his penetrating blue stare didn't waver as he replied, "Alessandra's fine. Just had a bit of a shock."

"She damned well better be fine."

"I promise you, she is."

"Oh, you *promise*, do you?"

"I wouldn't have dragged the two of you to safety if I were just going to kill you, would I?"

"Can't say I've ever understood what goes on in the minds of unhinged criminals."

"All we can do is wait for her to wake up and confirm it." The man studied him for a second. "You're Atkinson's kid, aren't you?"

The statement—like any mention of his father—made Rush's chest compress, but he kept his reply as even as the other man's had been. "Goes to reason. Since I'm Atkinson, too."

"More specifically, you're Sergeant Ken Atkinson's son. Now that I'm looking at you, I don't know how I didn't see it before."

"If you're trying to trick me into saying something, you should give up now."

"Your dad was a bit prickly, too. I don't think he really cared much for working with the unhinged criminal himself."

Something about the way the man said it—like it was fond memory—struck a chord with Rush.

"Who are you?" he asked, his tone now more curious than angry.

"I'm Randall Rivers. Lessie's father."

Chapter 18

This time, consciousness didn't seep in. It roared. And it was accompanied by the statement Alessandra already knew to be true.

Lessie's father.

She opened her eyes and silently stared at the two men standing a few feet away. Even if she'd been able to speak, she wasn't sure what she would've said. How did someone greet the father they'd believed was dead? How did a person even begin to acclimatize to the idea that he was still alive?

They don't...that's how.

Her brain didn't want to deal with it at all. So instead, it focused on the conversation.

"You expect me to believe that?" Rush was saying.

"Doesn't matter what you believe." Her father's reply held a shrug. "Still true."

"And you here in Whispering Woods is what...a happy accident?"

"Of course not."

Rush sighed. "You have fifteen seconds to convince me."

"Fifteen seconds isn't much time," Alessandra's dad pointed out.

"Twelve seconds."

"Fine. What can I tell you? Her birthday is on Christmas, but she pretends it's in July. She loves the ocean, and when she's mad, her eyes go the same color as the sea hitting the shore. I taught her to fire that same old gun you stole from me, and her mom didn't talk to me for a week because of it. Any of that ring a bell?"

The air was silent for a moment, and then Rush said, "Start at the beginning. And don't leave anything out. I want to hear it all."

As her dad began to talk, listening became less of a distraction from thought and more of a genuine interest in what he had to say. Alessandra closed her eyes to listen.

First, he explained some details she was already familiar with—that before he met her mother, he'd lived a shady life. Petty crime, mostly, but interspersed with some things he was more ashamed of. He told Rush how meeting his wife changed everything. It gave him a new purpose and a reason to go straight. So he did. Adding Alessandra to the mix only reinforced that it was the right thing to do. And he stuck by his right-side-of-the-law lifestyle for years.

His first relapse—as he called it—came when their little family was hit with a massive hospital bill. Alessandra was about three at the time, and she vaguely recalled the days her mother had spent recovering from an illness they never did define. She also kind of remembered her dad being unusually pensive, only because he was normally so jovial. But it made sense now, hearing him say that he'd taken a job running some stolen goods, and how unhappy it had made him. Once it was done, he swore he'd never go back. But then came the first round of blackmail. If he didn't join his buddies, they'd turn him in. And the threat became a recurring event. A year would go by. Sometimes two. Once even four years passed. Then the crew would "need" him.

But he finally had enough, and he went to the police on his own. He expected the worst—an arrest and conviction. It didn't happen. Instead, three cops who were working on a big bust requested a meeting. It turned out that they'd been chasing a particular man for a year. He was an overseer of some kind. Always behind the scenes, but in charge of a whole whack of other small crews, which included the one that was blackmailing Alessandra's father. The three cops were putting together a case, and it was very hush-hush. They wanted an inside man. Her dad leaped at the chance. Not only would it get him off the hook for the crimes he'd committed, it would also let him give back. A little bit of instant karma. But then things went wrong.

Someone figured out his confidential informant status and tried to kill him. They sent someone to the Riverses' family house to perform a home invasion that was supposed to result in Alessandra's father's murder. But the timing was off. No one was home, and the would-be murderer was caught in the act. So the three officers came up with a new plan. The big bust was only a month away, and they'd keep Randall in witness protection until then.

But that didn't work out, either. On the way to the safe house, another vehicle ran him and the officer driving him—a man posing as a cabbie—straight off the road.

At that, Alessandra almost gasped. The accident he was describing was the one that had supposedly killed him. She could recall the grief of it like it was yesterday. The urgent call down to the high school office. The policeman standing there, trying to look stoic, but just seeming sad as he explained. Her father, who was supposed to be heading to England for a monthlong course, had perished in a crash.

But the course was a ruse, she realized. *A cover for the witness protection.*

"They took advantage of it," her dad told Rush, his voice tinged with regret. "They used my 'death' to pursue the final bit of their case."

"But it was a setup," Rush replied. "Garibaldi told me about it."

"That's right," her father agreed, his anger audible.

Then Rush cleared his throat and asked a question that was on Alessandra's mind, too. "Why didn't you go back to your family after that?"

A heavy sigh preceded the response. "I tried. But I needed to time it right. I needed things to settle."

"Except they didn't."

"No. The bomb at the station came pretty damned quickly."

"Courtesy of Jesse Garibaldi."

"Smart, sneaky little sociopath, even if I didn't know it then. Let his own father die for the sake of the game. Not to mention the loss of *your* father and those two other perfectly good officers."

Rush was silent for a moment, and Alessandra knew

he must be hurting. She wished she could reach for him to offer him comfort. But she was sure now wasn't the right moment to interrupt. And he was already moving on anyway.

"And after that?" he asked.

"I was *ready* to go home," her father said.

"What stopped you?"

"I got caught by an old acquaintance. I was drowning my sorrows in a Freemont bar, trying to decide what the hell I was going to do, when it happened. A man I knew walked in. Thought he saw a ghost, but came walking straight up to me anyway. Guy's name was Stuart." There was a pause. "I take it from your expression that you know him?"

"Not personally," said Rush. "But my partners saved his daughter's life. I know he drove professionally for the senior Garibaldi first, and later for Jesse. I also know Jesse *killed* Stuart because the man was collecting photographic evidence against him."

"All true. But that came later. Do you know why Stuart started driving for Jesse in the first place?"

"Assumed he just got passed down. Like a family heirloom."

Her dad let out a chuckle—a sound that Alessandra never thought she'd hear again, and it distracted her so badly that she almost missed what came next.

"Hardly," he said drily, then turned serious again. "Stuart stuck around for the same reason he started taking pictures. Jesse threatened his family, and he was damned scared the kid—he was only seventeen, remember—would follow through. And why wouldn't he believe it after everything else? Why wouldn't I believe it, too? His dad. The cops. He was happy to sacrifice anyone to save himself. Stuart warned me that if I even *thought* about going home again, Jesse would find a way to get to all of us."

"I'm sure the caution was valid."

"You say that, but I can tell that you're thinking that a man who loved his family couldn't leave," stated her father. "But I'm telling you right now, if the stakes are higher if you stay, you do whatever the hell you have to. You tell me you wouldn't sacrifice your own happiness for the life of someone you love. And I tried my damnedest to come back. I sat around for that entire year after the explosion, waiting for Jesse to go to jail. I thought if he was behind bars, he might not be able to get to my girls. But you know what happened next."

"Better than most." Rush's reply held a hint of understandable bitterness.

"I'm guessing that's true. I'm very sorry for your loss, son."

As her father made the statement, a strange sensation struck Alessandra. The exchange she was listening to was a metaphor. It was Alessandra's past meeting her future. The man she'd loved as a child, and the man she was falling in love with now.

I need to see it, she thought, lifting her lids and tilting her head.

She found them in an odd pose. They stood face-to-face, with maybe two feet between them. Her father had one hand on his head, the other on Rush's shoulder.

"Your dad was an excellent cop and an excellent man," her dad said gently. "He loved you. Talked about you all the time with his buddies. So much that I don't think he even realized he was doing it. I know he worried about how you'd turn out. But I think he'd be proud."

"Thank you," Rush replied, his tone sincerely grateful.

"Can I ask you something?"

"Sure."

"You care about my daughter?"

"I do."

"A lot?"

"Honestly? I only met her a day ago, sir. But the moment I laid eyes on her, something changed, and I kind of wonder how I lived the last thirty-one years *not* knowing her."

"Good."

"Good?" Rush's echo was tinged with concern.

"I know it's been a long time since I've had any say in her life," her father said, "but I feel better knowing that someone else will love her as much as I always have."

"I'm not following," Rush replied.

"Fifteen years ago, against the instructions of the Freemont PD, I wrote my wife a note right before I went into the witness protection program. I took that note to her house—to *our* house—with the intention of leaving it, but I had second thoughts, so I tore it up. I had the pieces in my hand when my wife came home far earlier than she should have. I panicked. Tossed it all in the trash. Then I sat outside for hours, waiting for her to leave so I could undo my mistake. It never happened. She found the note. She taped the damned thing together."

And Alessandra suddenly saw what her father was planning, and she sat up, the blood rushing to her head and a protest on her lips. "Dad, no!"

Both men turned her way, and Rush hurried to her side. "Red."

She shook off the hand he put on her shoulder. "He's going to leave," she said. "He's going to confront Jesse."

Her dad confirmed it with a nod. "I should've done it years ago. And it's my fault we're in this situation to begin with."

"Dad, it's *not*."

"If I'd just walked away completely...never written that damned note..."

"You were just trying to warn Mom."

"And I endangered both your lives in the process. There's nothing I can do for her. But for you, Lessie... I can make this right."

"You probably won't even find him," Alessandra said desperately. "He told us he was leaving town."

"I'll find him," he promised.

"Jesse will kill you. Literally *kill* you."

"I'm going to do my damnedest to make sure that doesn't happen."

"Dad. Please."

"Jesse already thinks the two of you are dead," he replied. "You should take advantage of that."

Then he leaned down and pushed back a strand of her hair, and grief slammed into her. It closed her throat and cut away her breath, stealing any more words she might've added as her father turned and spun on his booted foot. He strode toward the car, slid into the front seat, then fired up the engine. And before Alessandra could even get to her feet, he was gone. She turned to Rush, and she collapsed into his arms, tears overtaking her.

Rush stroked Alessandra's back and stared after the disappearing car. He was torn.

Part of him was overwhelmed with the new revelations. Who the hell would've guessed that Randall Rivers had been a CI, let alone that the man was still alive? He couldn't help but wonder how he would feel if he were in Alessandra's shoes.

Pissed off, he thought automatically.

It was true. He tended toward hostility in situations like this. He'd be furious at being misled. Angry at being made to grieve. And that wasn't even factoring the current abandonment in the woods.

But part of him understood, too, how the other man had come to the decision. The woman in his arms was more than enough motivation. What wouldn't he do to save her life? Would he hide himself away for fifteen years? Would he give up the chance to hold her like this? Possibly for good?

Yes.

It would break his heart, dammit. Crush him like nothing else. But he would still do it, if it was the choice between keeping her alive and risking her life.

In that moment, he both hated and loved Alessandra's father. He'd be eternally grateful to the man for doing what had to be done to save his daughter's life. And he'd be eternally incensed at him for making her hurt not once, but twice.

"Red," he said, his voice rough.

"Please don't," she replied against his chest.

"He's going because he loves you."

"I know that. And I know you're going to say that you get why he did what he did all those years ago. And you're going to tell me we should listen to him and run away, too."

"Red," he said again. "I think we should—"

She didn't let him finish. She shook her head, her red locks flying.

"Honestly, I get it, too, Rush. I'd hide to stop you from

being killed. But I'm not dead, and you're not dead, and he's not dead. Not yet. But Jesse won't…" She broke off in another sob.

He held her for another few moments, his thoughts rolling around. He put himself in her shoes once more. What if he had the chance to know his own father all over again? What if he could see the end coming?

I can't let this happen, he thought, drawing in a breath that burned. *I have to think of way to stop it. But first…*

"Red," he said, his voice firmer this time.

She leaned back and stared up at him, her beautiful face streaked with soot and tears and pain and hope. "Yes?"

"You know how I feel about you."

"I know how *I* feel about *you.*"

He couldn't help but smile. "I suspect it's about the same. Do you want me to say it first?"

She stared at him, those blue eyes of her wide. "I don't think we should say it."

"No?"

"Not yet."

"What are we waiting for?"

"A moment where it doesn't feel like saying it is going to be goodbye."

He reached up to swipe a thumb over her damp cheek, bent to kiss her dirty lips, then murmured, "Tell me what you'd like me to do."

She kissed him back before tremulously replying, "Nothing too big. Can you just save the whole world?"

"Well. Maybe not the whole *entire* thing. But I'll go after Randall, if that's what you want me to do. I might not be able to beat him to Jesse, but I can sure as hell try."

"That just scares me even more. If something happened to you, Rush…"

"Two against one might be a safer bet."

"But it's *not* just two against one. It's two men who mean *everything* to me…and it's pitting them against a murderer who has his own mercenary army."

Her words brought an idea to mind, and he smiled again, more widely this time. "What would you say if I offered to bring in my own mercenary army?"

Alessandra sat up a little straighter. "Your partners?"

"Pretty sure they'd be happy to help."

"It won't ruin your case?"

He almost laughed, but settled for shaking his head instead. "You're worried about my case?"

She frowned. "It's your case. Of course I'm worried about it."

He kissed her, then threaded his fingers through hers. He stared down at their clasped hands, overcome with emotion. Everything about the woman in his arms felt right. Like coming home. Like his future. Like every damned thing he'd ever wanted, but had never known.

Like all those sappy love stories people tell, and I never believed were true.

He shook his head ruefully, marveling at the fact that he'd almost left Alessandra on the side of the road. He couldn't wrap his head around what might've happened if he'd done it. But then he just as quickly reasoned that things would've turned out the same. That's what happened when something was meant to be. A thick lump was forming in his throat, and he couldn't seem to clear it away.

He lifted his eyes and spoke even though it came out scratchy. "Alessandra?"

Her gaze was as warm as he was sure his own must be. "Yes?"

"This isn't goodbye."

"What do you mean this isn't…oh." Her cheeks went pink under the grime. "You're not saying it."

"You asked me not to. So I'll wait. But I can still think it."

"Me, too, Rush."

"You know I mean it."

"Yes."

He pushed to his feet, then offered her his hand again. "So let's do this. I'll place a call to Harley. He'll use his magical powers to find a way to slow things down between your dad and Garibaldi."

She let him pull her up, but her shoulders sagged as soon as she was on her feet. "He's going to have to have *real* magical powers. Because we don't have a phone. Or a car to get a phone."

"Right. But we can—" He paused abruptly and looked up as a familiar, not-too-distant whir came to life.

Alessandra lifted her eyes, too. "Is that a helicopter?"

Sure enough, a spinning, rumbling speck in the sky was getting bigger and louder by the second.

Chapter 19

Alessandra thought maybe she should be past the point of being surprised. After all, the last few weeks had been one stunning moment after another. The note. The death of her friend at the police station and the loss of her store. Then Rush. Falling for him so hard and so fast it barely seemed real. And the confirmation that Jesse Garibaldi was some kind of evil genius. And the pièce de résistance. The shocking revelation that her long-dead father wasn't dead at all.

I should be numb.

But as Rush pulled her back into the trees, and the black-and-white helicopter got nearer, Alessandra's mouth still wanted to drop open. That it was police issue was obvious. The coloring was a dead giveaway. And even if it hadn't been, it only took a few moments to get close enough for a good view of the logo on the side.

When it turned in the sky, she could also see that the initials FCPD were embossed over the front. It only took a second to place what the letters stood for.

"Freemont City Police Department," Alessandra murmured with a glance toward Rush.

He looked just as surprised as she felt. But he was smiling a little as well. She opened her mouth to ask if he knew what was going on—because he sure looked like maybe he did—but the air was suddenly far too loud for questions. And the propeller-induced wind was kicking up dirt and leaves, too, forcing Alessandra to close her eyes. When Rush slung an arm over her shoulder and pulled her into a protective embrace, she gratefully buried her face in shoulder, waiting out the noise and the flying debris. But the calamity no sooner ended than a new one took its place. Masculine voices filled the air, and when Alessandra opened her eyes and blinked away the dust, she found the source of the chaos in the form of three very different-looking men. Rush gave her a squeeze, then jumped straight into the friendly fray.

"Atkinson, you cranky old SOB," hollered a clean-cut guy with sandy brown hair. "You look like hell."

"Your mother would wash your mouth out with soap if she heard you cursing like that, Brayden," Rush replied, a grin in his voice and his hand out for a shake.

The other man—Brayden—bypassed the extended palm and dragged Rush in for a hug. "She'd forgive me, seeing the state you're in."

A second man—this one shorter than the first, but twice as wide—shoved the first out of the way and embraced Rush, too. "We thought you might be dead."

The third man, who was tall and blond, and sized between the first two, gave the second one an eye roll.

"Thought we agreed we weren't going mention his funeral plans, Harley."

"Nah," said the stocky man. "*I* just agreed to not killing him if he was still alive. Besides that, you were the one saying you were laying claim to his Lada if he'd kicked the bucket."

Rush turned to the tall blond. "Oh, *really*? My Lada, huh, Anderson?"

The blond shrugged. "She needs someone who can love her properly, Rush. Neither one of the Maxwell boys appreciates a car the way you and I do."

"Yeah," Rush grumbled. "But you could at least wait until my body's gone cold."

The blond man clapped him on the back. "Speaking of cold bodies...when did *you* start talking to real women?"

As every eye turned her way, Alessandra's face heated. She had an urge to pat down her hair and demand to be allowed to wash her face before they all started scrutinizing her. But it was too late. Each one of the men was already giving her a thorough once-over. She wondered what they saw when they looked at her. Her messy red hair? The dirt and soot caking her skin? The torn clothes? Or maybe just a crazy woman who was in love with their friend after knowing him for a day?

But Rush just chuckled and pulled her back against his chest.

"All right, all right, guys," he said. "She already knows about my woeful lack of ability to form lasting relationships outside the office."

Both of Anderson's eyebrows went up, and all three men were staring at her again. This time, there was a slower, more speculative feel to their examination. Like they'd realized that their jokes might have some merit.

And now, rather than wanting to straighten her hair, Alessandra wanted to pull out her credentials. Maybe show them her business degree and résumé. And invite some friends to testify on her behalf.

She straightened her shoulders and said, "So…which one of you is starting the interrogation?"

Immediate, booming laughter filled the air, and Alessandra relaxed.

"Okay," said Rush. "Before we get into me begging for your help and asking how the hell you found me in the first place, I'd like to introduce you to this living, breathing woman here. Gentlemen—and believe me, I use that term lightly—this is—"

"Alessandra Rivers," filled in the tall man who'd first greeted Rush, stepping forward and sticking out his hand. "Nice to meet you. Brayden Maxwell."

Puzzled, Alessandra put her palm in his and shook. "Hi, Brayden."

He let her fingers drop, then pointed to the tree trunk of man standing beside him. "My brother, Harley."

"Hi," Alessandra said again.

"And the tall, ugly guy is Anderson," Brayden added.

She turned to look at the blond man—who was more underwear-model good-looking than ugly—and offered him an awkward wave. "Hey, Anderson."

He nodded and gave her charming smile that lit up his eyes. "Good to meet you, Alessandra. Sorry you got caught up in our mocking. But I honestly don't think Rush has ever had a girlfriend who wasn't a part of an undercover sting."

"Hey, now," Rush protested.

"C'mon, buddy," said Harley. "You know it's true."

"I'm starting to wonder why I wanted you here," Rush said.

"Think it has something to do with saving your butt," Brayden replied. "But we should probably talk and fly. Captain wasn't all that thrilled about giving us the chopper, and if we're gonna track down Alessandra's dad without getting fired, we need to move."

"How did you know about my dad?" Alessandra blurted.

Rush slid his fingers down to hers. "I suspect that's what we need to talk about."

Frowning so hard it made her head ache, Alessandra let him lead her over to the helicopter. She climbed into the seat he gestured to, then held still as he brought down a harness and strapped her in. He gave her a quick kiss, tightened the belts, then handed her a headset.

"Put this on," he said. "Only one person can talk at a time, but the noise canceling is pretty good, and everyone will be able to hear."

"So no secrets!" Harley joked as he climbed in across from her and donned his own headset, then dropped his voice and whispered into the mic, "I mean it."

Rush gave his friend a playful shove and joined them inside, and Brayden quickly followed. Anderson, though, made his way into the cockpit.

"He's flying this thing?" Alessandra, her own voice echoing through the earphones.

Brayden smiled and spoke into his own mic. "Better him than the rest of us. Anderson is a man of many talents."

"Good to know," she replied drily.

Then the engine rumbled to life, and for a moment, everyone went silent. Alessandra clung nervously to

Rush's hand, but the helicopter lifted smoothly into the air, and it was obvious that Anderson was a capable pilot. When they were up and moving, Brayden's voice filled the headset.

"You remember Captain Rohan?" he asked. "Big guy. Birthmark in the shape of a star on his forehead?"

"Sure," Rush replied. "Retired right before the you-know-what hit the fan."

"That's the guy," said Brayden. "Right before he re-tired—I mean *right* before…like twelve hours before he handed over his service weapon—he happened to walk into a room at the station. The officers investigating the bombing were in there, viewing all these surveillance vid-eos. Hundreds of 'em, I think. Anyway, they were playing this particular one from outside a bar, and Rohan spied some guy standing on the stoop. He recognized him. Wanna guess who?"

"Randall Rivers," Rush filled in.

Brayden nodded. "Yep. Only problem is…the guy's supposed to be dead." He paused and offered Alessandra an apologetic look, then went on. "But Rohan's certain it's him, and he makes a big deal about it. For twelve hours, anyway. Tries like crazy to figure out if Rivers is somehow still alive. Dead ends everywhere. The new boss tells him it's just a doppelgänger. So Rohan retires and has to let it go. But for the next fifteen years, it's al-ways on the back of his mind."

"The case that got away," Harley interjected.

"Exactly," Brayden said. "But he carried on. Traveled with his wife for a while, then ran for city councilman. He's held his seat for the last decade, but was just about to *re*-retire."

"Let me guess…" Rush said. "In twelve hours?"

Brayden grinned. "Five, actually. But this morning, he got a call."

"From my dad?" Alessandra asked.

"In a roundabout way," Brayden told her. "He actually left a message for *our* captain. Identified himself as a CI and said he had information about Jesse Garibaldi. And—thank God—there was a coincidental overlap. Current boss happened to be in that room all those years ago when Rohan made a fuss about Randall Rivers."

"Hell of a thing," Rush stated, his awe audible even through the headset.

"No kidding," his partner agreed. "Knowing we were still working on this, the captain reached out to me. Very kindly added some resources to our otherwise limited budget. Hence our ability to get here so quick. And the chopper, of course. Unfortunately, the number Rivers had left didn't get an answer, but we *were* able to trace the call. Harley took that and used his networking skills to figure out where Randall was living, then used his magical powers to figure out he was here in Whispering Woods."

"I used the magic of technology," Harley corrected. "Which is the same way I found Rush and Alessandra."

"You see it your way, bro, I see it mine." Brayden grinned, then added, "Been trying since this morning to get a hold of you, Rush. Couple hours in, and we thought it was best to bring the party here."

"Glad you were thinking of me, *Mom*," Rush replied.

"You complaining?" Harley asked.

He shook his head and smiled. "No. Glad as anything to have you guys here. But I'm also pretty damned curious about how you found us way the hell out here."

"Good old-fashioned triangulation with a dash of thermal imaging," his stocky friend explained. "Traced your phone to the cabins. Found some interesting stuff. But not *you*. So we went back up, and Anderson had the brilliant idea of using the thermal cameras. Found you on our first sweep."

Alessandra had to admit that the whole thing was impressive. The quickness of Rush's partners' reaction and arrival. The way they'd put the puzzle pieces together and tracked them down. And there was more than a small part of her that was pleased that her father was the catalyst behind it.

Smiling to herself, she settled back in her seat, eager to hear what the plan was for moving forward. But before anyone said another word, the headset crackled in an odd way, and an unfamiliar voice filled her ears.

It only took a second for Rush to realize that the choppy incoming message was a broadcast from the local police.

"Any and all available units," said the unknown female voice, sounding more worried than a typical dispatcher. "Please respond to a report of a code twelve-thirty. Two vehicles involved, suspects unknown."

Rush exchanged a look with Brayden and Harley, but it was Anderson who replied to the call.

"Dispatch, this is Detective Anderson Somers with the Freemont PD," he said, then reeled off his credentials and asked, "Did you say a twelve-thirty? Dangerous driving?"

"Yes, sir," replied the woman on the other end. "Two vehicles sped through town. One took out a stop sign. I wasn't sure what else to call it, and there's no one to respond." She paused, then let out a sigh that made the headset pop in a wince-inducing way. "I'm sorry, Detective. It's my first day on the job."

"It's all right," said Anderson in his usual nice-guy way. "It can be overwhelming. Give me a recap. Why can't anyone respond?"

"Everyone's attending the warehouse fire in the industrial district."

Rush tossed another look toward his friends, then squeezed Alessandra's hand. She squeezed back.

"Tell me a little more about the two cars," Anderson said into the radio. "And give me a location. We'll attend."

The dispatcher muttered something that sounded like, "Oh, thank God," then said, "Both vehicles are making their way to the main road out of town. Vehicle one is an older sedan, light blue or gray in color. Vehicle two is described as a black town car. None of the complainants— there were four—got a look at the drivers except to say they thought the person in vehicle one had a beard."

Randall Rivers.

Alessandra's hand tightened in Rush's in silent agreement of his unspoken thought.

"Copy," Anderson replied. "We're on our way."

"Thank you, Detective."

The radio crackled again, then went silent.

"Anyone in here doubt that the two cars belong to Garibaldi and Rivers?" Anderson asked.

There were no murmurs of disagreement, so Rush said, "Only one way in and one way out of town. And a helicopter makes a pretty good blockade."

"Agreed," said Brayden. "Anderson, can you take us out past the edge of town and set us down across the road? We should be able to surprise our targets and eliminate any kind of collateral damage at the same time."

"You got it, Maxwell," Anderson replied.

Rush felt the helicopter shift, and a quiet couple of minutes later, they were completing their descent. The helicopter touched down on top of a winding piece of road—the topmost point before the road found its way back to the other side of the mountain that held Whispering Woods—and the four men quickly worked out the details.

Brayden and Harley would flank the chopper and prepare for the likelihood of an assault on foot.

Anderson would stay inside and use the helicopter as armor if he needed to.

Rush would take Alessandra up the road and find her a safe place to hide in the woods until it was over.

"Gonna fight me on that one, Red?" he asked as he helped her unbuckle the sticky clips of her harness.

Her blue eyes met his gaze. "No. So long as you're not going to fight me on staying with me."

He bent to kiss her lips. "Nothing I want more than to be your personal bodyguard."

From outside the helicopter, Harley snorted. "Bodyguard, he says. I'm not sure that's the word he's looking for."

Rush shot a dirty look toward his friend. "You're a serious pain in the—"

A furious, extended car horn in the distance cut him off.

"Dammit," Anderson swore. "I think they're going to get here quicker than we thought they would. Let's move."

Not wanting to waste any time, Rush slid his hands to Alessandra's hips and lifted her straight up. As he moved toward the open door, though, he realized he didn't really *have* any time to waste. The two cars were already visible just down the hill, and it was easy to see why they'd arrived so much faster than expected—they were traveling at breakneck speed. They'd be there in mere minutes.

Rush watched for another few seconds.

The light blue sedan was visibly rattling with the effort of the speed, but it still managed to keep up with the slick town car. As the two vehicles rounded the bend, the sedan actually smacked into the town car's bumper and sent it careering back and forth. For a second, it almost looked like Garibaldi was going to go off the road completely. After a moment, though, the town car regained control. And now Randall's sedan had dropped behind.

Damn.

Without checking on his partners—he knew they'd be moving into position already—Rush belatedly grabbed Alessandra's hand and tugged. She came easily, following him to the forest that lined the road. He kept going for a few more feet—until they were safely out of view of the road—then stopped, wrapped his arms around her, and strained to listen. For a second, there was nothing. Then came the competing car engines and the sound of tires spinning against dirt. Rush tensed, and he felt Alessandra's hand land on the small of his back. The roars grew louder and louder.

They should be stopping, he thought. *Or at least slowing down.*

Both Garibaldi and Randall should've spotted the helicopter by now, and they should've been adjusting accordingly. But the revs were only getting higher.

"Are they still speeding up?" Alessandra whispered,

her eyes widening as the engine noise seemed to rise all around. "Oh God. They *are* speeding up? *Why?*"

The question brought the answer straight into Rush's head, and he voiced it aloud before he could think to stop himself. "They're not *trying* to stop. They're playing a glorified game of chicken."

"But…" Alessandra trailed off in a quaver, then drew a breath. "My dad really *won't* stop. Not if it means letting Jesse win. If he thinks he can bait Jesse into crashing…"

"I know."

"We have to do something, Rush. He could die."

His mind was already churning with the possible directions the situation could take, the most probable one taking root.

His partners would soon—if they hadn't already—note the lack of a decrease in speed, and they'd come up with a defensive plan. Evasive action, likely, because Garibaldi would happily plow straight through them. Hell. Rush wouldn't put it past him to drive into them on purpose, then try to steal the damned chopper.

And Alessandra was right about her father. Even the brief interaction they'd had was enough to make Rush sure that the other man was utterly determined to make amends for the years he'd lost. He *would* keep going, and whether he hit the helicopter or the tree line, disaster was the only outcome.

What will *get him to stop?*

Knowing the answer, but dreading it, too, Rush turned toward Alessandra.

"Kiss me," he demanded, his voice a little rougher than he intended it to be.

Alessandra blinked, visibly startled by his tone. Her

mouth opened, but he didn't wait for her to say anything. Instead, he pulled her in and slammed his mouth to hers in a fierce kiss. He counted to five—it was all the time he dared take—before he let her go.

"Rush," she said worriedly as he pulled back. "What's happening?"

He couldn't meet her eyes as he reached down and unbuckled his belt. "Promise me you'll stay here."

"Stay here?"

"Please."

"I can't do that."

"I need to know that you're going to make it out of here alive."

"And you expect me to do what? Just accept that you're going to *die*?"

He slid the belt free, then reached for her hands. She tried to jerk back, but he was quicker. He slapped the strip of leather to her wrists and wound it around, steeling himself against her vehement protests and attempts to get free of his grasp. He was done in moments, and he pulled her to the nearest sapling, then haphazardly lashed her to it.

"I'm sorry, Red," he said. "Really."

"You're *sorry*?" she replied incredulously. "You're tying me up!"

"*Tied* you up," he corrected as he stepped back.

It wasn't tight, and he was sure she would be able to get out of the bonds in minutes. But he still felt like crap.

"For the love of God, *why*?" she asked.

"Because I know it's the only way you'll stay behind."

"What if someone comes? What if one of Jesse's men finds me?"

He heard the desperation in her tone, and he knew she didn't believe it was a possibility any more than he did.

"They won't get here any quicker than you can get yourself out," he said gently. "Not unless they have their own helicopter."

"Rush."

"Red."

"Please."

He wanted to kiss her again. To apologize again, too. And to beg for her forgiveness. But he couldn't. Not yet. He needed to act on the realization that had popped into his head—the fact that the only thing that would stop Randall Rivers from his current kamikaze mission would be knowing it would directly hurt his daughter. And Rush had to make sure Alessandra didn't figure that out and do something rash on her own.

He gave her a final regretful look, then spun on his heel and took off at a run.

Chapter 20

For a few stunned seconds, Alessandra stared after Rush. She didn't know what he was planning, but she knew whatever it was, it couldn't possibly end well. Undoubtedly, he was headed back to the helicopter and right into danger. And that hurt as much as being tied up.

This is going to be bad. She shoved off the overly obvious thought with a mental scoff. *Oh, was that fact in doubt? Him leaving you tied up wasn't enough of a clue? And speaking of which…maybe you should do something about that instead of standing here staring blankly.*

She shook her head and turned her attention to the belt. It was loose enough that it didn't chafe, but not so loose that she stood any chance of sliding her hands free. She gave it one yank, then another before realizing her actions were only tightening it more.

Gritting her teeth and trying to keep from crying,

Alessandra looked around for another option. When none immediately presented itself, she decided her best bet was to go feral. She bared her teeth and tried to drop them to the belt. Her hands wouldn't lift high enough. *Still.* She wasn't going to give up. She started to crouch down, figuring if she couldn't get the belt to her mouth, she could do the reverse. But as she made the move, her sandals—for the first time ever—failed her. The front edge of one caught on protruding root, and with a cry, she fell forward. Her knees smacked the ground, and her mouth met the mud.

Spitting out bits of dirt and twigs between her words, she muttered, "You…phh…can't…phh…be…phh…serious."

She tried to push to her feet, but pain shot through her legs. And her palms stung like nobody's business, too. A glance down told her why. Her hands had landed straight in a prickle-covered bush.

A prickle-covered bush. Realization hit. *My hands.*

She lifted them up and stared down. She was free of the belt. Somewhere in the middle of the fall, it had come off completely.

Elated, she started again to stand. But halfway up, a series of horrible noises filled the air and froze her to the spot. First came a screeching, metal-on-metal noise that made every part of her cringe. Next came a *boom-smash-boom* that she swore bordered on supersonic. Then came the unmistakable *crack* of a discharging weapon.

Alessandra forgot about her fall and her pain. She bolted back toward the road, ignoring the shoe that stayed behind and oblivious to branches that whipped into her with each stride. It was only a seconds-long run. Logically, she knew that. It'd only taken them moments to get into the woods. But getting out felt like an eternity. And when she burst through the trees and neared the road, she found no relief. She slowed to stare. The scene in front of her was chaos, and the blare of a car alarm reigned over it all.

Alessandra didn't even know where to look, let alone what move to make. Where was Rush in all the craziness? And her dad? There was smoke and yelling and the *thump* of feet. Though she knew she only took moments to glance around, time still moved with the same slowness as her run. Each second dragged on, a hundred times lengthier than normal.

Her eyes landed on the black town car first. It was upside down, its roof partially crushed. A long skid lay out behind it, clearly indicating that its flip had happened a couple dozen feet away, and that the car had kept moving. It was also an explanation for the god-awful noise. But then she saw something else. In spite of the car's placement, the driver's-side door was somehow open.

No, Alessandra realized. *Not open. Broken off on the hinges.*

And Garibaldi wasn't inside. But at least that particular fact gave her a purpose. She scanned the area in search of him. The frantic look around was made more difficult by the oily black smoke that somehow billowed from nowhere and everywhere at once.

A flash of movement to her left caught her attention, and she swung toward it. By the time she turned, whatever it was, it was already gone. But she noted belatedly that she was standing just a few feet from the helicopter. And inside, lying facedown on the floor, was Anderson.

Alessandra's throat closed up. She took a small, automatic step toward him. But she no sooner moved than the tall blond man shifted ever so slightly, making her sure he was positioned that way on purpose.

Alessandra exhaled and moved on.

The light blue sedan—her father's car—sat to the side, perpendicular to the road, and with the front wheels hanging precariously over the ditch. The rear tires, on the other hand, appeared to be almost flat. That fact had probably halted the forward momentum. Which was a good thing. Because another two inches, and it would've tipped right in. The rest of the car was in rough shape, too. The passenger side was crushed in, and it was covered in scrapes of black paint.

As she stared at the damage, a decade and half's worth of nightmares came flooding in. How many times over the years had Alessandra woken in a cold sweat, tears on her face, the smell of smoke lingering in her imagination? How many times had she had to block out thoughts of what her dad's final moments would have been like?

And here it is...all laid out. It would've looked just like this.

Alessandra opened and closed her eyes in a slow blink, then forced herself to remember that none of it had really happened. The nightmare had been a lie. She willed this moment to have the same falseness, and she dragged her gaze from the exterior of the vehicle to the interior. And she wanted to cry with relief. Like the town car, the sedan was empty. Then, as quickly as it had come, the relief swept away. Because while her father might've escaped the crash, he wasn't safe. Not yet.

And she still didn't know where Rush was. So she moved on.

Aside from Anderson, all of the other men were con-

spicuously absent. Neither Harley nor Brayden was anywhere to be seen.

Wondering how it was possible that five men had suddenly become completely invisible, Alessandra took a
small step forward. And the world finally sped back up.
Not to normal speed. To turbo.

From somewhere to her right, someone yelled her name.

A *thump-thump, thump-thump* came from a place behind her.

She started to turn.

But the air around her cracked.

Arms closed around her waist.

Searing pain marked her shoulder.

A flash of black caught her eye.

And then Alessandra hit the ground.

The impact winded her, and for a second she was im-
mobilized. She couldn't do anything except stare up in
surprise at her father's blue gaze. She could see that his
mouth was moving, but what he was saying was a mystery. And after a futile moment, he gave up. His lips
stilled, his fingers shot out, and Alessandra found herself being yanked unceremoniously across the dirt road.
But the sensation only lasted for a heartbeat—not even
enough time to suck in much-needed breath—before a
pair of hands slid under her body and lifted her from the
ground. And instead of staring into her father's eyes, she
was gazing at the espresso darkness of Rush's irises. He
looked angry, but she didn't care. She was too relieved
to be anything but glad—so busy, in fact, that she barely
even noticed they were moving until they stopped.

The soul-crushing feeling in Rush's chest didn't lessen
as he knelt down behind Randall's blue car. The vehicle

provided a small amount of shelter from the town car's alarm, and a shield from Garibaldi, but it did nothing to ease his worry as he examined the burn mark on her shoulder. It had cut through her shirt and left a welt as big as his thumb on her skin. It had to hurt. More than hurt. But she was damned lucky. In all his years of police work, and in all his years of working side by side with thugs and quick-draw scoundrels, he'd never once seen a grazing wound like this one.

Concern, fear and frustration filled his heart as he lifted his eyes to Alessandra's blue gaze. He was stunned to find her *grinning* back at him. Utterly pleased, dammit, while he sat there, thinking she'd been about to die.

"Stop smiling," Rush growled in a low voice close to her ear.

She reached up and touched his cheek and whispered, "You're okay."

"Yeah. *I* am. But *you* just got shot."

"I'm fine."

"I told you stay behind," he said.

"You tied me to a tree with a belt," she corrected.

"You *what*?" The startled near-exclamation came from Harley.

"I told you I secured her," Rush grumbled. "And how did you even hear that over the car alarm?"

"It's the kind of thing that carries over even the shrillest noise," said his friend. "And by the way... I didn't think you meant secure *literally*."

"Aren't you supposed to be watching for Garibaldi?"

"Multitasking."

Rush muttered a curse, then turned his attention back to Alessandra. "Red..."

She shifted a little in his arms, and with the situation

as dangerous as it was, her movement was distracting and pleasant. His anger dissipated, and he sighed.

"Have a look around," he said.

She obliged, and he watched as she took in their very limited space and the circumstances that occupied it.

Harley and Brayden crouched at one edge of the car, weapons drawn, their defensive stance obvious. Randall was there, too. He had his back pressed to the vehicle, and his breaths were coming heavily with the exertion of running for Alessandra.

A task you *should've performed,* Rush told himself.

It was hard to be resentful, though. The older man had spotted her just a moment before Rush had, and he'd been quick to react. While Rush was still hollering a warning and getting to his feet, Randall was already diving in. *Thank God.*

He squeezed her a little tighter, the ache in his chest growing even sharper. Then sharper again when he realized Alessandra's eyes were back on him again. She'd finished her brief perusal of their barricaded area, and she was looking at him expectantly. Waiting for an explanation, Rush knew.

Her father spoke up first, saving him from having to admit to his own reckless plan.

"Your boyfriend thought jumping in front of my car was a good idea," said the other man.

Alessandra's face filled with concern as she flicked a look from Randall to Rush. "Are you completely insane?"

"I knew he'd see me and stop," Rush replied.

"Lucky I *could* stop," Randall grumbled.

"Hell of a lot better than plowing straight into a helicopter. Don't make me out to be the bad guy."

Alessandra expelled a breath. "You're both crazy. Neither of you needs to run around being all heroic and trying to die for the sake of…" She trailed off, her face reddening.

For the sake of her.

Rush knew it was what she'd been about to say, and he wished—pretty damned fiercely—that they were alone so he could explain that he *did* have to do it, and why. His words weren't the kind of thing that needed an audience—especially not one that included her father. But once again, Randall saved him anyway.

"Of course we do, Munchkin," he said, his voice gruff with emotion. "Either of us is willing to make whatever sacrifice is necessary to keep you safe. Heck. I would've tied that belt myself if I could've. Probably tighter than Rush did."

"Dad!"

"All right," Brayden interrupted. "Now that we've established that you two are nuts…can we get back to figuring out how to make this standoff end in our favor?"

"Standoff?" Alessandra echoed.

Rush nodded. "Your dad hit the gas, then swerved and braked, which forced Garibaldi to do the same. Only Garibaldi's clearly been letting his stunt driver do most of the work, because he lost control and flipped. Managed to come out hot, though. Fired at the damned helicopter and sent everyone running for cover. Now he's holed up somewhere out there. He can't head this way because we'll see him. Helicopter's blocking the way out. And Anderson's got a rifle with a scope, so trying to sneak into the woods isn't much of an option, either. First bit of movement and he'll use his mad-crazy sniper skills to send in a shot."

"Speaking of which…" Brayden interjected. "Why didn't Anderson fire back a minute ago? Direction of the bullet should've made it easy to approximate a location."

"Because he would've had to risk hitting Alessandra in the cross fire," Rush reminded him. "And shooting after the fact would be a waste of bullets."

"Right," said his friend with a sigh. "So now what? Not exactly a starve-him-out situation. And when the local PD catch up, the chaos'll give Garibaldi an advantage."

"We need to flush him out," Harley stated.

"What do you think? Should we throw a damned rock and hope for the best?" Rush was only half joking; they badly needed a leg up.

"Rush?" Alessandra's soft voice drew his attention then, and he turned his attention away from the continuing discussion.

He belatedly realized that throughout the exchange, she'd gone noticeably quiet. And when he met her eyes, he could see that it was because she was holding something in.

"What is it?" he asked, his tone as gentle as hers had been.

She breathed out and said, "I think I know where he is."

Rush's eyebrows went up. "You do?"

"Yes. But I'm afraid to tell you, because I don't want you to run out there and try to sacrifice yourself again."

Rush ran a hand over his beard. "But you know you have to."

She swallowed. "I know. I'm scared, Rush. I don't want to lose you before I even get a chance to really have you."

He closed his eyes for the briefest second. He knew

exactly how she felt. After all, he'd literally tied her to a tree to try to keep her safe. But their feelings weren't going to help them with this particular fight. With a sigh, he tugged her close and kissed her forehead.

"If you don't tell me," he said, "*none* of us might make it out of here."

A resigned sigh accompanied her next words. "Right before he shot at me, I heard a noise come from behind me, and when I fell, I saw something black."

"Something black?" Rush repeated.

She nodded. "And now that I'm thinking about it, I'm ninety-nine point nine percent sure that what I *heard* was someone moving around on the ground, and that what I *saw* was the door from Garibaldi's town car. I'm even almost positive that the door was leaning up against something out there."

"The perfect place to hide," Rush said, hope percolating under the surface. "We just have to figure out a way to let Anderson know."

She bit her lip, then spoke again. "How focused is he?"

"What?"

"Would he be easily distracted from finding his target?"

"Unlikely. Why?"

"Because I think I know how we can draw Jesse out. But it might be a little noisy."

"I'm all ears."

Chapter 21

Even though she'd come up with the hastily explained idea herself, Alessandra still wanted to hold her breath as they put it into action. With each movement, she was sure Jesse would somehow figure out what they were up to. He hadn't gotten as far as he had in his criminal enterprises because he was a fool.

But we're being careful, she reminded herself.

And they were. Almost painfully slow, when it really felt like something should be happening quickly. Shots should be ringing. Shouted threats should be flying. Hostile negotiations, maybe. But there was none of that. The only sound was the ongoing car alarm, and Alessandra was already so used that particular unpleasantness that it almost felt normal to hear it.

And there really wasn't much of a way to speed things up, anyway. Not if they didn't want to draw attention to the fact that their movements had purpose.

Brayden still held watch over the rear of the car, while Rush and Alessandra had been inching their way toward the front—and more importantly, toward the ditch. And as they did their thing, Alessandra's dad was waiting to get to work on carefully opening the front passenger-side door.

"Alessandra?"

Her name was an urgent hiss from ahead, and she realized Rush had crawled forward again. Inhaling, she closed the three-inch gap between them. Then she waited as he made a new gap. She closed it. Then again. And again.

Hurry, hurry, Alessandra thought, even though she knew it wasn't an option.

The nearly flat tires meant there was little space between the undercarriage of the car and the ground, but Rush had said he was still worried that Garibaldi might be able to see something. And there was no room for taking chances.

Alessandra breathed out as they finished crossing the path of the door. From behind, she heard her dad shuffle, and she knew he was repositioning himself. Next came a light *click* as he found the handle and lifted it. And even though she knew it couldn't possibly have been audible from where Jesse was, she still tensed. She braced for the impending *squeak* or a rusty *squeal*—a noise that might actually carry—but there was nothing.

"Alessandra?"

This time, hearing her name made her realize she'd closed her eyes. She dragged them open. Rush was already at the ditch now—already *in* it, to be more accurate—and he was looking expectantly up at her. He was on his knees. He had to be, in order to avoid being seen over the top of the front end of the car. A hysterical giggle threatened, and Alessandra had to push her lips against each other to keep from letting it out.

Keep it together, she ordered silently.

She gave herself a mental headshake and moved forward. This was the spot where she had to exercise extra caution. The front end of the car was only a couple of feet long, and any miscalculation of the space could expose then.

But that's not going to happen, she told herself.

As she settled back and swung her legs around, Rush's hands landed on her knees.

"You okay?" he murmured.

She nodded. "Yes."

"Your shoulder?"

"Stings. But it's not bothering me."

"You're sure?"

"Yes."

"All right. It's a little awkward getting in. It's only about three feet deep, so bend your legs as you slide forward or else you'll wind up standing straight up." He smiled reassuringly. "We don't want that, do we?"

She couldn't quite smile back. Her heart was thumping too hard. And she barely managed to answer in a steady voice. "Okay. I'm ready."

But when he slid forward, she discovered that she wasn't quite as prepared as she'd claimed. Or maybe *Rush* wasn't quite ready. Because as Alessandra pushed over the lip of the ditch, she lost her balance, slammed straight into him and flattened him to the bottom of the ditch.

Rush's chuckle filled her ear. "You know that before I met you, I'd never once been stuck in a hole with a girl. But with you... I guess I should prepare for a lifetime of it."

She pulled back, prepared to find his mouth curved up with amusement and a teasing sparkle in his familiar brown eyes. Instead, what she found was utter seriousness.

A lifetime.

It was crazy. Impossible. Over-the-top, Ken-and-Barbie stuff. But it was true nevertheless. She *wanted* a lifetime with this mud-spattered man. She couldn't remember at all why she'd been holding back on expressing her feelings. Or why she'd asked him to do the same.

She opened her mouth to say as much, but Brayden's boots suddenly hit the ground on the other side of Rush's head, and then a noisy mechanical groan overrode both her words and her thoughts.

Rush dropped a curse. Not because Brayden jumped down near their heads and sent a splash of mud in his face. Not because the blue sedan tipped forward into the ditch near their feet, or even because the crash was too close for comfort. No. Those things were a minor inconvenience. The source of his swearing was the fact that he was damned sure that Alessandra had been about to say the three little words he longed to hear. The words he was holding in at her request. The words he'd never thought about any other woman, and which he was certain he'd never say to another. And the stupid car had ruined it all by cooperating and doing exactly what they'd planned for it to do.

Dammit all to hell. Can we just reverse time for, like, two minutes?

"Rush!"

Alessandra's urgent, whispered cry drew him back to the moment. She was clambering to a sitting position.

"Where's my dad?" she asked.

The idea had been simple. Randall was meant to put the car in Neutral and give it a nudge. The moment the vehicle started to move, Brayden was supposed to jump into the ditch with Alessandra's dad right behind. The crash that followed was intended to draw Garibaldi's attention, and the empty space they'd left behind would make him bold enough to expose himself.

But if Randall isn't where he's supposed to be...

Rush pushed himself up and whipped his gaze to the side. The car had done its bit and created a noisy distraction, and it now sat at a crazy angle, half in, half out of the ditch, its rear end sticking up. Harley and Brayden were exactly where they were supposed to be. Alessandra's father, on the other hand, really was nowhere to be seen.

Cursing again, Rush grabbed the edge of the ditch and leaned forward. He immediately spied the problem. Randall Rivers *hung* from the inside of the car. His hips and legs dangled out while his torso was sprawled over the passenger-side floor. He had his left arm bent awkwardly up, his hand flailing on the edge of the seat. On the right side, only his shoulder was visible, but it was obvious that he had the rest of his arm extended. It didn't take a genius to figure out that the other man was stuck. It took even less of a genius to conclude that at any moment Garibaldi would see him. Possibly take aim. Anderson would fire back, but it wouldn't do much good if Garibaldi hit Randall first.

Rush had no choice but to act fast.

He tightened his hands on the ground, yanked himself to his feet and propelled his body out of the ditch. He heard Alessandra call his name, but he didn't have time to turn and assuage her fears. He didn't even have time to turn and look at her. Seconds were the difference between Randall living and Randall dying. And the difference between two other things, too—starting his life with Alessandra with her father's death hanging over them, or starting it with her father walking her down the aisle. It wasn't even a choice. It had to be the latter.

Rush darted over the packed dirt and positioned himself beside the older man.

"You shouldn't be out here," Randall said right away.

"Neither should you," Rush countered. "So why don't you tell me what the problem is, so we can both get back to safety?"

"Sleeve's stuck on the gas pedal. Can't reach it with my other hand."

"Not for long."

Rush slid his own hand up to the sleeve and pedal in question. A quick yank, and Randall dropped to the ground. But they no sooner ducked and turned to run toward the ditch than three rapid-fire bullets hit the ground where their feet had just been. As they smacked the mud, Rush waited for the answering fire to come from Anderson. Instead, it was his friend's voice that carried to him.

"Garibaldi wants me to tell you he has some questions. He'd like you to file out, one at a time, with your hands on your head. And he'd like Alessandra to come first," he announced. "But if you want to just shoot him and let me die, I promise not to haunt you over it."

A kicked-in-the-gut feeling hit Rush immediately, but he made himself answer in an even voice. "That last bit's not a *terrible* offer."

"That's why I made it," Anderson replied. "Always called me Mr. Nice Guy, didn't you?"

"You earned it, fair and square," he called back.

Rush turned to the group in the ditch, hoping one of them would give him an indication that they were planning something. Harley had his hand on his sheathed gun and Brayden had his weapon drawn, but each of them gave him a quick headshake. Alessandra was standing close to her father, and Rush was grateful that the older man had a supportive hand on her arm.

Garibaldi's angry voice cut in. "If you're trying to buy some time…don't bother. In T minus thirty seconds, I'll shoot your blond friend. Then I'll shoot whoever comes out next. And I'll keep shooting until I can't shoot anymore."

Rush gritted his teeth and ignored the twist in his heart. He couldn't send Alessandra out, but he couldn't just let Anderson die, either. Garibaldi wasn't bluffing. He had Rush stuck. And there was no doubt that the other man not only knew it, but was enjoying it, too.

Garibaldi's next words—cheerful and threatening at the same time—confirmed it. "By my count, we're down to twenty seconds now."

"I'm coming!" Alessandra yelled suddenly.

Then—before Rush could process that she truly meant to do it—Alessandra ripped her arm free from her father's grasp and climbed out of the ditch.

And Rush was filled with a sudden vision of how it would go. He *knew* what Garibaldi's plan was. He knew why he wanted Alessandra to step out. The other man was going to shoot her on sight, because he knew it would cripple Rush and send things spiraling in his favor.

Rush couldn't let it happen. He leaped from the ditch and bolted, Alessandra's safety overriding everything else, self-preservation included. He reached her just as she stepped into the open. Vaguely, Rush was aware of other things. Like the fact that Anderson was lying on the ground, his eyes rolled back in his head. And like the fact that the distant wail of a very belated siren was blaring in the distance. But it was all secondary. The only thing that really mattered was Garibaldi and the way he was lifting his gun and taking aim.

Rush had no choice. He had to dive in, even if that meant becoming a human shield.

The air cracked with the echo of a single shot, and Rush's body fell to the ground in a heap. Alessandra couldn't stop a scream from erupting from her throat. It came out raw and full of emotion. A sharp contrast to the sudden lifelessness of her heart. Because without Rush, it had no real reason to beat.

Leadenly, she stepped forward. Then stalled. There was blood on the ground under Rush's head, and his eyes were closed. And she wasn't sure she could bear confirming what the evidence told her was true. The only man she'd ever loved had just taken a fatal shot. For her.

Chaos erupted around her. Harley and Brayden had surged out of hiding and were rushing in Jesse's direction. Alessandra's father was saying her name. Anderson was sitting up, a hand on his head. And a sobbing, wailing sound was coming from everywhere.

Not everywhere, said a voice in her head. *From you.*

She realized it was true. She was crying so hard that she was sure her chest had to be about to cave in. Her throat burned. But she couldn't stop the noise from coming. Just like she couldn't stop herself from collapsing to her knees as a stark reality hit her.

Over the last day and a half, she'd changed. Her world had exploded in the worst way. Yet somehow, in all of that, the things that really should've been most important—like the loss of her livelihood and the realization that someone she'd known her whole life was a murderer and the fact that her long-dead father was alive—came in second place. Because she'd found something more important. Something she hadn't even known she was looking for. He was the other half of her whole. And now he was gone. Before she could even tell him how she felt.

I love you.

"I love you."

Alessandra blinked, surprised to hear the words aloud. It took her a full ten seconds to process that it wasn't her own voice that had said them in the thick, needy way. It took another five to realize it sounded an awful lot like Rush. And she blinked again, thinking she'd fallen off into the abyss of Crazytown.

Alessandra's gaze slid over Rush's body. He was still pale and unmoving. Painfully lifeless. From his mud-covered jeans to his gun-holding fist to his closed eyes, there was no sign that he was drawing breath, let alone that he'd spoken. Alessandra's lids sank shut. But then the declaration came again, and it was too real to be an auditory hallucination.

"I love you, Red. And if you don't say it back now, I think you might never say it at all."

Her eyes flew open, and she found the impossible. Brown irises, staring back at her. Waiting.

"Rush," she breathed. "If you're only alive in my imagination, I'm going to kill you all over again."

His mouth twitched. "Did you hear what I said?"

She swallowed. "That you love me."

"And…"

"I swear to God, if—"

"Red."

"What?"

"I'm alive."

Tears spilled over, and she dived forward to press her head to his chest. His breaths were even and steady.

"Jesse shot you," she whispered.

"Actually, love, I think I shot him," he corrected, lifting the gun a little off the ground.

"But your head is bleeding everywhere."

"Banged it pretty hard, I think. Head wounds and all that."

She started to sit up. "I'll get your partners to call the paramedics."

His hand shot out and closed on her wrist. "Red?"

"What?"

"I'm still waiting."

"Oh."

"Well?"

Alessandra hesitated, suddenly nervous. "Every time I think it, something goes wrong."

Rush frowned. "What do you mean?"

"I think 'hey…this feels like forever'…and then the world implodes in helicopters and shootings and falling into holes."

She waited for him to protest. Or argue. She even *wanted* him to do both. But his mouth twitched instead.

Then he turned his head a little and yelled, "Hey, Brayden!"

The reply was immediate. "What's up?"

"Is it over?"

"Yeah, man. Hard to believe. But I think it is."

"Thanks." Rush's chocolate gaze sought Alessandra again. "See? There you have it. My man Brayden never lies. He's far too Goody-Two-shoes for that. Case closed."

She stared down at him. At the face that she hadn't even known existed until two days earlier. Less than two days earlier. She thought of the way her mom's eyes looked when she'd talked about true love and just knowing. And she knew, without a doubt, that the same sparkle had to be in her own.

"I love you, too, Rush," she said, her voice thick with emotion.

He grinned. "Thank God. Now about that doctor…"

Epilogue

Fifteen months later

The four men stood together, companionable and comfortable in spite of the closed quarters. From his position in front of the mirror, Rush stole a glance at each of his friends.

Harley sat on the window, adjusting the rose on his lapel in an attempt to cover the splash of paint that he'd accidentally flicked onto it earlier in the morning. Rush shook his head a little at the typical Harley mishap. Who else would think that painting something was a good idea on this particular morning?

Anderson was sitting on top of a desk in the corner. He had an open textbook in his lap, and he was studying intensely. That made Rush smile. Back to school for the teacher's fiancé. It seemed very fitting.

Brayden stood with his back against the wall. Unsurprisingly, his suit was perfectly pressed, his hair freshly trimmed and his face as clean-shaven as they came. When he shifted a little, though, Rush spied a Frost Family Diner menu in his friend's pocket, and he had to bite back a laugh as he turned his attention to his own reflection.

He gave his bow tie a tug and a dirty look, then sighed and faced Brayden. "All right. I admit defeat."

"You?" mocked the other man as he reached up and made the necessary adjustment. "The great and mighty Rush Aaron Atkinson has been bested by a bow tie?"

Harley piped up from his spot, "I don't think it's the bow tie, bro. I think it's looooove."

"Shut up," Rush muttered good-naturedly. "What are you…twelve?"

"I know you are, but what am I?" Harley said.

"And there it is," Rush replied. "Proof that at least one of my groomsmen is a child."

"This particular groomsman is a full-fledged business-man and a homeowner," Harley corrected.

"Seriously?" his brother asked. "When were you going to tell us?"

"I didn't want to say anything because I didn't want to spoil your big day, but I have a feeling Liz is going to get into the champagne and tell everyone anyway, so why not, right? Consider yourselves the first to know that we'll be officially reopening Liz's Lovely Things next week. We bought the building. Strictly opiate-free, of course."

"Very funny," Brayden said.

Rush smiled at his friend. "Hell. That doesn't spoil anything. Congrats, man."

Anderson cleared his throat. "Well, then. Guess I might as well tell you *my* news."

All three men turned his way, and he clapped his book shut, then scrubbed a nervous hand over his head.

"Nadine is expecting," he announced. "She's due two weeks after I officially finish the paramedic course."

"Dammit," Harley replied.

"What?" said Anderson.

"That's almost an upstage of my stuff."

Rush laughed. "Yeah, but are any of you getting married in three minutes?"

"Oh, right," Brayden said. "We're supposed to be *doing* something."

"That's right, Captain," Rush replied. "Something. Unless of course *you* have an announcement, too?"

"No news on my end. And I keep telling you not to call me that," Brayden protested. "Whispering Woods PD doesn't actually *have* a captain."

"And *we* keep telling you it's close enough," Harley responded. "Top-ranking official and all that."

"T minus ninety seconds," Anderson reminded them.

Chuckling, they started to file toward the door, but Brayden stopped them with a question. "Do you think they'd say we did it right, even with things turning out the way they did?"

Their laughter died off. None of them had to ask what—or who—he meant. Their pact, made as a promise to their fathers more than sixteen years earlier, had been thoroughly derailed by Jesse's death on the way to the hospital. And it wasn't even Rush's bullet that had done it. The cause of death was ruled as sudden cardiac arrest. An inevitability, the coroner had told them, based on the physical state of his heart. So they couldn't even lay claim to that particular dark victory.

They'd never found out if the murderous crime boss

knew who they were or what their purpose in chasing him down was, and they never *would* find out. It wasn't exactly the result they'd been looking for. Though they'd managed to arrest and convict the man with whom Garibaldi had made his deal, Jesse himself wasn't behind bars. Yet Rush hadn't ever felt robbed by the end result. If anything, he felt like he'd gained more than he'd lost.

"I think…" he said slowly, "that our fathers would be happy for us. They'd tell us that life isn't cut-and-dried, that Garibaldi got what he deserved, and that everything that happened over the last few years brought us to this moment right here. I'm getting married. Anderson is having a baby. Harley is *already* married and is a stepfather extraordinaire. And Brayden is basically running a town."

They all went silent, and then Harley cleared his throat. "So. Like I said. It's looooove."

There was another moment of silence, and then they all burst out laughing and started talking over one another. And none of it had to do with the stress and fear and sadness of the last sixteen years. It was time—officially—to move on. They could be the men they'd always been meant to become.

* * * * *

*Look out for Melinda Di Lorenzo's
next heart-pounding romance,*
First Responder on Call
*available August 2019 from
Harlequin Romantic Suspense!*

*And don't miss out on the rest of
the Undercover Justice miniseries:*
Captivating Witness
Undercover Protector
Undercover Passion

*Available now wherever
Harlequin Romantic Suspense
books and ebooks are sold!*

Get 4 FREE REWARDS!

We'll send you 2 FREE Books plus 2 FREE Mystery Gifts.

Harlequin® Romantic Suspense books feature heart-racing sensuality and the promise of a sweeping romance set against the backdrop of suspense.

FREE
Value Over
$20

Rebel asked more seriously, "How should a woman be treated, then?"

Avi smiled broadly. Now they were getting somewhere. "It would be my pleasure to show you."

She leaned back, staring openly at him. He was tempted to dare her to take him up on it. After all, no Special Forces operator he'd ever known could turn down a dare. But he was probably better served by backing off and letting her make the next move. Not to mention she deserved the decency on his part.

Waiting out her response was harder than he'd expected it to be. He wanted her to take him up on the offer more than he'd realized.

"What would showing me entail?" she finally asked.

He shrugged. "It would entail whatever you're comfortable with. Decent men don't force women to do anything they don't want to do or are uncomfortable with."

"Hmm."

Suppressing a smile at her hedging, he said quietly, "They do, however, insist on yes or no answers to questions of whether they should proceed. Consent must always be clearly given."

He waited her out while the SUV carrying Piper and Zane pulled up at the gate to the Olympic Village.

Gunnar delivered them to the back door of the building, and Avi watched the pair ride an elevator to their floor, walk down the hall and enter their room.

"Here comes Major Torsten now. He's going to spell me watching the cameras tonight."

"Excellent," Avi purred.

Alarm blossomed in Rebel's oh-so-expressive eyes. He liked making her a little nervous. If he didn't miss his guess, boredom would kill her interest in a man faster than just about anything else.

Avi moved his chair back to its position under the window. The hall door opened and he turned quickly. "Hey, Gun."

"Avi." A nod. "How's it going, Rebel?"

"All quiet on the western front."

"Great. You go get some sleep."

"Yes, sir," she said crisply.

"I'll walk you out," Avi said casually.

He followed Rebel into the hallway and closed the door behind her. They walked to the elevator in silence. Rebel was obviously as vividly aware as he was of the cameras Gunnar would be using to watch them.

"Walk with me?" he breathed without moving his lips as they reached the lobby. Gunnar no doubt read lips.

"Sure," Rebel uttered back, playing ventriloquist herself, and without so much as glancing in his direction.

It was a crisp Australian winter night under bright stars. The temperature was cool and bracing, perfect for a brisk walk. He matched his stride to Rebel's, relieved he didn't have to hold it back too much.

"So what's your answer, Rebel? Shall I show you how real men treat women? Yes or no?"

Don't miss
Special Forces: The Operator *by Cindy Dees,*
available July 2019 wherever
Harlequin® Romantic Suspense books
and ebooks are sold.

www.Harlequin.com

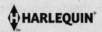

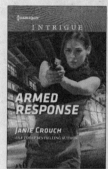  

Love Harlequin romance?

DISCOVER.

Be the first to find out about promotions,
news and exclusive content!

Facebook.com/HarlequinBooks

Twitter.com/HarlequinBooks

Instagram.com/HarlequinBooks

Pinterest.com/HarlequinBooks

ReaderService.com

EXPLORE.

Sign up for the Harlequin e-newsletter and
download a free book from any series at
TryHarlequin.com.

CONNECT.

Join our Harlequin community to share
your thoughts and connect with other
romance readers!
Facebook.com/groups/HarlequinConnection

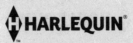

HARLEQUIN®

**ROMANCE WHEN
YOU NEED IT**

HSOCIAL2018